Praise for An Accident of Dragons

"A miracle of the cozy and the numinous: a truly alien dragon, glitteringly silver, with a bunch of human characters you just want to hang out with so you can try on clothes and talk about life together."

—**Ellen Kushner**, award-winning author of *Swordspoint*

"Delightful—I was all-in from the very first paragraph and could not put it down. I read it in one sitting. Such a light touch is hard to find, and Radke pairs her excellent world building with characters I found difficult, if not impossible, to resist. I will be watching eagerly for more from Cheri Radke."

—**Caroline Stevermer**, author of *The Glass Magician* and co-author of *Sorcery and Cecelia* with Patricia C. Wrede

"What do you get when an overly dramatic but charming, reluctant hero (who just happens to share his chaotic mind with a dragon) is yanked into a swashbuckling adventure to save the daughter he loves? *An Accident of Dragons*. Fantasy readers will enjoy this frolicking tale that marries dragons, the love of an unconventional family and the notion that discovering your true (and better) self can happen entirely by accident."

—**J. Penner**, author of *A Fellowship of Bakers & Magic*

"A witty confection of a tale, as if Oscar Wilde turned his pen to writing high fantasy. Charming and original, *An Accident of Dragons* will appeal to anyone looking for their next cozy, queer fantasy romp!"

—**Kimberly Bea**, author of *The Changeling Queen*

"Brimming with heart and humour, *An Accident of Dragons* is equal parts a cozy tale about love and acceptance, and a page-turning adventure on the high seas, full of twists and turns. Prepare to fall in love with the wittiest, messiest rake of a main character!"

—**Genoveva Dimova**, author of *Foul Days and Monstrous Nights*

"Radke writes with precision and empathy, tracing a history of grief and love with exquisite care. The protagonist is wonderfully flawed, resilient, and deeply human, and I especially appreciated how Radke flirted with tropes but always did something unexpected with them. And, of course, the dragons are wonderful!"

—**Jenn Lyons**, author of *The Sky on Fire*

AN ACCIDENT OF DRAGONS

CHERI RADKE

an imprint of Kensington Publishing Corp.
erewhonbooks.com

EREWHON BOOKS are published by:

Kensington Publishing Corp.
900 Third Avenue
New York, NY 10022

erewhonbooks.com

All Kensington titles, imprints, and distributed lines are available at special quantity discounts for bulk purchases for sales promotions, premiums, fundraising, educational, or institutional use.

Special book excerpts or customized printings can also be created to fit specific needs. For details, write or phone the office of the Kensington sales manager: Kensington Publishing Corp., 900 Third Avenue, New York, NY 10022, attn: Sales Department; phone 1-800-221-2647.

Erewhon and the Erewhon logo Reg. US Pat. & TM Off.

ISBN 978-1-64566-246-4 (deluxe trade paperback edition)

First Erewhon deluxe trade paperback printing: May 2026

10 9 8 7 6 5 4 3 2 1

Printed in China

Library of Congress Control Number is available upon request.

Electronic edition: ISBN 978-1-64566-247-1

Edited by Diana Pho
Interior design by Kelsy Thompson
Images courtesy of Icongeek26 and Saeful Muslim via Noun Project, and Fiona Hesh

The authorized representative in the EU for product safety and compliance
is eucomply OU, Parnu mnt 139b-14, Apt 123
Tallinn, Berlin 11317, hello@eucompliancepartner.com

For Sally

An Accident of Dragons

PART ONE

A BAD FIT

THE FIRST SIGN OF SOMETHING AFOOT WAS IN THE fit of my favorite evening jacket. It was not too tight across the belly, mercifully, but rather too tight across the shoulders and even in the arms. Many men would perhaps take a sanguine view of this development, but I confess I found it disconcerting. When a man is on the wrong side of forty, I suppose he has simply gotten used to the shape of his own body, allowing of course for seasonal fluctuations and changes of habit. Of late I had done nothing more strenuous than twirling ladies about the dance floor, so I harbored no delusions that this sudden muscular growth was of my own doing.

My dragon was having her own way with me, it was clear. I had known such things might occur when I entered my contract, but seven years had passed with no obvious changes to my person. I had rather thought I was too old to be affected so, that such gifts were the province of men and women who were born dragon-touched. Where would it end? Could my clothes be let out, or would I require an entirely new wardrobe to be made for me? On second thought, that did not sound so bad.

Still, I could not help but wonder about the why of the thing. Did the dragoness Summer feel I would need strength in the days to come? I did not hold with the idea that dragons are prescient in any way, but there was no question that Summer often knew a good deal more about the world and its happenings than I could ever fully account for. If she wanted me girded for a fight, well, I didn't much savor the thought. I've never been a fighter. I attempted to reach out to the dragon and ascertain what she meant by all this, but she was napping and utterly disinclined to acknowledge me. So that was that.

By the time I accepted that the jacket would fit as well as it would fit for the present, I still had some leisure time ahead of my dinner engagement, so I thought I might check in on my wife. A ball to celebrate the equinox was coming up, and as we would be expected to appear prominently, I had several logistical considerations to discuss with her. Her apartment was one level above my own in the palace, so I trotted up the stone stairwell and let myself in. Though the apartment was mostly underground on three sides, the severity of the white stone walls was cheered by colorful hangings, and the furnishings reflected a practical good taste. From the western-facing wall of windows, warm golden light spilled over the scene before me.

My stepson Brook was there, a lad of sixteen—no, seventeen! I'm sure he was seventeen—studying some text or other in a focused manner. I could swear he got bigger every time I looked at him, and he now struck me as comically oversized for the delicate settee he lounged across. My own darling little Zinnia, only five years old, played on the rug with a gray tabby cat. The particular animal was not familiar to me, but I was unsurprised by its presence. Cats were always following me and Zinny around. It all looked quite homey.

Canna—that's my lady—sat at her desk going through our official correspondence, but she set it aside at my entry and turned her attention to my thoughts on the ball. She was as capable as ever in absorbing the necessary details, despite my own rather chaotic style of imparting information. She even reminded me that we'd already gone over most of this, perhaps with an air of puzzlement over why exactly I had bothered to come. I think she suspected that I sometimes showed up out of boredom and loneliness rather than because I had true business to discuss, though that was not fair at all. Canna placed less importance on these shows of pageantry than I did, but I felt it was incumbent upon me to put on a good show for the people of Summer. It was truly the least I could do.

Canna's only concern about the festivities involved the gown I had chosen for her. "I know I told you to pick whatever you like," she said to me. "But I went for my fitting yesterday, and well, don't you think it's a bit much?"

"I've no idea what you mean," I said, all honesty.

"It's very close fitting and low-cut, isn't it? Won't I look a bit ridiculous, dressing like a young thing?"

"Nonsense!" I told her. "You've a figure as fine as anyone. I don't see why you shouldn't show it off. And it's in fashion."

"If you really don't think it will look odd . . ."

"If you won't be comfortable in it, of course we can choose something else," I told her. "But ask yourself—why should I wish to make my wife look ridiculous? I assure you, it's perfect, and you will look a marvel dancing in it."

I took her hand and spun her about the sitting room, and she laughed in almost girlish delight. I always loved to make Canna laugh, for a rare pleasure is all the more to be savored.

"Besides, no one will be looking at you anyway. I'll be right beside you, and I promise my outfit will be twice as outrageous, and I'll be twice as pretty." I winked at her.

Canna laughed even more. "*Teddy!*" she mock-chastised me.

I always liked it when she called me by name, and I was feeling rather good about the whole thing—until I caught a glimpse of Brook frowning at me. Well, let him. Why should I feel guilty about flirting with my own wife? In fact, I had a sudden inclination to spend more time with her.

"You know, I feel it's been an age since I left the palace," I said to her. "I thought I might go out sailing tomorrow."

"That sounds nice," she replied without much interest.

"Perhaps you'd like to join me?" I persevered.

"Oh." She looked a bit quizzical. "Wouldn't you rather take a . . . *friend* out with you?"

I knew what she meant—she was thinking of me having a lover to entertain—but I rather resented that she'd reference the idea in front of her son. The boy hated me enough as it was, and he surely knew what she was getting at as well as I did. It was all a little unfair anyway. For all my reputation as a libertine, I hadn't been with a man in months.

"I don't have any friends," I ended up saying. And that was perfectly true on both the literal level and what I'd meant to convey, though it came out quite a bit more pathetic than I had intended. Still, I am nothing if not swift to recover from social missteps. "But it's no matter. I'll take Zinnia. You'd like to go sailing with me tomorrow, wouldn't you, Zinny?"

Zinny looked up at me from the floor and nodded slowly, like a queen passing solemn judgment. You never knew what you were going to get with Zinny—impish terror or tranquil sage. It varied by the moment. I'd been told this was the way of things with dragon-touched children. Her little upturned face was in some ways like a perfect miniature of mine, but also entirely her own. She never ceased to amaze me.

"Good, then. Perhaps I could come back after dinner to collect her?" I asked Canna. "She can stay at mine tonight so that we can head out in the morning. And I'll make sure to wash her hair before I bring her back."

"Noooo," Zinny objected. She meant about the hair, of course. My daughter would as soon let her hair turn to brambles and invite birds to nest in it, but I saw to it that the wild crown at least got washed and detangled, even if she wouldn't let me do anything else to it. No one in Summer knew how to handle a tight curl such as ours, so I trusted no one but myself to manage her hair for her. I ignored her objection.

Canna agreed to my plan with no trouble, so with a quick kiss for Zinny and an even briefer peck for Canna, I was off.

My dinner engagement was in the Abalone Room, another three levels up, and my legs started to ache by the second stair. That was no doubt another sign of a change, for I was well accustomed to all this trotting up and down the levels of the palace, the vast underground warren built into the cliff face. Twelve levels stood between my rooms and my dragon's sea caves, and I managed that jaunt almost daily. I wondered if I were simply dreading the dinner so much that my body rebelled.

Each quarter, the various high-ranking officers of the Sea Guard and the Home Guard gathered to discuss their state of affairs, and they all absolutely loathed having me there, quite as much as I loathed being there. I couldn't say if the officers had always resented including Lord Summer in their discussions, or if it was just me (or perhaps a healthy dose of both). But what could they do? Claim that the monumentally massive dragon snoozing under the palace was somehow not a relevant factor in the protection and defense of the island?

As for that, well, I had my own doubts whether the dragoness Summer was as reliable a guardian of the land of Summer as most of its denizens liked to imagine. She obviously *could* defend the island from almost any threat, don't mistake me. I'd no doubt she could tear a fleet of ships to pieces as casually as I might swat aside a flock of angry coots. But would she bother? Well, probably. Yes, most likely. It was not much worth worrying about, was it? And certainly not worth talking about, not by me of all people. My role was to make people feel like the dragon was friendly and under control.

The Abalone Room had once been dazzlingly grand to my eyes. A mosaic fashioned of thousands of polished abalone shells formed one continuous image of my dragoness, glittering in iridescent splendor as her sinuous form wound across the walls, the ceiling, and even over the surface of the long stone table. How important I had felt the first time I attended a council in such a room! But that sense of awe had long since given way to the banality of business.

I was the last to arrive and cursed myself for forgetting that these military types are all frightfully punctual. I wasn't truly *late*, not by any civilized standard, but I imagined that they did not take such a charitable view of the matter.

Admiral Rostrum scrutinized me with particular scorn, I thought. A square-jawed, gray-haired, solidly built man, the admiral no doubt had little tolerance for my sort and scarcely made a secret of it. Very little provocation was required to prompt him to expound upon the vital importance of traditional family values to ensure the continued stability and prosperity of Summer, as if all that weren't due to the dragon anyway. If the admiral weren't so damned competent and well-liked, I might have been tempted to throw my weight around for once and force his early retirement. But the admiral knew his business, and truly it was none of mine, so I tolerated him on the occasions we had cause to interact.

As I took my seat at the head of the table, I made my apologies for keeping everyone waiting.

"No doubt you had other important matters to attend to, Lord Summer," Admiral Rostrum observed as he let his gaze wander over my clothes and my perfectly coiled curls. I pretended not to catch his implication and smiled as charmingly as I could manage. Imagine being accused of being too fussy about sartorial matters while actually wearing an ill-fitted jacket.

A great deal of their business remained a mystery to me, so I knew the greater part of wisdom would be to stay silent as much as possible and absorb what I could. It was not always easy for me to abstain from conversation, but it was made simpler that day by my seemingly insatiable appetite. I could scarcely talk with my mouth full, so I ate and listened and ate and listened.

Our military was a bit of a pathetic showing, if I'm to be honest. Half a dozen ships rounded out a fleet whose main function was to chase away pirates and small-time raiders. A sparse land-based militia served even less obvious purpose, but was nevertheless well supplied with all the shiny weapons and smart-looking uniforms they could desire. Considering how unlikely it was that any nation would ever launch a full-scale assault against us and risk engagement with the dragon, this little show of military theater was deemed more than sufficient by most in Summer. But needless to say, these officers took it all very seriously.

On this occasion, they had some vague concerns about cults rising and gaining power in the otherlands, but I'd heard all that before. I'd spent some time in the otherlands myself before becoming Lord Summer, and I well knew the way those types of manias came and went like changing seasons there. The otherlands weren't like Summer—which was steady and predictable and always comfortable—but the general malaise of such places was nothing new and nothing to fuss about.

At some point I became aware that a veritable mountain of empty oyster shells and various crustacean husks had grown in front of me, and it was attracting some curious stares from around the table. Somehow I had consumed enough for five or six men, and the worst of it was that I was still hungry.

I normally have a light appetite, so I had never known this particular mortification before. Fortunately, I was intimately acquainted with so many other forms of embarrassment that I could rise to the occasion with equanimity. I offered only a chagrined shrug to the glances until the evidence could be mercifully cleared away.

The business of the evening wound down, and the officers turned to more casual conversation. Still, it was mainly centered on ships and companies and things that I had little involvement with, so my attention wandered as I sipped my brandy.

"I heard that your son is going to be joining the roster of the *Godwit* before long. You must be quite proud." Captain Grace was speaking to me, without doubt, and yet I had a hell of a time making sense of it. First I had to divine that she must mean Brook, since there was no one else who might reasonably be called my son. Then there was the idea that he was joining the Sea Guard, which was very much news to me.

To cover my obvious surprise, I niggled over a detail. "The *Godwit*? Not the *Avocet*?"

"As far as I am aware, he never approached my mate regarding serving on the *Avocet*," Captain Grace replied cordially—and of course she would know, as it was her ship.

"Ah, well, I must have simply assumed then, seeing as it was his late father's ship and all," I replied. "But then I believe in letting young people manage their own affairs as much as possible."

"I quite agree." Captain Grace smiled at me.

"He'll do well on the *Godwit*." Admiral Rostrum joined the conversation in a genial tone. The *Godwit* was his ship, the flagship of the little fleet. "A fine strapping lad like that ought to flourish once he can live among men and get out from under the skirts of coddling women and . . . others."

That could scarcely be allowed to stand, but must be handled with tact. It would be best to swallow him whole and spit out the bones at leisure. No, no, that wouldn't do at all! But I was already talking. "Oh, yes, I've no doubt that the best way to get a boy to 'man up' is to surround him with sweaty, half-naked men all day and all the night too."

Silence did not so much settle over the gathering as strangle it in its tracks. Captain Grace covered her mouth with her napkin, which might have been covering a chortle. The rest of the table was less ambiguous in their disapprobation. I could recognize when it was time to clear the stage, so I made my excuses and pushed off. I did give the admiral a wink on my way out, just to see his flabbergasted face.

After that minor rout, I needed something to ease my heart before I faced my daughter. It was late for a visit to the tailor, but I thought old Reed might still be at work in his little shop, and it was on the same level of the palace. Besides, it was important to make sure my outfit for the equinox ball would still fit properly in light of recent changes to my person. The shop was closed up, but Tailor Reed opened at my rap and let me in with a cheerful air.

First things first: I explained Lady Canna's hesitations about her dress, and we discussed if it were possible to make it a bit more conservative without spoiling the overall effect. Reed was brilliant about such things and offered several quite sensible suggestions. I told him to do whatever Lady Canna liked best.

I could not keep him from the scent of the true difficulty for long though; Reed perceived at a glance the trouble with my jacket. He took my new measurements with a mournful air. So distraught was he that I began to suspect all his apparent affection for me had more to do with the way my slender frame held clothing than any other virtue of mine. "For once, I had a Summer who was easy to fit," he moaned. "Still, I suppose this isn't so bad yet. You're not going to keep going with it, are you?"

"I've no idea," I told him. "I don't control it."

"Surely you must have some influence with her?" he pleaded.

Now that was touchy territory for a tailor. The whole mystique of being Lord Summer required some, shall we say, finesse on the topic of just how much influence I held over the dragoness.

"Well, you know, it's complicated. Perhaps in my heart I wanted to change. I will endeavor to make clear that this is quite enough though."

"Yes, yes, quite enough. You don't know the struggles I went through with Leo all those years, or with Jack after him."

I wished he hadn't mentioned Jack.

At once I knew that I would find no further comfort in this familiar ritual, and I was eager to be gone. Reed must have sensed my change in mood, for he hurried the remainder of the measurements along and spoke but little more. I thanked Reed for his efforts, apologized more heartily than I ought to have for the inconvenience of changing shape, and headed home. That is, I headed for my wife's home, of course, to collect Zinnia.

While I walked the white stone corridors, I tried once more to reach out to Summer. I knew the dragon was awake now, for I had felt her stir and shift out of her sea caves at sunset as usual. And of course she'd touched my mind at least once at dinner. But she continued to ignore me, and I could only sigh.

My lack of influence over the dragon surely could not be attributed to a general deficit of the Summer scheme, which had been bumping along smoothly for hundreds of years. It must be my own failing. When had there last been a Lord Summer who had come to it in middle years, rather than being born and bred for it? Would I ever be able to form a bond as strong as everyone in Summer seemed to imagine it ought to be? Even in previous times when the line had been broken, my understanding was that the replacement had usually been quite young, and thus perhaps more malleable of mind.

Perhaps I needed to brood more. Previous Summers had been famous brooders—the furrowed brow, the faraway stare, the hunched posture. Surely I could manage that. But no, no, it wouldn't do at all. I looked ridiculous when I attempted it in the mirror. I could pout quite fetchingly, but I had no knack for brooding.

At least Zinnia would be able to get things back on track when her time came. Once she came of age and entered her own contract with Summer, I needn't worry about my own failings anymore. So I had done something right there. I supposed so anyway. I was aware that some places in the world would count it a bad thing to promise your firstborn child to a dragon—most places, actually. But this was Summer.

At Canna's apartment, I asked her about this business of Brook joining the Sea Guard. (The boy was not around.)

"You knew about it," she told me in a decidedly exasperated tone.

"No, I did not! If it was ever mentioned to me, I'm sure it was only as some vague idea that might someday come to pass, not as a course of action already decided."

"He's seventeen. When did you think he would do it? And what else would he do? It was his father's occupation."

She had a point, of course. Summer's obsession with nothing ever changing and everyone following in the family line made it all but inevitable that Brook would join the guard like his late father. Still. "But why the *Godwit* then? Why not the *Avocet*? Captain Grace is a very capable commander, while Admiral Rostrum is . . ." I scarcely knew what I wished to say of the man, except that I did not trust him with Canna's child.

"The flagship is more prestigious, and it's what Brook decided. What do you care anyway?"

There was another fine, solid point. Why did I care? The boy was bound to me only by my sham marriage, initiated for the sole purpose of creating an heir of Summer, which was long done. And surely a solid, normal lad like Brook had nothing to fear from someone like Admiral Rostrum. If he had chosen Rostrum's ship, he likely admired the man, as many did. Perhaps, as the admiral himself had implied, Brook was eager for a more masculine atmosphere, denied to him since his father's death, for I certainly had not sufficed to fill the gap.

No doubt I had simply been embarrassed by not knowing anything about the matter and vexed at being needled by the admiral. That was all.

"I suppose I don't," I replied to Canna. "Is Zinny ready?"

On cue, Zinnia came running out of her room, three cats hurtling after her. I picked her up and tossed her into the air. She squealed in glee, and my heart lifted. I really had done something right with her.

AN EGG

THE WATER WAS CHOPPIER THAN I'D HOPED THE next morning, but Zinnia was undeterred and determined to get out there. What could I do but oblige? Even if we tipped, I had little fear of drowning. Summer could be surprisingly fast to rouse herself, and she moved through water like lightning. If it came to it, a dousing wouldn't be so bad on such a warm day. I was due to reset my curls anyway.

A large white tomcat followed us on to the boat with calm assurance of its reception, and I didn't bother to boot it. I just hoped it knew what it was about. As we got underway, it settled in contentedly near the bow and somehow managed to be in the way at all times.

Zinny laughed as the swells rocked us and the spray hit her face. She asked a million questions about the boat, the sea life we saw, and various meteorological phenomena. I had fewer answers than she might have liked, but she nevertheless seemed to enjoy herself as thoroughly as I might wish. And I suppose I handled the boat adequately enough; Jack had always been the better sailor, but I had learned from him, and I made do.

The views of Summer were as spectacular as always—sheer white cliffs rising out of the sea like walls of cloud. From the water, you'd hardly know what a rich and verdant land lay above the cliffs: a bucolic paradise of fields and orchards unfolding over the rolling hills, complete with cozy villages nestled in the valleys. The island of Summer was as gentle to its people as it was forbidding to outsiders—and all thanks to the bounteous blessings of my dragoness, so they say.

As we sailed past where the palace was inset into the cliff face, I tried to engage Zinny in guessing which windows and balconies belonged to which parts of the interior of the palace, but she had no care for the game. Her big saucer eyes fixed on the jagged openings of the sea caves below.

"Let's go see Summer!" Zinny suggested, or perhaps demanded.

"Of course. When we're back in the palace," I told her.

"No, now!"

"You mean, you want to sail into the sea caves? My darling, that's not possible."

"Yes, it is!" she insisted, clearly annoyed to be contradicted when she felt confident she was correct. "I've seen it lots of times."

This was no doubt information Zinny had gleaned directly from the dragon Summer's memories, though she may or may not have fully understood that. Since she had learned to talk, which had been early and often, she had said things that a little girl couldn't possibly know, but an ancient dragon might. I supposed eventually such children sorted it all out and came to understand which parts of their mind were their own.

In theory, an heir's connection to the dragoness should not be as strong as that of a full contractor like myself. Zinny's link to Summer was merely the price of my contract, not a contract in its own right—not until she made her own commitment to the dragon, thus continuing the cycle for her own firstborn child. Yet Zinnia always seemed to be more in tune with Summer than I was: no doubt further evidence of my own inadequacy.

"The way the waves crash about those sea caves looks frightfully dangerous," I told my daughter. "Aren't you worried we'd be squashed all to jelly?"

"Not if we go in the right way."

"I really rather think we ought to stay out of the sea caves and visit Summer later."

Zinnia looked straight at me in her most unnerving way and said, "She wants us to come *now*."

And then I could feel it too. How had I missed it? All at once it was imperative to sail into the sea caves immediately. In fact, I wanted to. It sounded so fun, so easy. It was the work of a moment to change our direction, and the wind favored us. Of course it did. It was as easy as breathing to bring the little boat right into the mouth of Summer's cave. The cavern's stony embrace was cool and quiet, and reflections of the waves played across the great dome of the ceiling in an endless dance of light.

Zinny pointed out a particular channel, and the next wave pushed us right up onto a little underground beach. The only effort I had to exert was to drag the little boat up out of the reach of the surf once we'd alighted.

Coil upon coil of dragon cluttered the floor of the cavern, rippling like a shimmering silver sea, so one could scarcely tell where her colossal contours began or ended. Zinny scampered barefoot up over the serpentine silver-white form without a moment's hesitation. Of course, I was not scared of Summer either, not anymore. Not much. She was a part of me, after all. How could I be frightened of the physical form of a being that already occupied my mind night and day? I wasn't. Of course not.

I followed Zinny as she unerringly made her way to

where Summer's head rested on her own coils. The dragoness dozed during the day, but her eyelids breached lazily at our approach. The eyes appeared almost completely pale white today, like the moon in a daylight sky.

Any questions I might have put to her died on my lips. One does not simply interrogate a dragon about her ways and her desired ends, at least not this dragon. Looking into her eyes always filled me with an indescribable sort of awe and joy. In ages long gone, her eyes had looked upon marvels and beauties that we no longer know, but it was all there still, in her memory, and would be for ages hence. Long after my bones are dust, so shall I be there, with Jack and with Zinny too.

"Look, Daddy!" Zinny called to me, pointing at something.

An egg nestled in a hollow amidst Summer's coils. Its presence was astonishing, for I was sure I had never heard of such a thing occurring in all of Summer's past, not as long as we had records to tell, and my limited sense of Summer's mind did not lead me to think our records spoke false. Never before had she produced an egg, not in all her centuries.

The egg looked small there, next to Summer, but it was big enough to hold a creature the size of a bloodhound. As Zinny climbed down beside it to look it over, the egg dwarfed her easily. At first glance it appeared filmy and insubstantial, like the surface of a soap bubble, but under my fingertips it was as hard as any of Summer's scales. Thinking of a little hatchling coming forth out into the world made me grin like a fool. The egg was stunning and precious, and I was overwhelmed with protectiveness for it.

And it needed to be disposed of.

What? That was not my thought at all, and so much was it in discord with my native state of mind that it made me dizzy. I sat down on Summer and tried to sort it out.

At this point I should perhaps say a word or two about how Summer communicates with her contractors. Many assume that it is like a voice in my head, not so different from hearing a friend's voice out loud, which plainly belongs to another entity and could not be confused for one's own thoughts. It is not. Summer's mind was entangled with my own, and her thoughts were as much a part of me as my own—or rather, if she wished them to be? I was not entirely sure how much she was in control of the process, for I certainly did not feel that I was.

Take the example from dinner the night before. If I look at Admiral Rostrum and think to myself that I would like to swallow him whole and spit out his bones, it is safe to say that some part of that thought is originating with the dragoness, for obvious reasons. Yet what is Admiral Rostrum to the dragon but another puny little figure striding a wooden deck out on the sea? She has no reason to hate the admiral except that I hate him. So it is my thought too that brings us to the conclusion that the admiral would best serve the world as a light snack before moving on to more pleasant matters.

As far as I understand it, the more time we spend together, the more intertwined it all becomes, and there's no end to it. If I were to die tomorrow, Summer would most likely still hate the admiral, and she would still love any that I loved. That was of course how I ended up here in the first place. When Jack had been Lord Summer, he had loved me—so I had been told, that he must have truly loved me—and thus Summer had loved me. And when Jack had died without giving her an heir, Summer had wanted me when she wanted no one else.

Thus all the land of Summer was stuck with me, however inadequate a lord they might think me. That was of course the third part of the triad, the part I understood the least. Summer is Summer is Summer, so they say, and I could see well enough how the lord and the lizard approach being one and the same. But what of the land? I loved Summer, a jewel amidst the sea, the only place I had ever truly called home. But I felt no differently toward the land and its people than I ever had. The forests and fields had gained no new charms for me. No mystical bond had grown between me and its often obnoxiously insular inhabitants.

I have strayed from my point again. Where was I? Right, so there was this beautiful, precious egg before me, and Summer felt that it must be disposed of. I let the thought unfold in my mind.

Procreation had never been an appealing end. To give life was to be beholden to that life, and such an unpayable debt in both directions held a sort of horror beyond reckoning. Far better to be clear in one's obligations and contracts. For long I'd lived perfectly contentedly without ever thinking of breeding, until I had been obliged to it. But Zinny had turned out to be such a blessing—no, wait, that was my own thoughts slipping in again.

Summer did not regard the egg as a blessing, and she had no intention of interrogating her own thoughts on the matter. For someone who had lived a hundred lives or more through her contractors, she remained remarkably rigid when she wished to be. It was plain to me now that this egg was the result of something that must have occurred during that business seven years earlier when a horde of singing drakes had descended upon the island for a spell. Summer was evidently not pleased with the reminder of that time and all that had come with it.

"Well, what do you want me to do about it?" I complained aloud. "If you want it gone, can't you simply pick it up and drop it to the bottom of the sea?"

A deep well of rage opened in me, and I squeezed my eyes closed as if to shut it out. Of course that did nothing, and I had to live with the emotions burning through me for as long as she wished to subject me to them. Anger was not the only thing there, of course, but the sadness and fear and horror and regret were all near-drowned by the crushing roar of it—anger at the nobles for their stupidity, at the drakes for besting her, but most of all at Jack. I little wished to dwell upon Summer's judgments concerning Jack; I pushed the thoughts away and at last rejected Summer's barrage of fervor.

"What's wrong?" Zinny asked.

I almost snarled at her to leave me alone, but I swallowed that back and tried to recenter my mind on my own thoughts and feelings. "Ah, well, I'm not sure what Summer wants me to do with this egg. She's . . . a bit conflicted. Do you feel it?"

Zinny shook her head. That was a relief at least. I scarcely thought my five-year-old daughter was ready to handle such feelings. I scarcely thought I was ready to handle them. "What's wrong with the egg?" she asked.

"Nothing. The egg itself is fine, I'm sure. But she doesn't want it. It brings up memories that she would as soon forget, and she never planned for such a thing. But she doesn't want it destroyed either."

The furrows on Zinny's little brow revealed that she was thinking very hard about the matter. It was adorable. "We should take it away, but keep it safe."

That seemed reasonable enough. Let Summer calm down without the reminder in front of her, and give me some time to think it over. I nodded. "There are other sea caves, smaller than this one. Shall we take it to one of those and hide it?"

Zinny approved, so we set to work. Or rather I set to work, since Zinny couldn't hope to help with shifting the egg. Was this why Summer wanted me stronger? To lift heavy things for her? Certainly I needed the extra help. The egg must have been well over half my own weight, and even with rolling it part of the way, I was hard put to lug it onto the boat. Once it was loaded, I began to fear for the vessel's seaworthiness with the two of us as well.

The white tomcat apparently shared my concerns, for after watching me struggle to move the egg, it unceremoniously abandoned our party. With a swish of its fluffy tail, it turned around and headed deeper into the cavern, no doubt aware that it could make its way back to the palace on the inside of the cliffs. It occurred to me that the animal had a point.

"Zinny, maybe you ought to head back home by the usual way, up the stairs," I suggested to her. "I'm loath to overload the boat, and I can handle getting the egg somewhere safe by myself."

She considered, nodded, then skipped off after the cat. One less thing to worry about then.

"And don't tell anyone about the egg!" I shouted after her. Could she keep a secret? I had no idea, but it would no doubt help that it was Summer's secret. The dragon would have her own ways of keeping our mouths shut.

WITH A GREAT DEAL of swearing and sweating, I managed to complete the necessary task and get the egg settled in a small, unobtrusive cave along a particularly inhospitable stretch of cliff. I noted a twisted tree on top of the cliff as a landmark to find the place again. The only casualties were to my wardrobe, as the jagged rocks of the cave snagged viciously on the delicate fabric of my shirt.

The lads on the docks gave me some funny looks as I returned the boat, but I was well enough acquainted with stares to give it little thought. It was only when I was halfway back up to my rooms that it occurred to me what they were thinking. I had set sail with my young daughter in the morning and returned alone with torn clothes and no mention of her absence. But of course they hadn't dared to question me on it. Oh, well. They'd learn soon enough that little Lady Zinnia was still very much alive and well.

But that brought me to another consideration. When I'd sent Zinny up the stairs alone, it had seemed only sensible that it was much safer than returning to the choppy seas in an overloaded sailboat. She knew the route through the caverns and vaults very well, and I'd had no doubt she'd be fine. Yet on reflection, it occurred to me that some might not regard it as the epitome of parental judgment to send a five-year-old alone through catacombs filled with vermin and human remains.

I had told her to go home. Would she have gone to my apartment or Canna's? I scarcely liked to contemplate what Canna would think of her returning alone. And if Zinny had heeded my enjoinder to keep the egg a secret, she would not even be able to account for why I had done so.

The worst of it was that Canna would *not* give me an earful about it. We would not have it out and say all kinds of unpleasant things we didn't mean. We would not dig up ancient arguments to accuse the other of having done far worse at one point or another. And we would not tearfully make up and admit that we were both just worried about our daughter. That was what real husbands and wives did. Canna would probably just give me a look, shake her head, and I would go back to my own suite alone.

But it never came to any of that. When I got back to my apartment, Zinny waited for me with her usual gaggle of feline companions, and she assured me that no one was the wiser. What a marvel she was.

Unfortunately, her loyalty was paid back with the cruelest betrayal she could conceive, for I made good on my threat to wash and detangle her hair. Many tears were shed and recriminations cast in my direction. I made no headway at all on my continued campaign to convince her to let me braid it. She only cheered up when I allowed her to help with washing and twisting my hair. I believe she took a sort of vengeful glee in imagining the process was as torturous for me as it was for her.

After all ablutions were finally complete, we snuggled in quite cozily together in my bed. Normally having Zinnia with me helped me to feel content and fall asleep, but on this occasion I found myself restless and uneasy at heart.

As much as I tried to banish it from my thoughts, the egg returned to my mind over and over. Why had Summer entrusted it to me? What did she think I ought to do with it? Such an unprecedented event in Summer's history represented a more weighty responsibility on my shoulders than I quite liked. And even apart from all that, the egg itself tugged at me, nagging at my thoughts and occupying my dreams.

Indeed, my dreams took strange shapes and brought me to corners of Summer I was sure I had never been in waking life, fixating on small matters I had never consciously given any mind to. I dreamt myself a shepherd anxious for a sickly lamb, rubbing the tiny creature's limbs against the cold. Then I was a weaver woman fat with child, struggling to reach the loom over my swollen belly. Were these moments a manifestation of my apprehension over my new responsibility for the egg? Or perhaps a sign of guilt that I was not taking enough care with the everyday business of Summer? I could not say.

Thus I slept fitfully that night without much in the way of true rest—which made it all the more disconcerting to be woken by Admiral Rostrum banging on my door.

A FAMILY MAN

CONSIDERING THE UNGODLY HOUR, I ASSUMED THE knock at the door must be from Canna wanting to check on Zinny. It was nothing unusual for me to keep Zinny for days together, but she may have heard something about me returning from sailing alone that would worry her. As such, I barely shrugged on a dressing gown and didn't even bother to remove my hair covering as I blearily opened the door.

The sight of Admiral Rostrum was sobering, for his presence at my door could only reasonably be explained by some sort of urgent situation threatening the island. Certainly the admiral had never called on me at home before. He looked me over with apparent confusion. "You were still sleeping?"

I gestured him in but ignored the question, since the answer was quite obvious. Before I became Lord Summer, I had maintained a more regular if lackluster acquaintance with the hours immediately following sunrise, but it had been years since I'd felt much inclination to renew the connection.

Zinny peered out from my bedroom, and I said to her, "Why don't you run over to your mother's rooms for now, darling? I'll come see you later."

"My apologies, Summer," said the admiral as he watched her dash away. "I did not mean to intrude."

"It's quite alright, and there's no need for pleasantries, Admiral." I sat down and began to unwind the scarf from my head. "Please, tell me what's going on."

The admiral stared at me in a most unsettling way. I knew I must look a fright, unshaven and half-dressed, but surely he had more important things on his mind? "You go by Teddy, don't you?" he asked.

Not what I expected. "With my *friends*, yes." I acknowledged my given name with unambiguous emphasis.

But the admiral didn't seem to pay much mind to that. "You know, I was surprised that you spoke of expanding the military the other day."

Had I said that? It was true that I was often anxious about how much Summer relied upon the dragon for its defense, so I very well might have dropped such a comment. My tongue gets ahead of me sometimes.

"Most Summers are quite obstinate that it's not necessary," the admiral continued. "But it's long been a goal of mine to see more investment in our defense. Such a rich nation as we should have a mighty fleet at our disposal. Think what we could do then!"

I had no notion what he thought we might do then, but his tone uneasily gave me the impression that he was thinking of expansion and subjugation, not mere defense.

"Of course the trouble, besides allocating the funds, is with recruitment," he went on. "The supply of young men is never what it ought to be, what with the birthrate problems on the island. Even allowing women into the ranks has only just managed to fill out our current rolls, and surely no one could deny that it hurts us in the long run. How are we ever to get the birthrate up if the young women are out on ships instead of at home with husbands where they belong?"

"The fecundity situation in Summer has been unchanged for hundreds of years," I pointed out. "I doubt that restricting women to their homes would cause them to suddenly start popping out more babies."

The admiral seemed unconvinced. "Hmm, well, I wasn't really suggesting we stop allowing women to enlist anyway. As I said, we need more souls in the military, not less. The other option, of course, is otherlanders. They're tricky though, as most of them are not very inclined to hard work by nature." He continued to expound upon the flaws of otherlanders and the methods by which he thought they might be compelled to work harder. None of his methods seemed to involve positive inducements.

If I hadn't heard it all for myself, it might have been difficult to credit that the admiral could sit in my chamber, look me in the face—my quite obviously foreign face—and say such things. Nor did he even seem to think he said anything remarkable! There were any number of things I might have liked to say back, but I realized that would only prolong the conversation, and the more pressing question rising in my mind was why we were having it.

"Forgive me, Admiral," I cut him off, "but is this what you came here to talk about? I had rather thought there must be some sort of emergency."

"Oh," he said, and looked a bit abashed. He stared at me in that strange way again, and then to my alarm, he started to babble. "Well, as for that, I know you and I haven't always seen eye to eye, but I got to thinking, well,.thinking that maybe we ought to work more closely. I saw you in that sailboat yesterday, you know, and I thought you did quite well handling it. Very impressive! We have more common ground than you might think, I should say. Though I do apologize again for disturbing you this morning. I didn't know you'd be . . . indisposed."

His gaze lingered then on the open neck of my dressing gown, and I abruptly understood. I felt a fool for missing it, honestly, except that I loathed the man so much that I'd assumed the feeling was entirely mutual. You would think I'd have learned never to underestimate the hypocrisy of such a fatuous jackass. Or my own charms.

Had the admiral taken my behavior at the dinner as a sort of invitation? I swear people let their ideas about me run rampant in their own imaginations, regardless of what I actually say or do. And they should know by now that I flirt with everyone; it's not meant to be serious. Taken from a purely aesthetic view, the admiral was not an unattractive man, if one went for rugged, rough-hewn features and a broad, bulky build (which, of course, I did). But the repugnance of his soul quite overwhelmed such considerations—or at any rate, it ought to have.

The dragon surged in me, but I tried to shove her down. She always tended to assert herself at times when I felt agitated or threatened, and the heat of her vehemence burned so hot it made it hard to focus. She had her own notions of what I ought to do in any given situation, but I knew I should handle this in my own way.

I stood up, and the admiral stood too. He came towards me, and it took everything in me to fight the urge to strike out and bite at him, as the dragoness would be likely snap up any impudent drakes who tried their luck with her. So instead I just stood there as he grabbed the back of my neck, pulled me in, and shoved his mouth against mine. The sharp bristle of his whiskers scraped at my face, and the musky smell of him filled my senses.

Now, I want to make one thing very clear. I have no wish to duck responsibility for any of my actions by blaming them on the dragon. In this case, it's true that without her interference, I might have done better at evading that—well, I hesitate to call it a kiss, but I suppose I must. But that is as far as it goes.

Nor was it too late to extricate myself, not at all. Naturally the admiral would never have attempted to force the thing. He may have been an ass, but he was not imbecile enough to attack his superior, and he was not suicidal so far as I knew. Any show of violence against me would be met with a swift and zealous form of draconic justice that was likely to overshoot the eye-for-an-eye principle by a wide margin.

All this is to say that it was me—my choice and no one else's. I can't say I'm unashamed, but I will own it. Why, you might ask? Surely almost anyone else would make a more suitable lover, you are no doubt thinking? Well, since Jack's death, I had tried other lovers—nice, charming men with perfect bodies who were only too happy to fall into bed with Lord Summer. I had felt nothing for them, and it did nothing for me but to open a great nothing in my soul. Loathing is a poor substitute for love, but it is *something*.

Yet I think that if the admiral had come to me the day before, I would have turned him away as I ought to have. Some restlessness had stirred in me, a feeling growing and unfurling since I'd found that egg in Summer's cavern. For no reason I could define, I now felt hemmed in by the staid routine that my life had become, endlessly trapped playing a role I could not quite pull off. The admiral's rough and rude handling of me perhaps promised a comforting return to the role I was meant for, and I responded to it in spite of myself.

Summer was all attention for this assignation, which was new to me. In the past, I had suspected that she had, well, assisted me when it came to conceiving an heir, if you know what I mean, but I had never detected her presence in my other forays at coupling. Now I suspected that she had simply been too bored with my lackluster lovemaking to bother with paying heed. It was quite different with the admiral. Summer was like an echo chamber in a way, taking my passion, letting it resonate through her, and passing it back to me tenfold. The resulting intensity was unlike anything I'd ever felt.

When it was done with, I was inclined to kick the admiral out straight away, but he was too obviously flushed and sweaty to turn loose on the palace. So I had to let him stay there while I shaved and took my hair out of the twists. The admiral watched me closely throughout, which was deeply unsettling and unwelcome. I thought it could scarcely be more uncomfortable, but then he started talking.

"You ought not to live here by yourself," he instructed me quite authoritatively. "It's not healthy for a man."

"I don't. Lady Zinnia is here half the time."

"Your daughter? No, that's not what I mean. The way I see it, just because you have needs that can't be met in your marriage, it doesn't mean you should hold yourself apart like this. You need to recommit to your wife and live as a family."

"I don't suppose it matters what she thinks of the idea?"

He scoffed. "Why should a woman object to having her man at home? It's the natural way of things, isn't it? I'm sure she'd like having another little one underfoot too, before her bearing years are over. You managed the first one quickly enough—quite impressive, really! You might try for a son this time."

"Thank you for the advice, Admiral."

"You know, my friends call me Ros."

"How nice for them."

The dryness of my responses did little to deter the admiral, and I began to suspect that he did not quite understand sarcasm. Indeed it made me question whether I had perhaps misinterpreted any number of his comments over the years. Remarks I had taken for subtle jabs at me might have been more genuine than I realized. This revelation did nothing to improve my opinion of the man.

His manner was rather more at ease than I might have anticipated for the circumstances; it would seem he was scarcely new to such pursuits. Yet perhaps that was not wholly surprising. Most in Summer did not count it significantly more debauched for a man to spend time in other men's beds than to frequent the beds of women who were not his lawful wife. And now that I thought about it, I could not recall the admiral ever being quite so specific in his disapprobation of dissolute lifestyles. His hypocrisy perhaps had *some* bounds.

An orange cat jumped up on the bed, and the admiral frowned and moved as if to shoo it off. I caught his wrist. "The cat can stay. You're leaving." We briefly agreed that if questioned, we would say that we had been discussing a possible scheme to expand the military. And if he wished to come again, he would make an appointment for a reasonable hour. The admiral already seemed keen on another rendezvous, and I confess I was not wholly indifferent myself.

At least I would be able to count on the admiral's discretion, I thought. I rather doubted that his wife and grown sons were fully informed of his views on the prerogatives of a family man. Nor did I think he would much relish the thought of his colleagues and subordinates learning of his proclivities. So at the time, it was some comfort to think that no one would ever find out.

WITH THAT ORDEAL OVER, the egg returned to the fore of my thoughts. It was growing on my mind, I felt, worming its way through me, nudging me to do something. I little knew whether that was merely my imagination or an actual phenomenon, since it seemed at least conceivable that a dragon's powers to infiltrate the mind could begin in the egg. It occurred to me I might be better equipped to decide what to do about the egg if I knew more about dragon reproduction and dragon hatchlings.

Loremasters of Summer could no doubt provide exhaustive knowledge about such topics, but if I sought their wisdom, I feared I would tip my hand. I felt quite sure that

Summer did not wish for the people of Summer to know about the egg yet, if ever, and any mention of an egg would be sure to attract a good deal of attention, seeing as Summer had never before produced an egg.

That left only the library.

On my way, I pondered whether the admiral might have something in the vicinity of a point regarding Canna. Not the way he put it, of course, but I had long suspected that she had come to regret our arrangement. She had been so practical about the matter when I first proposed it to her, but after six years, the reality no doubt had begun to tell. Perhaps the approach of the end of her "bearing years," as the admiral had so obnoxiously put it, might indeed be weighing on her. Even if Canna had all the children she wanted, it must be a difficult time for a woman, to see the possibilities of life shrink before her. It would make anyone more reflective of the lot life had offered them.

In selecting a wife, I had been quite intentional in choosing a mature woman who had already been married and experienced a good bit of life. I had insisted upon it, in fact, as various nobles attempted to advance the idea that I ought to marry Jack's much-younger half sister for the sake of continuity to the previous line: a notion that horrified me on more levels than I liked to contemplate. Canna had seemed a much wiser choice, and I had felt some affinity in that she also was bereaved of her first love, the much-esteemed and well-lauded Captain Ash. I had imagined that age and experience might make the situation easier to accept. But when it comes down to it, I suppose no one is truly ready to give up on love and happiness and the life they truly want.

I arrived at the library with no small amount of apprehension. I was acquainted with the layout of the library from when Jack and I used to play hide-and-seek among the stacks there as children, but that was about as far as my understanding went. All those rows and rows of books felt intimidating now. I wandered down an aisle and frowned at all the gilded spines with their glittering titles.

"Teddy?"

I was so unaccustomed to being called by my name that for an instant I feared that the admiral had somehow followed me there, though the voice was nothing like his. I spun about to find that Brook had come up behind me. My stepson was one of the few who might use my name, though I could not recall the last time he had addressed me at all.

Loose strands of hair framed his face in defiance of the sloppily fastened hair tie, and his little wire-rimmed reading glasses perched awkwardly on the bridge of his nose. The spectacles had suited him well enough as a boy, but looked faintly ridiculous on the tall, broad-shouldered young man standing before me.

"Oh, hello," I greeted him. "I'm just having a look around."

"Is someone hurt?" Brook asked earnestly.

"Hurt? Why would someone be hurt?"

"You're in the section on medicines and herbals."

"Oh! No, I was just looking around."

"So you said." He took me in with a narrowed gaze. "Are you sure everything's alright?"

"Of course it is." His scrutiny flustered me, and I felt it was time to turn things around on him. "And what are you doing here?"

"I come here all the time," Brook said, "to read about history. I've never seen you in here before though."

"History? What, the history of Summer? I'd have thought it rather boring, what with the dragon preventing anything from ever happening or changing."

"There's more to it in the details than you'd think," Brook said. "But I'm actually more interested in the otherlands, only there's not much about them here."

"You've never asked me about the otherlands," I pointed out. He surely knew I'd spent over a decade away from Summer, traveling the otherlands with Jack, and thus would be better informed than most on the island.

"Oh, well, I . . ."

This was the perfect time to eel away. He would not question a sudden departure while he himself was eager to be free of the conversation. But instead I kept talking.

"Is that why you want to join the Sea Guard, to see other places?"

"I suppose so. I know they don't usually stray far from Summer, but at least they see otherlanders and interact with them."

"And kill them."

I don't know why I said that. I suppose I meant it as a sort of joke, but how would it be funny to someone actually embarking on that path? Instantly I could see Brook stiffen and pull back from whatever sort of tenuous connection we had established.

"And what's so wrong with that?" he asked, indignant in the way that only the young could be. "If they attack us, what else are we to do? Don't they deserve to suffer the consequences?"

"Oh, yes, quite. I know there's no real alternative. Though as for what they 'deserve,' I scarcely think I can say. A lot of people out there are hungry."

"You mean, hungry for riches and power?"

I stared at my stepson and for a moment wondered how I had missed that he was an idiot. But I had to remind myself that he was young and that he had never left Summer. Even in my own rather chaotic childhood in Summer, I generally had more or less enough to eat. Brook had probably never even conceived of going to bed hungry. Yet he would scarcely appreciate a lecture on the less fortunate.

"That's not *exactly* what I meant." I hastened to change the subject. "Say, you wouldn't happen to know where the books on dragons are?"

Now Brook looked at me like I was the idiot. Turnabout is fair play, I suppose. "It's that whole wing over there," he said, pointing.

"Oh, I see. Yes, I suppose the enormous stone dragon sculptures do offer a bit of a hint, don't they?" I edged away, though I could not shake the feeling that Brook continued to watch me.

There I found lots of books, so many books, more books than anyone could possibly read in a lifetime. It was hard to believe there could possibly be so much to say about dragons. Before wandering that wing, I had felt that I pretty much knew the essentials about dragons, but clearly I must have been missing a few details.

The basics of dragon life and reproduction were, of course, well known to me. A dragoness would continue to grow in size and power for the entirety of her life, which had no natural end as far as we were aware. She would establish herself in a place that suited her, hoard whatever baubles pleased her fancy, and enjoy the fear and respect of all passersby. A drake, on the other hand, would never grow much larger than a draft horse, and his life was likely to be brutish and short. Without a fixed abode, he would wander the world upon the wing as something of a minor menace, until mischance or mating put an end to it.

A drake seldom survived his attempts to mate, and his only chance of accomplishing it was to woo the much larger dragoness into the mood with a unique mating song. If his melodic efforts failed to impress, the drake would be best advised to make a swift departure and take to wing if he did not wish to satisfy any of his lady's other appetites.

If any eggs resulted from the match, my understanding

was that the dragoness would guard them zealously while they remained in the shell. Only after they hatched would she force the hatchlings away from her sight to make their own way in the world. However, it would seem I must in some way be mistaken about that, or that Summer was behaving in an atypical fashion, for she was not guarding her egg. She had turned it over into my keeping instead. That seemed like the most important thing to understand.

A feline librarian spotted me as it rounded on patrol, but continued on with its own cat business. Moments later, however, a human librarian appeared, almost as if the cat had alerted him to my presence (though I'm sure that's ridiculous). The librarian fussed around me a good deal and struggled to conceal his vexation that I would not be more specific on what I was looking for. He assured me several times that librarians have some sort of code of discretion, but I persevered in my secrecy.

Eventually I managed to select a few volumes that appeared most closely related to the topic of reproduction and took them with me back to my rooms. I set them down by my preferred chair, where they made quite a pretty little stack with their fine leather bindings and gilded spines. I read nothing that evening though.

The stirrings of a black mood began to nudge at me, such as I had not felt in some time, and I found myself more inclined towards ruminations on the past as I sipped my wine. The conversation with Brook had set me to thinking of my childhood and how I had often scrounged and scavenged for food all around the countryside.

Such was the bounty of Summer that few had objected to an urchin like myself filching a few plums from their orchards, poaching rabbits from their fields, or even hooking trout from their streams. Most people in Summer were quite kind to me as a child, and now that I can see my features replicated in little

Zinnia, I count it little wonder. I must have been an angelic creature, and my precocious manners readily charmed all but the most stubborn disapprovers. Most looked with an indulgent eye on my trespasses and scavenging, often adding a gift of an extra sweet or a cast-off toy of their own volition.

With my scrounged contributions supplementing Alice's income, most of the time there was plenty for both of us. I can recall only one stretch of time when things felt lean: the summer when Alice was pregnant, which would have been when I was about twelve. Alice couldn't work in her condition, except at small handicrafts in the home, and she did not excel at those. So we had very little in the way of money that summer, for Alice refused to let me work so young, and I wasn't getting any money from Jack yet.

At the time, I was determined that Alice should get as much as she needed of everything, to be certain that the baby would thrive. I frequently begged off the food we had with the claim of having little appetite, though it was far from the truth. I was still growing and could have eaten quite voraciously. Yet despite being often hungry, in some ways I count that summer as one of the happiest and most carefree in my life.

I recall one evening in particular when we sat together by the hearth of our little cottage, which was on the outskirts of the village nearest the palace. While Alice spun yarn, I was engaged in attempting to mend a pair of shoes that had come to a sad state. Alice had warned me not to buy them, for they were more fashionable than practical, and she predicted that I would regret it when they fell apart. I had not heeded the warning, and yet I stubbornly refused to regret. As I puzzled over the detached soles, Alice laughed softly into her spinning and shook her head. I stuck out my tongue at her and persisted with a pout.

I was already adept at repairing and adjusting clothing, especially at reworking other people's castoffs to match the current fashions. More than once, folk had failed to recognize their own discarded clothes when they saw me sporting them at the village festivals and would wonder aloud at how I came by such fine things. But shoes presented a greater challenge, what with my limited supplies and Alice's complete lack of sympathy for my struggle.

As she became more obviously bored and frustrated with her own task, however, Alice's attention wandered back to me. She told me that she'd happened into a conversation with a midwife who had declared quite confidently that the way she carried presaged that she was certain to have a girl.

"Good!" I replied heartily. "We wouldn't want some beastly, dirty boy, would we?"

Alice laughed. "If boys are so beastly, what does that make you, little brother?" She called me "brother" sometimes, but do not imagine there was any deceit or misunderstanding in the matter. I always knew she was my mother.

"I—" I began but paused for dramatic effect, as such flourishes were already in my repertoire, "am one of a kind. But you mustn't hope to be so lucky a second time."

"I'm not sure one person could handle so much of such luck," Alice parried with a smirk.

"Exactly."

"A girl would be nice," Alice agreed. "Though I suppose she's not likely to have a happy time of it, any more than you or I."

"But we are happy," I said absently, still focused on my task.

Alice looked on me with a smile, which threatened to turn sad but instead veered towards the mischievous.

As I held up a bit of leather that I thought might do for a new sole against my bare foot, Alice tickled it, and she laughed as I shrieked in protest. I retaliated by tickling her armpit, and she readily dropped her spinning to flee the attack. We ended up on the bed, which we shared, laughing and shrieking in turn until we fell into an exhausted heap.

Despite what many might think, I do count myself as having had a happy childhood, free in my roamings and secure in the affection between Alice and me. But it could not last forever, and that summer was perhaps the end of those pleasant days, though I little knew it at the time.

That fall, the baby was born dead—a boy, in fact, though I did not hold that against him. I buried him under my favorite willow tree, which had often been a refuge for me. I hoped it would bring comfort to him too. Alice named him Lucky, and she said it was for the best that he didn't live. Perhaps she was right, though I wondered why this little tragedy should have to befall us, when so many other babes in Summer were born hale and whole. Or why Alice should have had to suffer through the horrors of pregnancy at all, when so few women of Summer bore more children than their families desired and had use for.

Never again did I feel that our little household was so cheerful as that summer. Most likely, however, the stillbirth was only a final marker of the era coming to an end, not the cause at all. That was the last summer in which I felt like a child, or perhaps I should say the last summer in which people treated me as a child, for I felt no strong shift within myself so much as I saw it in other's eyes. My childish beauty transformed into something more dangerous and subversive, and with it, the kindness and indulgence to which I had become accustomed cooled. My old tricks failed me, and I would have to learn new ways to charm people, with much less certainty of success.

As for Alice, I think it likely that her childlike manner in this time was only a mirror of my own. Briefly she was given the chance to live out a second childhood through me, after her own had been cut short by my arrival. But when I grew up, at last she had to put aside childish things for good.

A BUSY WEEK

NOBLES FROM AROUND SUMMER BEGAN TO ARRIVE for the equinox, and quite a few would count it an insult if I did not greet them or show my face at various preliminary festivities. Thus my days were filled with flitting around to this group or that, with quite a wide variance of enjoyment out of the engagements.

Many of the nobles liked me well enough at this point. They recognized that I had settled down from the more brazen excesses of my youth, and they could allow that I was an affable enough fellow. Some even considered me a refreshing change of pace from the normally brooding and serious line of Summers. Older women in particular were easily charmed, since I shamelessly flattered them and flirted with them. I've always loved to flirt, so long as it doesn't mean anything.

On the other hand, a few of the stuffier and more self-important nobles gave the distinct impression that they still called me a whore as soon as my back was turned (or even not quite!). Yet they nevertheless expected me to make time for them. Everyone in Summer wanted to be known by Summer if at all possible. How else could they feel that the blessings and bounty of the dragoness Summer would visit upon their lands and their people?

But even these sort let it be known that they appreciated my more hands-off approach to the role of Lord Summer. I knew that many previous Summers had taken a much more active part in the day-to-day management of the island, but I could scarcely see how I might improve upon the nobles' judgments in dealing with their own lands. I preferred to restrain myself to the core of my role: being a liaison to the dragoness and fulfilling a ceremonial position for the people. The last thing I desired was to get in anyone's way.

Among the arrivals were Canna's parents from their villa on the north shore. As social obligations go, they were usually easy to manage. I simply brought Zinny along and let her entertain her grandparents for me. Canna was their only child—a common enough circumstance in Summer, regardless of preference or effort—so they had been delighted to gain this unexpected second grandchild. Canna's mother was usually fairly chatty, if a bit scatterbrained, and I could fill the time with talk of what Zinny had been up to.

On this occasion, however, Canna's mother begged off with a claim of being unwell, so I was left with her more laconic father. Thankfully, they had brought with them a gift of libations from the fruit of their renowned vineyards, which I eagerly sampled during the visit. One has to be polite, you know. Effusiveness in praise of these lovely gifts came easily and perhaps smoothed things over a bit.

The books I'd taken from the library remained in their tidy little stack all that week, giving me a jolt of guilt every time I glimpsed them on my way in or out of the apartment. Why had I even bothered to collect them? I knew I would not read them, at least not while I was so busy. Yet the egg still nudged at my thoughts, still pecked at the edges of my mind when I laid down to sleep. I promised myself that when the equinox was over and the nobles began to return home, I would attack the problem afresh.

Of course I did not neglect to make time for Summer herself in that week. The dragoness became quite cross if I went too long without seeing her, and any excuses about human engagements simply would not do. I had the sense she was ever on the lookout that I might abandon her altogether, as she felt Jack had done, and if I went two days together without a visit to her cavern, her suspicions grew. Her suspicions could take very strange shape and character, so it was best not to rouse them to begin with.

Now this is not to say that she desired anything in particular of me. The important thing was that I was there. She liked to have me where she could see me with her own eyes and touch me with her own claws. It comforted her, and that was, after all, my most vital role in Summer—to keep the monster content. Sometimes I worked on my hair. Sometimes I spoke to her of whatever was on my mind, or I composed dreadful verses in honor of her beauty. Sometimes I talked of Jack.

She liked music, which suited me. Summer was at that time my sole audience for playing and singing, except the occasional lullaby for Zinny of course, for I found it perfectly dreadful to play for a human crowd as Lord Summer. The nobles all felt the need to fawn over me with obsequious praise, a tiresome charade that didn't touch my vanity. I knew perfectly well I was a middling musician, competent enough on the lute to play passably and let the expressiveness of my voice carry it off, for I have a decent range and a genuine joy in music. Summer, on the other hand, expressed the proper level of disdain for my skill married to appreciation for my natural charms that made it an easy pleasure to play for her. She preferred sentimental ballads.

If I felt disinclined to play, then I simply lounged in her presence, basked in her beauty. In my blacker moods, I was silent. I leaned against her, drank wine out of the bottle, and I stared up at the cavern ceiling. The stalactites continually dripped, dripped, dripped down towards their stalagmite mates below. For a thousand years they might continue to reach out at every moment of the day, growing just a tiny bit closer with every drop, and yet most of them would never meet.

The admiral too paid me more visits that week—in the evenings, thankfully—and I cannot deny I began to look forward to his visits. With Summer's support, my endurance and capacity for repeated efforts seemed to have no limits, and I found myself keen for things I'd never had much taste for before. The admiral proved to be game for almost anything if he thought it would please me.

It was, of course, increasingly difficult to ignore that the admiral was fully smitten with me. I wondered if it had anything to do with the dragon's glamour, which I had heard could make people more easily enamored with contractors. Yet even if that were the root cause, I knew the feelings would be no less real. On one hand, I felt I ought to put an end to it for the admiral's sake. But on the other hand, it wasn't as though I even liked the man. What did I care if I broke his raisiny little heart? If ever I began to feel guilty about it, then every time the admiral spoke, it made it that much easier to bear.

Yet as satisfying as those encounters were, when the admiral left, I always seemed to sink back into my black moods, which were coming on more and more often now. Like the rain making its way back to the sea, my thoughts turned to Jack.

It was strange to think that Summer had been there with Jack all those years as she now was with me. He'd told me as much, of course, many years ago when we were both lads of about fifteen or sixteen. He meant it as a sort of warning, I suppose, in case the idea of the dragon's presence made me too uncomfortable and I wanted to back out of going to bed with him. Fat chance of that.

I was wild about Jack for years before we became lovers, and to have the chance to be with him had seemed a boon beyond all reasonable expectation. For long I'd had no notion that he saw me as anything but a childish playmate, to whom he bestowed his kindness in the spirit of charity and nostalgia. I knew no better until the very moment he kissed me, though I suppose he must have known my feelings all along. Certainly he was confident in his reception as he pulled me in for the kiss, if not in how to continue from there. That was alright though, for I knew what to do. I remember everything about that first time with him—not particularly good, of course, but so sweet and precious in its way. I know it was Jack's first time, and it pleased me inordinately to see his shy delight in it.

Afterward I went home and promptly told Alice all about it—eccentric, I know, but such was the nature of our relationship, so much more like close siblings than mother and son. I expected her to be pleased for me, as I was so pleased, but instead she was somber and perhaps a little severe.

I recall that she asked some very odd questions—or so they seemed to me at the time. Did he pull my hair? Choke me? Hurt me in any way? I was horrified, as you might imagine, and fiercely defensive of Jack. Haughtily I assured her that he'd done nothing of the kind—that he'd been gentle and generous, and that everything was wonderful. Why couldn't she be happy for me?

Then she smiled sadly and said that of course she was happy if I was happy. And then she asked the question that definitively threw cold water on the whole business: "How much did he give you for it?"

I told her that it wasn't like that.

"Oh, Teddy, you mustn't let people take advantage of you. You needn't give it away just because someone says 'love'."

"He didn't say he loved me," I told her, meaning it as a further defense of Jack, that he hadn't tried to deceive me with any such grand pronouncements.

But pity filled her eyes. "That makes it worse, doesn't it, little brother?" she said. Alice advised me on how to broach the topic next time—to be casual about it, as if it were only a matter of course—and she assured me that he would give me no trouble over it.

I took Alice's admonition to heart, in a way, but still I couldn't bring myself to speak of money the next time I saw Jack. Instead I avoided telling Alice that I'd seen him again. The third time I was with Jack, however, the matter resolved without action on my part, for Jack brought it up himself.

With much formality and distance in his manner, Jack apologized for being remiss and told me that he planned to arrange for a stipend to cover my living expenses and further suggested that I might have quarters in the palace if I wished them. Until all that could be fully sorted, he hoped the following sum would suffice, and he handed me a rather hefty purse. He added that the terms should be sufficient to ensure that I need not have other clients, which I took to mean that my exclusivity was expected.

Thus I thoroughly regretted that I had not brought it up myself, for if I had, I would never have known whether Jack saw our assignations on such terms or not. I still knew nothing of what drove him to offer the money. Had he spoken to someone else about the matter, as I had spoken to Alice, and thus been advised to remedy his behavior? Or had he come to it on his own?

Alice, at least, was delighted when I related the details. A regular stipend and housing was far more than she had hoped, and the liberality of the initial offering encouraged her to think that the stipend would be generous indeed (which, of course, it ended up being). She quite warmed to the idea of my affair with Jack and congratulated me on securing so fortunate a patron.

Never again was I quite so close to Alice after that, for I could not abide the way she spoke of Jack even when she praised him, and Jack was soon to become my whole world.

Do not think though that I was ever truly naive about it. From the first, I knew my love for Jack was doomed. Heirs of Summer often took lovers of the same sex while they were young, even if not wholly inclined that way, for their first issue was too vitally important to risk on a casual dalliance. This I knew. I had accepted it in that spirit and known my place, fully expecting that I would one day be replaced with a wife.

Even as the years went by and that didn't happen, even as Jack fled Summer to avoid being hounded about marriage, I had been certain that one day Jack would screw his head on straight and do his duty. How could he not? I had only hoped I might still have a place in his life when he did.

Of course then the story had gone all wrong. Our love was indeed doomed, but not at all in the way it was supposed to be. My lifelong preparations to fade into the wings of Jack's life had not in the least prepared me for him to die and leave me alone. I little knew how to live without him, nor how I was meant to structure my life if he were not at the center of it.

In the end, I suppose that's the true reason I decided to accept the call to become Lord Summer. For all the considerations that I'd weighed, the flat truth of it was that I'd had no alternate scheme to consider. I could be Summer, giving me a tie to Jack that would last forever and ever, or I could go off on my own with no notion of how to fill my days. I'd never had much to recommend me but charm and beauty, and I was painfully aware of being thirty-three years old at the time. When a man is too old to be a whore, I suppose he might as well become a king.

A BALL

ALL OF SUMMER DELIGHTED IN MARKING THE TURN of the seasons with extravagant excess—perhaps because seasons served as a comforting reminder that nothing ever truly changed, even when they appeared to. Every village green on the island would be alive with music and dancing on the eve of spring this night, and the common folk would perhaps showcase even more zeal and devotion to the occasion than did the nobles at the formal ball. Village aldermen and alderwomen would re-enact the same ceremonies that I would lead in the palace, symbolically binding us all to the land—a mirror of my own unbreakable bond to the dragon. Whether there was any true efficacy to these ceremonies, I could not say, though it was lovely to think so.

The last time I spoke to Zinnia before the ball, I was occupied with getting myself ready. Even for such an important occasion as the equinox, I had no body servant attending me. I flattered myself that I knew my own hair and skin better than anyone in Summer, and I liked doing it anyway. I was aware the palace servants did not look too kindly on this eccentric attitude of mine, seeing it as both a form of snobbishness and a lack of gentility all at once. I suppose it was.

Zinny, along with several cats, perched on the back of a sofa to observe my progress. All those intent, gleaming eyes might have unsettled someone with less confidence in their vision, but I found the reserves to stay the course.

"Are you going to dance a lot?" Zinny asked me.

"I certainly hope so. Though it won't all be fun. I'll have to dance with plenty of dreadful people as well as interesting people, and not one of them will be a handsome prince."

Zinny nodded gravely, seeing the injustice there. "I'll go see Summer while you're dancing."

"No, darling, I'll take you in the morning." What was I thinking? That was far too ambitious. "Or rather, let's say early afternoon."

"I want to go tonight."

"Well, sometimes we have to wait for the things we want. Don't you think you're going to have fun with your minder? I thought you liked Pearl."

"So? I want to see Summer. She could be my minder."

"Don't be silly. Dragons can't be minders for little girls. Besides, Summer will be out hunting all night. You know that."

Zinny pouted in a way that looked so much like me that I laughed.

I counted myself so very fortunate that Zinnia had come to join my life. I had someone to love again, which is all I ever truly wanted. And yet once again, I knew it wouldn't last.

A parent's love is always doomed, for a child will never love a parent with the same intensity that the parent loves the child, and as the years go by, the child's love will only grow the fainter. If all goes as one must hope, Zinny would find her own love and quite nearly forget about me. Just as I always did with Jack, I knew I must prepare myself to fade into the wings of her life and watch her go on to live the life she was meant to. But not yet.

I applied the final touches of my cosmetics and stood up from the vanity. "Well, what do you think?" I asked my daughter.

My whole turnout was white, down to the boots of creamy white calfskin, but the spring spirit showed through with strategic bursts of color. Fresh flowers of purple and blue wound through my hair, which curled in perfect ringlets even more voluminous than usual. Embroidered flowers and vines crept over the arms and back of my jacket, and sparkling gems winked out from among the stitches. Painted-on vines framed my eyes, and my lips shimmered in glittering green.

"Like a sea monster!" Zinny offered enthusiastically.

Not what I'd expected. "Well, that's not very nice," I pouted.

"But I like sea monsters. Summer is a sea monster, and she is very, very pretty."

"Ah, so you're saying I look pretty?"

"Mmhm." She looked at me sideways with a sly smile. "But you already know that, Daddy."

I smiled and winked at her. I did, of course. "Perhaps it's time to see how your mother and brother are getting on. Shall we?"

So Zinnia and I made our way up to Canna's apartment, where Zinny would remain with her minder while I escorted her mother to the ball.

Unsurprisingly, Canna was ready when we arrived, for she was ever punctual and prepared precisely when she meant to be. The glittery green gown I'd chosen looked just as marvelous on her as I'd hoped; it contrasted nicely with her copper complexion, hugged her curves, and flowed with her movements. The elaborate beadwork winked and shimmered with each step and complemented the jeweled combs in her hair. I was aware that not everyone counted Canna a great beauty. The professional matchmaker I had consulted years ago had been almost hesitant to recommend her on those grounds alone, though she had met every practical criteria I had specified. But I had no patience with any who held such views. She was lovely.

"No changes to the gown?" I asked.

"Hmm?"

"I spoke to Tailor Reed about some possible changes to make you more comfortable, and he said he'd discuss them with you. But you didn't make any changes?"

"Oh, yes, he brought that up, but you said it was fine as it was, and I trust you. You haven't changed your mind?"

"Absolutely not." I grinned. "You look perfect. Just one thing missing." I leaned forward and carefully planted a kiss on her cheek, leaving behind a shimmery green imprint of my lips. I showed her the effect in the mirror, and she was more delighted than I expected.

Brook had apparently left already with the intention of going to the ball with his friends. Idly I wondered what he was wearing and if it would show him to best advantage. The boy had grown well into his natural gifts, if he would only stop slouching and wearing ill-fitted clothes—but I knew that he would scarcely appreciate my advice on such matters.

Zinny still looked a bit put out, but I couldn't worry about that at the moment. Though she hadn't said anything about it, I fancied that a part of her pique most likely stemmed from envy about not going to the party. I made a note to myself that for the solstice I might arrange to have her make a brief appearance early in the evening. She was old enough for that.

OUR ENTRANCE WAS TIMED to Summer's movements. The ballroom was on a lower level, close to the sea, and people would be gathering on the balcony at sunset to watch the dragon exit her sea caves. I waited until I sensed her departure, heard the gasps and exclamations of the crowd, allowed just enough time for people to make their way back in from the balcony to the ballroom, and then I entered—one Summer out, one Summer in. My appearance caused just the stir I was hoping for. I attracted nearly as many appreciative gasps as the dragon.

The banquet portion of the evening was mostly work for me, of course, but my ceremonial role was not of an unduly trying sort. All my parts had been well rehearsed, and I am not in the least of a nervous disposition about speaking to crowds, for I confess I quite enjoy the attention. I flatter myself that I made a good show of it, speaking with more expression and vigor than what I recall of Leo's performances in my youth. I don't believe Jack ever presided over any such occasions.

When it came to the ceremonial foods, I did encounter a brief obstacle in my intentions. I knew that most Summers made only a symbolic show of eating the ceremonial foods that were of the less appetizing variety, but I had always considered it better form to consume my full portion and clean the plate, no matter how bitter or strange the item. Whoever had arranged my plate had perhaps been unaware of this custom of mine when they'd placed on it a whole fish, about the size of my hand, with its head and scales intact. It would take an absurdly long time to eat the entire thing with a knife and fork when I knew everyone would be eager to get on with things.

The idea that came to me perhaps originated with the dragon, for Summer would not find it in the least bit disgusting, and from her came the assurance that it would be possible. When the time came to eat the fish, I acted without a single flourish to forewarn that I was about to do something unusual. I picked up the fish by the tail, tipped back my head, and dropped it down my throat. I swallowed it whole.

The stunned reaction was gratifying for someone who so delights in being provocative as I do. At least I knew I had given them all something to talk about, that the evening would not soon be forgotten. Daintily I dabbed my lips and smiled as the shocked whispers broke out across the room. It was only later it occurred to me that the little trick might engender a certain strain of humor on how I could manage such a thing without gagging. Yet I found I cared little, as long as the people were entertained.

The banquet came to a close, and the more enjoyable part of the evening could begin: the music and dancing.

I love a party. I love to watch people preening and posing, fluttering and flirting in their finest things. I love to dance and to sing and to drink far too much. I love to be the center of attention. I love having ladies vie for a chance at my hand on the dance floor. I love catching gentlemen staring at me and flirting with them until they blush. I love laughing about things that aren't funny with people whose names I can't quite recall. I love the way the room spins and tilts when I've been drinking all night.

A good deal past midnight, I was still dancing and in an exceedingly pleasant mood, when all at once I felt off. A chasm opened in my chest. I could not breathe, could barely move. I was aware of people gathering around me, asking if I was alright, but they felt somehow unreal. Someone guided me out onto the balcony. That was good. The balcony was closer to where I needed to be.

A man steadied me by the arm and said something about, "Fresh air will do you good." I flinched back.

Males were vile, revolting creatures that ought to learn their place. Well, that clearly wasn't my thought, at least not about human males. Was there a male dragon around? Hazily I lifted my gaze to the skies.

A shadow passed in front of the stars, and I knew there was only one thing it could be. No bird or bat could make such a large occlusion. Drakes may be tiny compared to the magnificent dragonesses, but they were still much larger than anything else that goes on the wing. And it was carrying something.

Zinnia.

The thought was not mine, but I knew the truth of it as clearly as if I could see it with my own eyes. Summer could see perfectly in the dark. The drake was carrying Zinnia in his claws, carrying her away from Summer, carrying her towards a foreign ship. I could just make out the dark outline of the sails far on the horizon.

I needed to get to that ship. I was already taking off my boots and my jacket, though people around me were trying to stop me. I shook them off easily enough. I was stronger than they expected, and who would dare apply real force on me? Perhaps I ought to have explained, ought to have accounted for myself in some way, but it all seemed so urgent. And those people were as insubstantial as mist, as insignificant as ants. Whether such a thought could truly be a product of my mind held no meaning at that moment.

I jumped off the balcony.

Did I mention I don't know how to swim?

PART TWO

A DEAL

SHOCKINGLY COLD, THE WATER HAD ITS SOBERING effect on me. My attempts to grasp at anything that might steady me yielded only sharp rocks that tore into my clothes and flailing limbs. I could see nothing. As I floundered in the freezing sea, I wondered what the hell I had been thinking. Everyone at the ball must have thought I had simply gone mad. I suspect my inebriation had made it easier for the dragon's thoughts and suggestions to take hold.

Hard, smooth scales pressed around me, and I relaxed into Summer's steely embrace. Her coils squeezed with just enough pressure to be comforting without quite crushing me. At times it seemed a close thing though. She gave me no time to feel at ease, however, before she dragged me along behind her through the sea. I still could not fill my lungs, but in her embrace it seemed a less urgent thing, and somehow I was sustained without breath. This scarcely made for an agreeable trip, but I nevertheless knew I was safe and I could trust her. Summer would never hurt me, and there was always comfort in that.

Completely silent, she arose out of the sea along the starboard side of the unknown ship, hugging the hull with her form. The ship's name was painted along the prow, but I couldn't make it out in the dark. She took me in her claws and pushed me up to where I would be able to reach the railing and pull myself over. Then the dragoness stopped, waiting.

It seemed she thought I ought to handle this on my own. Wonderful. I just needed a moment to catch my breath and also to become a completely different person.

Voices reached me from the deck.

"Never mind that. What was she doing in that cave? She doesn't even look like one of those people."

"They must steal children from the mainland and feed them to the dragon."

"What? Why even bother? The silver lady would scarcely notice so small a morsel, if even half the rumors are to be believed."

"Isn't it more than just the meat? The life gives strength to the serpent or some such?"

"Don't be ridiculous."

This was all rather encouraging in a way. Whoever these people were, it seemed like they had no idea who they had kidnapped. Nor had they even intended to kidnap a child. Maybe they'd simply give her back, if I asked nicely.

"Meow."

A black-and-white cat peered down at me from the deck with a single yellow eye. Being thus discovered, I supposed I couldn't delay my grand entrance much longer. I pulled myself up over the railing and onto the deck. I intended to land quietly, but that didn't go terribly well. Nevertheless, I straightened up and rapidly regained my usual poise. The one-eyed cat at least offered a warm reception; at once it rubbed up against my bare feet and twined around my legs.

A crowd of sailors turned to stare at me. They were a motley group, coming from a range of backgrounds and circumstances if I guessed rightly. Yet even so, a sameness pervaded all of their clothing and accoutrements, which I recognized as the result of machine-made textiles and standardized production techniques. Ghastly stuff.

Near the bow, a fully grown green drake about the size of a horse lay curled in a neat ball with its wings folded at its side. A slim iron collar encircled its neck. Against its breast sat Zinny, and its front leg rested casually over her lap, restraining her. A wave of revulsion passed through me at the sight of the male dragon touching my daughter, with anger following close on its footsteps. I little knew how much of it was my own feelings and how much was Summer's. The green drake looked at me and did not blink.

At the time, of course, I scarcely knew what I looked like, but I would later get a better idea. The flowers in my hair had been so well secured that the stems and leaves remained, but most of the blossoms had popped off or been torn to shreds when Summer dragged me through the water. The salty water had wilted the greenery, leaving the impression that my hair was tangled with seaweed. All my face paint had washed off except the bold green lip dye, sans sparkle. My soaking-wet all-white clothing clung to me in an ethereal, insubstantial way, torn ragged at the edges by my struggles when I first hit the water. I must have looked like some sort of ghostly sea sprite risen out of the depths.

I seldom count myself at a loss for words, but my best manners failed to offer up a suitable salutation for this particular situation. My head would not stop spinning long enough to formulate an original one. I settled on keeping it simple.

"I'm here for the girl."

The sailors scarcely seemed reassured, and most of them shrank back even further. A tall, well-built sort of man with prominent cheekbones and flat braids stepped forward.

"Who are you meant to be? How did you get here?"

"That's none of your concern. Just give me the girl, and I'll be on my way."

"I don't reckon we'll be turning over an innocent little girl as a sacrifice to the dragoness."

I restrained a sigh and a rolled eye. "She's not a sacrifice. I mean her no harm."

"Whatever she may be, I don't reckon she belongs on that island. Look at her! Seems neglected, what with her hair all matted and—"

"Oh, for pity's sake, her hair is not *matted*. It's not my fault she doesn't want anything done to it and lets it get so wild, but really, let's not get carried away. It's not that bad. I was going to wash it tomorrow as soon as I got a chance."

That was not *exactly* what I might have planned to say, had I had all my wits about me. Please recall that I was still very much intoxicated, and I had always been defensive about Zinny's hair. It was not the first time it had been commented on, though I'd often attributed the judgmental attitudes to the ignorance of the people of Summer about this type of hair. I scarcely thought to hear it from someone who had that texture of hair themselves—from a pirate, of all people!

"You're her father?" a sharp feminine voice asked. I had not noticed a woman's presence at first, for she was dressed much the same as the men. The woman possessed a certain resemblance to the striking man I'd been speaking with, though she kept her hair very short, cut close to the scalp. Tall for a woman, she was of a height with me.

"No . . ." I did at least make the attempt to dissemble, but it was obvious I was fooling no one. I'd made my relation clear enough. "Yes, she's my daughter."

"And the silver serpent brought you here to this ship?"

"I didn't say that."

"You didn't have to. You're obviously a contractor." She gestured to the feline at my feet, still furiously attempting to gain my attention. "And Crispin can sense there's a female about." She nodded backwards towards the green drake behind her.

So she was the one connected to the male. As far as I knew, drakes could not establish stable contracts with humans, but I understood there were other ways to control or manipulate them, at least for a short time. Perhaps it had something to do with that iron collar on its neck. I said nothing to her inferences.

"I'm Sally Hollow-Light, and this is my brother, Tom Hollow." She indicated the tall man beside her. Despite the physical resemblance between them, I was a bit surprised to hear her identify him as a sibling, for her manner of speaking was considerably more polished than his more rustic style. "It seems to me that we have something you want, and I suspect you have something we want."

I supposed she wanted me to ask, but I simply waited.

"We know there's an egg here. Crispin can smell it. Tell us where the egg is, and you can have your daughter back."

"The egg? Yes, alright, fine, you can have it." Their looks of surprise told me I ought to have played that differently.

"Just like that?" Sally replied with clear skepticism.

"Yes, yes, just like that. I scarcely care about the egg. I want my daughter first though."

"Even if we were to agree to that, there's no way to get her safely back to shore right now."

"That's fine. You can just pitch her over the side."

Sheer horror reflected on all the faces around me. I was coming to the realization that it might be unwise to negotiate with otherlanders while my brain was so thoroughly pickled in brandy and wine.

I attempted to clarify. "Summer will take her back to Summer." Somehow, that only seemed to cause more confusion, though it took me a moment to understand why, for it had felt a perfectly lucid sentence to me. I made one last stab at making myself clear. "That is, the dragon is called Summer. She'll take her back to Summer, the island."

Tom Hollow voiced the incredulity that had clearly permeated the crowd. "We ain't throwing a little girl overboard to a dragon!"

"She'd be perfectly safe, as safe as she could be anywhere in the world. She's been bound to the dragon all her life." Once again, it was the wrong thing to say, and I ought to have known better. Grimaces of disgust reminded me how people outside of Summer felt about contracts that involved the contractor's child. I was not endearing myself to them, but it vexed me that they'd judge me for something they couldn't begin to understand. And they were the ones who'd stolen my daughter! "Certainly she'd be safer than with that drake."

"Crispin isn't going to hurt her," Sally asserted.

"I'm scarcely inclined to take your word for it. Males are not safe or stable, and whatever you've done that makes you feel you have it under control, I don't trust it. I don't want my daughter near that thing." I knew that some places did not maintain quite so strong a bias against male dragons as in Summer, as less remote places were perhaps more accustomed to seeing itinerant drakes wandering about. But surely no sane person would hold that drakes were safe to be around children.

"Then you have plenty of incentive to help us get the egg," said Sally. "She stays right there until we have it."

"You'd still have me as a hostage. Put me next to that dragon and let her go."

"No. We'll need you to get the egg, while she stays here as assurance."

"Daddy, it's alright." I turned to Zinny's voice and saw her smile.

"Zinny . . ." I had nothing to say.

"I'm sorry I ran away from Pearl and ruined your dancing." She giggled. "I told you, you look like a sea monster."

In the corner of my eye, I saw the siblings exchange

glances. Sally put herself forward once again. "As you see, she's fine with Crispin. She won't come to any harm, as long as we get the egg."

"Whether you get the egg or not, I strongly suggest you let no harm come to her, if you have any care for your own lives. Concern for her safety is the only reason Summer has not already destroyed this whole ship and everyone on it. I assure you it would be quite a small matter for her."

"Of course, of course. We don't want to hurt the girl anyway," she said with a gesture that perhaps was meant to be placating. "But we need that egg."

"It's in a sea cave a bit further down the coast. There's a particular tree that marks the spot. I could draw it for you."

"No, you have to take us there. Otherwise you could say anything. When we have the egg, then you and your girl go on your way. Deal?"

I'd expected that and could scarcely refute it. It would have to do. Sally Hollow-Light extended her hand, and I shook it. I looked to Tom Hollow and extended my hand to him as well. Between these two, I was unclear who might be the true leader, but I would be sure that both were bound by the agreement. Tom took my hand more reluctantly, but he shook.

I told them to head north, and the sailors set about to make that happen. The men handled themselves competently as individual seamen, perhaps, but not as a crew that had long been together, at least not on this vessel. They got in each other's way and sometimes had to converse over who should do what. There seemed to be no mate giving direct orders. While most of the men were distracted, I subtly tried to edge my way closer to Zinnia. But Sally and the green drake both always seemed to be watching me.

Summer circled slowly in the water below, still shadowing the ship. Though I could feel her presence, I had no sense of whether she approved of my negotiations so far. She had been so angry and resentful about the egg, and she had given it over to my keeping, so surely she must not care for it? If she did object to the trade, she must have ways of making her feelings known.

When we were near the area, I directed them to stop but admitted that I couldn't see well enough in the dark to identify the cave. Dawn was not far off, so Sally determined that we would simply wait until there was enough light to see.

Zinnia, meanwhile, had taken up the task of manicuring the drake's dagger-like claws. Humming a little song as she worked, she carefully picked bits of grime from around his scales, while the creature remained still but alert under her ministrations. The cat too joined them and curled up at Zinny's feet. I little knew what to make of how well she seemed to be taking all this in stride. Zinnia had always been an odd duck, which can only be expected from a dragon child, but I wondered if there might have been more to it on this occasion.

With so little apparent need to comfort my daughter and nothing else to do for the moment, I moved over to the railing and set about extracting the weeds from my hair.

"I reckon you must be cold in those wet clothes." Tom Hollow spoke from behind me. I turned to find him proffering a blanket.

"I appreciate the thought, but I'm fine, thank you." Since I had entered my contract, I seldom felt the cold too harshly.

"Well, you ought to think about covering up anyhow, some might reckon. There's a lady present, you know." He spoke with a wryness to indicate he was not quite earnest in counting his sister as a lady, though of course he had a point that wet white clothes leave little to the imagination. He draped the blanket over the railing. "It's here if you change your mind, Mr.—what did you say your name was again?"

"I didn't. But you can call me Summer, if you must."

"Not a lot of names to go around there, eh? Well, here you are then, Mr. Summer."

I couldn't help but laugh. "Just 'Summer'. It's not a surname. People in Summer don't even use surnames."

"What, not at all? How do they keep track of folk if it's all just Tom, Dick, and Harry?"

"Summer is a small place when it comes down to it. They have a novel system in which everyone knows everyone else's business so thoroughly that there's never any confusion."

"'They'?"

"Hmm?"

"Oughtn't you be saying 'we', not 'they'? Ain't it your country?"

"Oh, yes, of course it is."

Tom looked at me speculatively, and I knew exactly what direction his next comment would take. "You don't look like you're from there."

"Really?" I responded with mock incredulity. "Never heard that before."

"It's just I didn't reckon they let immigrants in there. I didn't even reckon that they let in visitors. And I've heard naught of people from there traveling abroad much either."

"That's quite true." It had been such a long time since I'd spoken to anyone who hadn't known all there was to know about me, I scarcely knew what to say to account for myself. Perhaps I ought to have made the effort, tried to gain some sympathy with the man, but I couldn't find it in myself to care what he thought. "What's going to happen to the egg when you take it?"

"You do care then, do you?"

"No, I don't. A man can be curious, can't he?"

"We'll sell it."

"Oh, is that all?"

"That a problem?"

"It's not what I expected. With your sister having that little . . . pet drake, I thought maybe there was something else you wanted with the egg. More personal."

"Money is personal enough when you need it, I have found."

"I see. Well, good luck then."

"So you really don't care?"

"I beg your pardon, but did you want me to?"

"It just figures."

"What 'figures'?"

"That a man who will sell his own daughter to a dragon would sell his dragon's offspring just as easy."

My feelings on hearing this account of myself can scarcely be described, though perhaps can be imagined. This man had come here to steal our egg from us, had instead stolen our daughter, and somehow made us into the villain of the tale? Because we weren't crying over the deal we'd made? The audacity of these people to hold Zinny from me and make faces at my handling of her. Zinnia belonged to me, my own.

The ship rocked violently and listed to the side. Summer's tail flashed into view for but a moment before it vanished again beneath the waves.

Alarmed cries rose up from the sailors around us, and the cat yowled as it gripped the boards for purchase. Tom Hollow lost his footing and fell. I didn't. I stood over him and stared down at him sprawled on the deck. Summer's rage boiled up inside, a mirror of my own. "I could eat you."

His face contorted. "Huh?"

"Eat you. Swallow you whole. Know all your hopes and fears and dreams and anxieties, and watch it all go pop, pop, pop! Like bubbles. Like joints popping out of sockets as they squeeze down the gullet. Everything you are, then meat. I could just eat you."

All the sailors stopped to listen. You might think that this speech would have seemed ridiculous, coming out of my mouth as it did. It's not as though I've ever been physically imposing, and most of these sailors were indeed larger than me. But no one laughed. No one scoffed or cracked a smile.

Did I mean it? Hell if I know. We had never actually eaten a human in the past seven years that I'd been Summer, but I knew Summer wouldn't turn up her nose at it, and at that moment, I was willing to see how it would be. Try everything once, as they say. For a moment the gentle slosh of the sea bumping against the hull was the only sound in the night.

Sally rushed over from the other end of the deck, stooped by her brother, and hissed in his ear, "What the hell have you been saying to him, Tom?" Roughly she yanked him to his feet. He muttered something back to her, perhaps in his own defense, but she was having none of it. "Can't you ever just keep your mouth shut! There's a dragon the size of a castle under our feet, and you're getting into it with her contractor? Do you always have to antagonize *everyone*?"

Seeing the man get such a dressing-down from his sister dulled the edge of my anger. I scarcely think of myself as an angry man, but this whole situation had me quite on edge, and of course the dragon in my head didn't help. Or perhaps the dragon had less to do with it than I'd like to believe.

Sally turned to me and made an attempt to smile sweetly. "I'm sorry about my brother. He's an idiot."

I shook my head and turned away, for I did not trust myself to speak.

Twice this man Tom Hollow had provoked a reaction I had not intended, and both times it had been about Zinnia. I could readily admit that I was defensive about Zinny's wild hair, but was I really so defensive about her part in the contract?

When I decided to become Summer, I had considered

many angles of what it would mean for my life—that I would have to stay in Summer forever, that there would finally be a real place for me in Summer, that my mind would no longer be entirely my own, that I'd never be alone again, that it would be good for the stability of Summer, that I could live in ease and comfort, that I would have to marry a woman, that I would hold a connection to Jack forever.

Zinnia had not existed yet, and the idea of a child to come had not quite felt real to me. To the extent I had thought about it, it had seemed good. My child would be a lady and a ruler of men—not so bad for the son of a whore. Everyone in Summer accepted that these contracts were right and good: the proper way of things that ensured the island's prosperity and lent a special kind of continuity to the line of rulers. Certainly Jack always seemed to cherish his connection to the dragon, even as he'd attempted to reject other aspects of his role.

Now that she was here, it was impossible to imagine what Zinny would be like without her connection to the contract. In fact, she could not possibly exist if not for the contract. No possible scenario would have led Canna and me to have a child together if not to create the next Summer. So how could I possibly regret it or second-guess it? Zinnia's life was in every way bound to Summer and always had been.

OVER THE WHITE CLIFFS, the sky paled enough to let me make out the silhouette of a solitary twisted tree clinging to the jagged edge of Summer. It might have struck me as a lovely sight, if not for the dull hangover blossoming in my skull.

"That's it there," I called out to Sally. I pointed at the cave below the tree. "That's where the egg is."

She nodded grimly at the news, not at all jubilant as I might have expected. "I was going to send Tom in the boat with you, but I suppose I'll have to send someone else?"

"We need to row over there? I thought you were going to send the dragon like you did with the main cave."

"No. I need to keep him on the girl. Otherwise your silver lady could surely snatch her away, couldn't she? Unless I had someone hold a knife to her throat, which I'd rather not. Too much chance for accident, you see? So you'll row over there and bring back the egg for me, and I'll send someone to help you with it. Not Tom, since he's proved himself an idiot. Anyone else you'd like?"

I sighed. "Mr. Hollow is fine. Let's just get this over and done with." I looked over at Zinny and said, "I'll be right back, my darling, and then we'll go home."

Zinny nodded, unconcerned. She watched with bird-like curiosity as the little boat lowered over the side. I wondered if that drake were somehow keeping her pacified, or if perhaps Summer herself was. It still sickened me to see the drake touching her, but I was relieved she did not seem distressed.

I let Tom Hollow do all the rowing. He could think me a worthless dandy all he liked. But he didn't oblige by complaining or struggling with the task, which could have prompted a snarky comeback on my end. His well-muscled arms worked the oars with rhythmic precision, and he was otherwise silent.

"Do you have children of your own, Mr. Hollow?"

"I'm not meant to be talking to you."

"What, because your sister said so? Do you always do what she says?"

"Only when she's right."

"Well, there's a distinction without a difference. Don't you know women are always right? And besides, it was a simple question. Perhaps I'll be more offended that you won't answer. Or I'll be forced to suspect that you're avoiding the question. What are you hiding, Mr. Hollow?"

"I don't have kids."

I smirked. "Now that *figures*."

"I'm not meant to be talking to you."

I yawned and leaned back. Despite the situation, the sleepless night was beginning to tell on me, and the danger to Zinny all felt less real now that I was apart from her. The ordeal was almost over, and she would not come to any lasting harm. The sea at dawn felt peaceful in the little rowboat.

As we entered the cave, the little boat banged about a good bit against the walls, but Tom gritted his teeth and stayed the course, and the boat maintained its integrity. We pulled up into the tiny little landing without incident. The egg was exactly where I had left it, as beautiful and precious as I remembered. I didn't watch and didn't help while Tom loaded it into the boat. Annoyingly, he struggled very little with the weight of the egg compared to my difficulties, or at least he didn't show it.

As we emerged back out into the open in the boat, I took in the developing scene before us, and I swore. Tom spun around to see what I was looking at.

The *Godwit* and the *Plover* approached the foreign ship, closing in from opposite sides.

"Son of a bitch! You set us up!" Tom accused me.

"Why would I set this up? I was getting what I wanted."

Tom scoffed. "You sure agreed to give up the egg in a hurry. I knew that couldn't be right."

Something snicked together in my mind. "Is that why you were provoking me? Trying to get me to admit I cared about the egg?"

"Well, don't you?"

"It's complicated!"

"I don't reckon it's a fair negotiation, when one side can see when the other's lying and the other side can't," Tom added on a somewhat petulant note.

He referred to the well-known talent of contractors to

be able to tell when someone is lying, which, of course, I definitely knew how to do. It's such a basic skill of draconic influence that it would be absurd to think that a contractor of seven years wouldn't have mastered it. After all, even contractors of *much* less formidable dragons than Summer could boast this power. There was nothing to it really. I absolutely could do that. So naturally, I had known all along that the Hollows had been earnest in their negotiations. It went without saying. Obviously.

We both watched rather helplessly as the ships closed in.

"What do you think your sister will do?" I asked.

"It would seem she's running," Tom said in a flat voice, as if he were a mere disinterested observer to this phenomenon. Indeed the ship was putting on sail and turning tail. "The *Shadowcat*'s a much lighter and faster build than those old-timey buckets of yours. They'll never catch her."

"Perhaps not," I agreed as I watched the ship go, my heart going with it. Its construction did appear a good deal sleeker and more modern than that of our ships, and it soon began to shrink away towards the horizon. "It's a good thing we'll have you to tell us where they're going then, isn't it?"

I smiled grimly, showing my teeth. Tom Hollow did not.

A STORY

THE *PLOVER* PURSUED THE *SHADOWCAT* FOR A TIME, though it was quite obviously too slow to catch the sleek foreign vessel. Meanwhile the *Godwit* turned around to collect the boat Hollow and I occupied. The crew of the *Godwit* was all astonishment at finding me in the boat, and even more astonished by the egg. Gasps and exclamations murmured through the crew like a wave, and everyone stopped to stare as the egg was hoisted aboard. So much for it being a secret.

As I clambered on to the deck, Admiral Rostrum rushed over, still in the dress clothes that he had worn to the ball.

"Teddy! You're alright!" he called out in desperate relief.

"You address me quite familiarly, Admiral," I returned harshly. I realize, of course, that this rebuke was entirely unreasonable. It must have been plain to everyone that he spoke from the heart and meant no disrespect in calling me by name, and I could only have come across as high-handed to call him on it. But the last thing I wanted at that moment was the admiral cozying up to me in public view.

"I apologize, Lord Summer," the admiral replied. He stopped well short of me and dipped into a sort of chastened half-bow, though it was not counted the correct form to bow to Summer. "I forgot myself. We all feared the worst when no one could find you in the water near the palace."

"I have been where I wished to be," I informed him. "But the worst *has* come to pass. Lady Zinnia was on that ship that you just let get away."

The admiral's eyes widened in horror. "How can that—?"

"Zinny! What do you mean Zinny was there?" someone else cut in.

It was Brook. The presence of Canna's child was a surprise that I could not seem to grapple with just then. "What are *you* doing here?"

"I allowed him to join us, Summer," the admiral jumped back in to explain. "Even though he's not officially joined up yet, we could use the extra hand, and it only seemed right to let him help, as he was naturally most concerned for your welfare."

I found it hard to believe that Brook had been taken with such genuine worry for me, but that was neither here nor there. No doubt he simply got caught up in the excitement and wished to be a part of it. "You should go home to your mother," I told the boy.

"How was Zinny on that ship?" Brook repeated more forcefully.

"I scarcely know. She must have slipped her minder and snuck down to the sea caves. That ship had a drake that grabbed her out of there while it was looking for the egg." I gestured vaguely behind me at the egg.

Both Brook and the admiral looked at the egg for a moment, but they turned back with blank, almost dazed expressions. Neither of them said anything about the egg. I realized that the whole crew now ignored the egg, except for two men still engaged in moving it to safety. Yet even they had a muted manner towards the egg; they handled it as they would any other bit of cargo. At length the admiral shook himself off as if from a chill and proceeded with the conversation.

"And who is this man with you?" the admiral asked.

I turned to consider Tom Hollow, who had come aboard behind me but had done his best impression of a piece of furniture since then. "This is Tom Hollow. He's the one who's going to tell us where that ship is headed. Aren't you, Mr. Hollow?"

I've seen fish on the hook that looked more at ease than Tom Hollow did as he looked around at the *Godwit* crew's staring faces. "Well, I, uh, I don't reckon I . . ."

"Mr. Hollow is perhaps a little shy," I said. "Could you get him situated somewhere private? I will want to have a chat with him shortly."

Directives were thus issued, and Tom Hollow was led down below.

"If we're to pursue this ship to some foreign port, we will need to lay in more supplies, Lord Summer," the admiral informed me. "We won't have enough rations on board for more than a couple days. That will be true for any of the ships in the fleet."

"How long will that take?"

"A few hours, at least." He must have read some sort of scowl on my face, for he added, "We'll be able to bring in clothing and personal effects for you as well."

"Is that supposed to comfort me?" I snarled at him. "*Clothes*?"

"No, I didn't mean—"

"Forget it," I cut him off. "If it must be done, it must be done. While you're at that, send the boy back to the palace."

"Hey!" Brook spoke up. "I don't want to go home. I want to go with the ship."

"This is no time to play at heroics. You don't belong here."

"I'm not a child. I can make my own decisions, and the admiral has already given me permission to be aboard. You wouldn't interfere for any other man, and I don't see why you should play at being my father all of a sudden."

I could remember a time not so long before when Brook had always seemed vaguely frightened of me, but he seemed to have gotten over that tolerably well. Perhaps when he became larger than me.

"And you would leave your mother alone at a time like this? Do you feel no obligation to her well-being?"

"Grandma and Grandpa are with her. I should be here. I'm supposed to join up next month anyway. Why should I have to miss an event of such historical significance by a few weeks? And Zinny is my little sister; I should be part of rescuing her."

The argument exhausted me. I scarcely cared whether the boy was there; I balked at it only for Canna's sake. How could I face her if I lost both of her children? But no, I couldn't even think that. I'd lost Alice, and I'd lost Jack, but I could not lose Zinny. I would get her back.

"Have it your way. I don't have time for this," I told Brook and turned away, dismissing him from my thoughts. "I need to speak to Hollow."

"About that," the admiral spoke. "Meaning no disrespect, Lord Summer, but are you sure you should be the one to interrogate the prisoner?"

Of course. I gave way on one thing, and now the admiral was back to questioning my authority and competence. Doubtless he simply didn't believe I had the grit for such a thing. "Do you have people here who are specially trained in interrogation, Admiral?"

"Well, no, not exactly—"

"Then for what cause do you imagine someone else could handle it better than I?"

The admiral gaped, plainly not in possession of a point that was not utterly insulting. Nevertheless, he made an attempt. "I fear you take too much on yourself, Lord Summer, and you are not quite yourself. You need to rest—"

"As far as I can surmise, no one here has rested since before the ball. If you're so worried about my alertness, perhaps you could fetch me some coffee."

The admiral backed off. I know I was crueler to him than I ought to have been, but I needed some vent for my frustration and anger. I blamed him for ruining my deal with the otherlanders, though even at that moment, I knew that was also unfair. The admiral had acted perfectly rationally based on the information he had had at hand.

If anyone could really be blamed for us working at cross purposes, it was I. If I had paused to tell people at the ball what was going on and why I was jumping in the sea, much might have been avoided. Or could that be blamed on the dragoness, who had clearly been prodding my thoughts and clouding my mind? But I could not take the dragon to task for that, and the self-recriminations were not yet ready to blossom into full self-loathing and misery. So I was left with the people in front of me. I did not like the admiral, and I knew he'd take it.

Perhaps that was in truth why I wished to be the one to question Tom Hollow. Unlike the admiral, Hollow could justly be blamed for Zinny's peril and would be a fair target for my rage. Did I hope that he would hold back, at least for a little while?

The admiral's turn for the literal did occasionally have its advantages, for someone—a young woman of energetic demeanor and a charmingly freckled complexion—actually brought me a mug of coffee. Then she led me down to where Tom Hollow had been stashed in a storage area.

Tom sat on the floor with his legs drawn up in front of him, his elbows resting on his knees. He looked up at me with wary distrust.

"Look, I'll tell you what you want to know—whatever I know anyway. I won't hold naught back. And I reckon you'll know I'm telling the truth. You'll know. So there's no call for anything funny."

So much for interrogation. I sighed and sat down on a barrel across from him. "Are you always this much of a coward?"

"The way I see it, why should I try to hold out? I know well enough that you're not about to give up and walk away. It's your daughter."

"That's quite true."

"And I already reckon you're cool blooded. What you said on the *Shadowcat* about feeding me to the dragon, I believed you. You've no call to convince me you're a monster. I know it. I believe it. There's no call for any of that . . . dragon stuff. In my head, I mean. I don't want none of that. Let's be civilized about this, yeah?"

Quite the charmer, wasn't he? It seemed vaguely odd that he was so worried about draconic power being turned on him while his sister worked with a drake, but then again, perhaps it was not. Those who truly understood what dragons were capable of had the most cause to fear them.

"Aren't you meant to ask me questions?" Tom asked after I had been silent for a time.

"You know what I want to know."

"Right. Well, I don't rightly know where Sal went. She always had more ideas than she let on, contingencies for everything, wheels within wheels, if you follow. I know where she might have gone though."

I waited.

"Oxeye. The fellow who funded this whole thing—the ship, the crew, all that—he's in Oxeye. Sally might've gone there to explain things to him."

"Who is this man?"

"Light. Mr. Lowell Light, that is. He owns the town, just about, all the factories there, runs the place to his liking."

I recalled that the woman had named herself Sally Hollow-Light, and I knew how surnames tended to work in the otherlands. I frowned. "You wouldn't by any chance be speaking of your sister's husband, would you?"

"Oh! Ah, they're not together anymore, not really. I never liked him, you know, never approved. But Sal, she's always had ideas. Always wanted to be someone. And she was good at that game—good at acting like she already was someone, you know?"

I did, of course. Before I became Lord Summer, I had had a good deal of experience with acting the gentleman while being nothing of the sort. So if Tom's take was to be believed, Sally and I were perhaps more alike than I had guessed. Yet that gave me no hope for us getting along and reaching an understanding more easily. People like me *hate* people like me.

"So when you said you were going to sell the egg, you meant to your brother-in-law?"

"Well, I mean, I put it that way to see how you'd react, I'll own that."

"And you think Sally will have gone to her husband to explain things at this juncture."

"Maybe. But she might think it'd be better not to, maybe to try to get a dragon egg somewhere else before she goes back. But the thing is, if she didn't go to Oxeye, I don't know where she will have gone."

I nodded. "What does this Mr. Light want with a dragon egg?"

"Oh, well, I reckon it's for the Kittevers."

"The Kittevers?"

"Yeah, the Kittevers."

"Are you going to tell me who or what that is?"

Tom was plainly taken aback. "You're telling me you ain't never heard of the Kittevers?"

"I haven't left Summer in seven years, but I'd never heard of them before that. Is it something new?"

"Oh, hell, I guess so. It would be, let's see, around eight years ago now we first started hearing about them—hard to believe that's all it's been. Damned if they're not everywhere now. You really never heard of 'em? Don't you have, uh, spies or what have you?"

"Summer's people have little care for what happens in the other—on the mainland," I said. "Please, tell me what they are and what they have to do with this."

"Ah, well, it's hard to describe. I reckon they started out as one of those dragon cults, you know, those loons who worship dragons—er, that is, not that there's anything wrong with that, if you, you know, if you have a—"

"People in Summer do not worship the dragoness," I interrupted him. That was perfectly true, even if I can allow that the level of reverence for Summer could easily be misconstrued. The otherlands, in contrast, always seemed to boast pockets of people who flat-out deified dragons. They usually remained firmly on the fringes of society, regarded as either unsound of mind or duplicitous of purpose. It troubled me to think that attitude might have changed.

"Oh, good." Tom seemed decidedly relieved, not just for the awkwardness of his imagined misstep. "But the Kittevers are more than that anyway. It's like a whole way of life, a whole mission or some such. And once they get to someone, they're all full-on fanatical about it. No half-hearted converts with them and no half measures neither."

"What is the way of life? What is their purpose?"

"Oh, ah . . . I don't reckon I rightly know how to put it."

"What do they have to do with this Mr. Light then?"

"Well, when the Kittevers move into a town, they take over everything, you know. Get all the folk on board and oust the old bosses if they don't toe the line. Mr. Light wants to keep 'em out of Oxeye, seeing as he's got it all the way he wants it. So he works with them, gives 'em stuff they want, and convinces them to give Oxeye a miss."

"So Light wants the egg to bribe the Kittevers to leave him alone, and the Kittevers want the egg for . . . ?"

"Damned if I know. I'd just as soon give the Kittevers a wide berth."

"Well then, perhaps you can explain what your sister stands to gain from all this."

Tom hesitated for a moment, as if wrestling with whether to tell me more, but then he added, "Well, he's got Sally's kids." He watched me closely after he'd said it.

"Light does? He's kidnapped her children?"

"They're his kids too, so he's got the law on his side, but I don't reckon he gives a fig about them. He's keeping them from Sal out of spite, you know? If she can get this thing for him, he'll give her a settlement and let her take them. Then she'll leave that town and never see him again."

"I see." I considered all he had told me. "One more thing then—how did your sister come by that drake? How does she keep it under control?"

"Crispin? Oh, uh, that's no business of mine, I reckon. That thing has been hanging around her for ages."

"You don't know how she controls it?"

He shrugged. "Sometimes dragons just befriend folk, don't they?"

I had little notion what to make of that, but I supposed I had enough to be getting on with. "Thank you, Mr. Hollow. I will see that you're treated well on board here."

WHEN I EMERGED, THE ship had docked, and supplies were being brought on board. The admiral stood on the dock conferring with the harbormaster and a few other officers who had shown up. Captain Lance of the *Cormorant* looked like the night had been rough on him. Captain Grace sported an unusual look; her hair and cosmetics were still done up for the ball, but she'd changed back into her usual uniform. Yet she pulled it off by seeming unselfconscious of it, always the key to any bold turnout. I supposed I looked far more strange than either of them, but I strove not to think of it.

I joined them and offered a summary of what had happened on the *Shadowcat* as well as the most salient points that Hollow had offered. The *Plover* had also returned and was able to confirm that the *Shadowcat* had indeed been headed in the general direction of Oxeye, though its destination could hardly be certain before they'd lost sight of it.

None of us gathered there had ever visited the town of Oxeye, but the officers knew its location from maps. Situated on a small peninsula that resembled an ox's head, it was one of many coastal towns dotting a narrow strip of arable land between the sea and a low but rugged range of hills. Though that coastal region as a whole was the closest part of the mainland to Summer, Oxeye in particular had never been one of our trading partners. Summer engaged in only a modest amount of trade with the mainland, for we could produce almost everything we needed from our own soil, and our traders were as averse to change as anyone in Summer. They seldom experimented with new routes once they had settled on a port that could reliably offer up the goods we needed.

The admiral estimated that it would take two or three days to reach the town. He suggested it would be best for the *Godwit* to be loaded with supplies as quickly as possible and set out at once, and then the *Avocet* and the *Plover* could follow when they could be made ready, in case we needed more muscle after we arrived. Since I was eager to leave as soon as possible, I readily agreed to this scheme.

No one talked much about the egg or how it might factor into the plan—almost as if they had trouble focusing on it. I supposed I had my dragon to thank for that. She has her own ways of keeping secrets under wraps, even for things that ought to cause a sensation. Everyone in Summer is under her glamour in a way. Most often it's best not to think too hard about that.

Next I inquired whether arrangements were already being made for my personal effects, or whether I needed to pursue it personally.

The admiral surprised me there. Although he confirmed that the order had indeed been issued for the palace staff to pack some of my things, he added in at the end, "You know, Lord Summer, you really don't have to join us."

"I beg your pardon?"

"I mean to say that you needn't feel an obligation to come along for the show of it," the admiral said. "We have this man Tom Hollow; we know where to go. We will have plenty of expertise and might to bring to the matter. Is it really wise to risk both Summer and the heir at once? What good can it possibly serve to have you along?"

Any lingering remorse I might have felt about my snappy treatment of the admiral evaporated all at once. "Admiral Rostrum, you make it plain you think me a wastrel and a dandy of little use. That is fine. I don't much care what you think of me. But I will ask you—once—to refrain from renewing any such suggestion in my presence. I am coming on this errand, and indeed I am in command of this errand. If that is not amenable to you, then perhaps the *Godwit* should not be a part of it. Not much has been loaded aboard yet, and these preparations could be easily shifted to another vessel. The *Avocet* would do just as well, I think, and I would be happy to place this mission in Captain Grace's capable hands."

Captain Grace started in surprise at being so named and looked uncomfortable.

The admiral's jaw tightened. After all the facetious jabs I'd made that seemed to have half gone over his head, I think I had finally gotten through to him. "That will not be necessary, Lord Summer," he muttered.

CANNA MADE IT TO the docks before we got underway. I worried for a moment that she too would insist on coming along, and there could be no reasonable counterargument to it. She had as much right as Brook or I to join the mission, and she was no less capable. But she had no mind for that at all, it seemed, and I certainly did not suggest it.

I little knew what to say to her. Zinny was the thing that bound us together, in every way, and we were nothing without her.

"I feel there must have been something more I could have done to stop it," Canna said.

"No, don't think that. She was determined to go down there that night, and you know how Zinny is when she's like that. I doubt even Pearl could reasonably be blamed for it." I could be though, given that Zinny had told me of her intentions quite clearly, and I had failed to take it seriously.

"I was almost the last to know that anything was even going on," Canna went on, as if she had not heard me. "I'd left the ballroom before you jumped in the sea and didn't even learn of it until almost dawn."

That was no great surprise. Canna often became overwhelmed at large gatherings and turned in as soon as it was polite and acceptable. "Knowing wouldn't have changed anything," I assured her. I put my arms around her, which felt strange at first but more comfortable as she accepted the embrace. "I'll get her back," I promised. "No matter what is necessary."

Canna lifted her head from my shoulder and looked into my eyes. She seemed vaguely suspicious, as if she feared I had some secret purpose in mind. "Don't be too reckless, Teddy. Your life is important too."

I nodded, for of course it was true that yet another premature loss of Lord Summer would pose a severe trial for the island—but in the long term, it would not be as devastating as losing the heir.

Then I left her to say her goodbyes to Brook, who I imagined was the true reason for her visit to the docks. I vaguely hoped that she might convince him to stay behind after all, but when I looked back, I knew that that was not the tenor of their conversation. Canna was tearful but proud as she bade her son farewell.

A Good Fit

THE ADMIRAL VACATED HIS CABIN FOR MY USE. I might have made a show of protestation about it under other circumstances, but I was too annoyed with the admiral. Despite my exhaustion, sleep held little appeal. Before I even tried to rest, I put forth the effort to get my hair into twists, and I looked through the luggage that had been packed for me. Of course I found it ample and all in order. At the bottom of the chest, clothes for Zinnia had been optimistically tucked away under my own. Her little dresses looked so very tiny in my hands. I refolded them all carefully and put them back where I'd found them.

The hasty packing would have been managed by Robin, the fellow who took care of my clothes and linens. Perhaps I ought to have brought him along as a valet, and then I would have had someone with me instead of sitting in the lonely cabin all by myself.

Seeing as I was setting out for the otherlands, I suppose it is only inevitable that I would have thought of Jack. He had always been preoccupied with the otherlands, much as Brook was now. Indeed, I suppose Jack would have been about the same age as Brook when he first started talking a certain way about places outside of Summer. That seemed strange, for it didn't feel so long ago that I could remember having such conversations with Jack, and yet Brook seemed incredibly young to me. Was there any chance we were as naive as he when we talked about leaving Summer? Yes, I suppose we were.

I recall one occasion when I was in Jack's room, lounging as we often did with no particular aim in the midafternoon. I was practicing a certain chord progression on the lute, which was a new instrument to me at the time, and I kept fumbling the same transition. My efforts were further hindered by a tortoiseshell kitten who kept attacking my hands with great gusto, much to the amusement of Jack.

He in turn flipped through a book which purported to give accurate travelers' accounts of the otherlands, often pausing to read aloud to me from certain passages that he found particularly astonishing or noteworthy. I can say now that the book was a lot of rubbish, from what I remember of it, but at the time we knew no better.

After a particularly enchanting anecdote, Jack said, "I wish I could go to all these places." I recall being somewhat startled, though it's difficult for me to say why. It seems now a perfectly pedestrian thing for a lad to say, but it felt oddly portentous in that moment, as indeed the rest of the conversation would prove.

"It sounds as though a lot of these places are very dangerous," I pointed out.

"Have you no sense of adventure? That's the *point*. Here, there's no danger, nothing changes, there's nothing to decide. It's all determined in advance. Don't you ever want to change it? Change your fate?"

I scarcely knew what to say. Of course there were times when *I* wanted to change my fate, but I knew Jack was not truly asking about me. The question was clearly rhetorical in that sense, but the implications for himself were too strange.

"Jack . . . are you saying that you don't want to enter your contract?"

That was unthinkable, of course. *Every* heir of Summer eventually entered their own contract, continuing the cycle by committing their own firstborn child to the dragoness. Most did it as soon as they turned twenty-one and were deemed to be of age, though it was not truly required that it be done at a specific age if the current Summer remained hale and hearty. But to not enter their contract at all was unheard of—no heir would even desire to avoid it, by my understanding of the matter. But I little knew what else to think.

"What?" Jack looked up at me, startled. "No. Of course I'm going to contract."

"I don't understand," I said. "If you intend to become Summer, how can you change your fate?"

Jack shifted a bit away from me, and I couldn't help feel he was annoyed at the question. "Well, obviously I can't just leave Summer. But I mean all the rest of it."

"I thought you said you did want to leave Summer."

"No, no, I meant the dragon. I can't leave the dragon. I want to leave the island."

"Doesn't it all go together?"

"Well, of course it does," he snapped at me.

Carefully, I suggested, "Perhaps you could travel a bit *before* you become Summer."

"As if my father would ever allow that," Jack huffed.

To that, I truly had nothing to say. No matter how carefully worded, no matter how much in agreement with what Jack had himself just said, no comment on Leo could ever fail to provoke Jack's temper. Leo was forever vexing him, for they seemed locked in a constant battle that no one else understood, and yet Jack would brook neither praise nor censure of his father from anyone else. I suppose he felt that no one else understood. No doubt that was true in my case, for

I couldn't say what the problem between them was, but I suspected it was at the heart of nearly all Jack's disquiet.

That is not to say that I was in doubt who to blame for their troubles. Leo was a cunt, and everyone knew it, so I had no hesitation in laying the fault at his feet. Yet I often wished I knew exactly what passed between them.

Jack sighed. "I suppose you think I'm such a spoiled brat, complaining about my lot to you."

"No . . ."

"You're a terrible liar, Teddy," he said, but he smiled as he said it. He took the lute out of my hands and set it aside, and he pulled me in and kissed me. We left the conversation behind.

It troubled me at the time, of course, but I supposed it the normal sort of youthful resistance to obligation. I did not seriously expect that Jack would behave in so reckless a manner as he ended up doing, accepting his contract and yet refusing to live in Summer or to produce an heir: perhaps the only true obligations of Lord Summer. Perhaps if I had taken him seriously earlier, I could have done more to stop him, to change his mind about things.

As you might imagine, I simply did not see it as my responsibility to worry about it. Jack was scarcely bereft of people putting pressure on him to stay the course—his father and stepmother did plenty to make him miserable in that way. I saw my role to be his reprieve from all that. And yet if I had tried harder to understand what he was feeling, who knows what might have been different? I still cannot claim to understand what Jack wanted.

These were the thoughts that circled my mind as I lay alone in Admiral Rostrum's cabin, until I eventually must have drifted off.

WHEN I AWOKE, I felt different, like something was missing. No, not missing, just fainter—like a star that seems less bright under the glare of the full moon. For the whole of the seven years that I had been in contract with my dragon, I had remained in Summer and never strayed far from her. Even a visit to the far eastern shore of the island was well within her normal range and field of influence. Now I moved further and further away by the moment, and Summer was still in Summer.

I had not given much thought to it before setting out, but of course she wouldn't follow the expedition. She never left Summer. It's not as though she had followed Jack around during all the time we had traveled the otherlands together. But then Jack had possessed many talents as a contractor that made him a formidable force to be reckoned with all on his own. I couldn't help but feel that I didn't amount to much without the dragon herself close at hand.

At least I could still touch her mind to some degree, and through her, gain some reassurance about Zinnia. Zinny was still alive, well, and not in any particular distress; that much was clear to me. Without that knowledge, I scarcely know how I might have functioned through the journey.

Shaking off my unease, I dressed and headed out into the late-afternoon sun. Everyone rushed around to and fro, busy with the thousand various tasks a sailing ship demanded, and I was the only one idle with nothing to do. To my surprise, I saw Tom Hollow at work on the deck with the other sailors. I spotted First Mate Caul and asked him about it.

"Do you not approve, my lord?" Caul asked. "There seemed little point to keeping the man cooped up. It's not as though there's anywhere he can go."

I acknowledged the logic of that and assured Caul he had done nothing wrong, though I approached Tom Hollow next. He looked up from his task and registered some surprise at the sight of me.

"You look different," Tom observed. He cocked his head to consider me in an admiring sort of way, I rather thought.

"Yes, I do generally practice the custom of appearing fully dressed in public, with shoes and everything."

"Your hair too though. You *do* know how to work it."

I had to suppress a laugh. What a strange set of circumstances had led this man to the misapprehension that I didn't know about hair. Plenty of folk seemed to think my head was mostly full of hair, in all senses. "And how are you, Mr. Hollow?"

"Oh, I'm fine."

"You're being treated alright? Not worked too hard?"

"Nah, it was my notion to work. Better to keep busy, I've always reckoned."

Perhaps there might have been a more subtle form of savvy in his choice. Working alongside the regular crew would surely lead to some level of camaraderie, which might gain him sympathy and allies in the days to come, whatever they might hold.

"And the food!" Tom continued. "Whoever heard of so much fresh fruit so early in the year? Or those flaky rolls? Tell you true, I've never had such good fare aboard ship."

"Are you a sailor by trade, Mr. Hollow?"

"Oh, nah, I don't reckon I have a trade, as you might call it. I've been a carpenter, a barber, a barman, done a bit of this and that, here and there. I do know my way around a ship alright though, even if this one's like a museum piece."

Was he subtly trying to sow doubt in me with his little jab at the ship? "Well, please do let me know if you ever feel you are mistreated aboard." I began to turn away, but Tom spoke again.

"I've been asking some of the sailors about you, you know. They gave me quite an earful."

That scarcely sounded promising, but I believe I smiled pleasantly enough. "I've no doubt of that."

"Is it all true?"

"Probably. I can scarcely commit myself without knowing what was said."

"Let me tell you then. Let's see, let me get this right . . ."

I could guess what had been said and did not much relish hearing it repeated back, but I suppose a grim curiosity tends to prevail in cases such as these. I nodded to let him speak. To my dismay, he drew himself up with a dramatic flair, like an actor delivering a prologue at the start of a play. Perhaps he'd left out a bit of time on the stage from his account of his varied career.

"Many years ago, a young woman—or more of a girl, really—arrived on the island all alone in a little rowboat, barely afloat, while a great storm raged all around. The girl was so exhausted that she fell into a faint at the oars, and yet by some accident of fate—or the blessing of the dragon, some say—the waves brought her boat ashore to a beach where some fishermen happened to be out securing their supplies against the storm. They fetched up the boat and found to their astonishment that the girl was in the throes of labor! On that very beach, she gave birth to a baby boy. And though people from the mainland were not normally allowed to come and stay, the girl and her newborn babe were deemed too pitiable to be sent back at the time. Rumor has it the girl even caught the eye of Lord Summer for her delicate and exotic beauty."

I can scarcely express my astonishment at hearing this tale and the mode in which it was expressed. Was it true? I had little notion. I knew that Alice had indeed arrived alone on

Summer with me as a stowaway in her belly, but she had never mentioned how far along she had been at the time. I'd assumed not very. Certainly I'd never heard about a storm or giving birth on a beach or other such melodrama. Nor had anyone during my childhood spoken of fate or the dragon in connection with our arrival. Far from it.

"I'm not sure I'd like to call it *many* years ago," I said to Tom. "But I'm afraid I can't otherwise comment on the veracity of some of these more extraordinary details, despite having had something of a starring role in the event."

"Well, there's more. I'll own this next part is a bit more confusing to me, but I reckon I can manage the gist. Now this part is thirty years on or so, and the Lord Summer of the time has died without an heir. If I understand rightly, this was counted something of a calamity in Summerland, since the people there actually want their lord to be a draconic contractor, and they count all their good fortune as due to the dragon's patronage. That right?"

At my nod, he resumed his more dramatic delivery style.

"But the dragon would accept no one. Countless nobles attempted to woo the dragon into a contract with no success. She blamed the nobles for what had happened to her contractor, I gather, and everyone feared that her wrath would soon turn against the people. Without the dragon's goodwill, crops would fail, pestilence would scourge the populace, storms would lash the island, the earth would shake, and fire would rain down from the heights! Or even if it didn't go that far, at any rate the island would no longer enjoy the life of ease to which the people had all become so well accustomed.

"The nobles were so desperate that they were willing to accept anyone who could contract with the dragon, no matter their birth. As it turned out, there was only one man she wanted, only one man she deemed worthy, only one she would accept as her bondmate—that very same child of the mainland whom the dragon had brought to the shores of Summerland some thirty years earlier. And so he became the king—or rather, Lord Summer, I should say—and returned the land to its blessed state of grace, and all has been well since then."

Tom Hollow watched closely for my reaction, and I cannot say what conclusions he might have gleaned from my face. "So is that all true?" he asked.

"I suppose it is, in a sense," I acknowledged with some reluctance.

"Well then, I reckon I've got my answer, about how you came to be where you are. Though I have to say, the sailors here were mighty vague about the thirty-odd years between your birth and you becoming the lord here." Hollow paused as if waiting for me to fill it in.

I did not oblige him. I had no doubt that if he continued pressing the sailors he would procure the tawdrier parts of the tale—that Alice, finding no place for herself in Summer, had turned to the oldest trade, as they call it, and that I had not strayed so very far from her footsteps in becoming Jack's kept boy. But I was not inclined to offer these tidbits to Hollow, and so I took my leave.

That the sailors had offered such a mythologized and sanitized version of my history amazed and perplexed me. Was it only because they had been speaking to an otherlander and wished to avoid sullying the reputation of Summer to foreign ears? Or did these young men genuinely think of me from such a lofty and fate-fueled frame of mind?

It was not possible that they were actually ignorant of my background, but they might, I supposed, have a romanticized view of it. It *was* romantic, after all—Jack really had loved me. I knew that now. So I had been informed by the foremost loremasters in the land. Everyone knew it, for the dragon would never have wanted me otherwise. Few could be so certain of their lover's regard as I, even if the realization had come too late to ever be more than cold comfort. So why should it seem so incredible to me that people might now think well of the story? Especially among those who might be young enough to have only known the end result. I couldn't say.

I stopped by the galley to get something to eat, but the cook registered some alarm at my casual intrusion. With a strange sort of obsequious insistence, he shooed me out with the assurance that a meal would be brought to me in my cabin. As I headed back there, I wondered again if I ought to have brought a personal servant to manage things for me. I knew well enough that it made many people uncomfortable when I wandered about on my own like a private man. The palace staff had simply gotten used to my ways, but the crew of this ship would not be.

To my surprise, Brook brought the meal to my cabin, though on reflection it was not surprising at all. He was new to the ship and untrained in the more technical tasks. Of course they would have him running errands like this. Still, it felt awkward to be served by him. I thanked him with perhaps more formality than was appropriate, little knowing whether to address him as a son or as a page boy. I was aware that a real gentleman would not trouble themselves over being correct in such an edge case, but I could not help but fret over such trivia. Certainly Brook took little notice and stood on no such ceremony.

"What are you planning to do to get Zinny back?" Brook demanded of me.

"Without more information, I can scarcely hope to hazard a plan," I told him. "It would more than half depend on speculation."

"You must have some idea," Brook persisted.

"There is a chance we may be able to trade Hollow for

Zinny, depending on how much they value him. If not, there's the egg. We might also be able to intimidate them with a show of force, since the *Avocet* and *Plover* will not be far behind us. Or with threats of unleashing the dragon on them, I suppose."

"Will they be easily intimidated, do you think? Do they fear the power of Summer?"

"That's difficult to say. The name of Summer is well known throughout the otherlands, but with varying degrees of accuracy in their understanding of our land and our strength. For many otherlanders, Summer is little more than a fairy tale. Some know a bit more, especially in coastal towns where they might have at least a smidgen of contact with our occasional trading ships. Since I don't believe we've ever traded with Oxeye, it's impossible to know what they will think of us."

"What if this cult has her instead by the time we get there? The Kittevers?"

I shrugged. "I suppose the same logic applies. I'd warn you not to get too caught up in the romanticism of the idea of a magic cult, like you see in melodramas. These organizations are generally . . . less impressive than they'd like you to believe. Ragtag groups of misfits playing at being great mystics."

"Mr. Hollow seems to believe they are very dangerous."

"I've no doubt they are, in their way. A desperate fool can often be more dangerous than a well-situated man of influence." Then the further import of Brook's words hit me, and I asked, "You've been speaking with Tom Hollow?"

"Everyone has. He's been pestering the crew with questions all day. He seems to take a very keen interest in Summer."

"About Summer? Or about me?"

Brook frowned and took a moment to puzzle over my

question. "Which Summer do you mean?" he asked eventually, and I understood his discomfort. It was vaguely taboo to ask for clarification of an utterance of *Summer*. Is it that to ask is to acknowledge that there's a difference? No great matter though, I suppose, considering how rarely it comes up. People of Summer are so adept at picking up the context.

"Either," I replied, which I think was true, and also held the benefit of relieving Brook's unease. "I know Hollow's been asking about me. I've been under the impression that he's been trying to draw me out—to judge my weaknesses, that sort of thing. From the questions he asked, do you think Hollow is also interested in our land, our dragon? Or is he only interested in me as a man?"

"I'm not sure. He did seem most interested in how you in particular became Summer. Sort of like he's incredulous about it." Brook mused to himself for a moment. "I almost get the impression that he thinks we ought to be snobbish about coloration or some such. A silly notion, isn't it?"

"Quite absurd," I agreed, wholehearted if a little amused. My stepson truly was a charming trove of innocence regarding the world outside of Summer. I nearly regretted that he might shortly become better educated in such matters.

I could see how Hollow might have gotten the wrong end of things. He logically surmised that such an insular island nation was likely to be hostile to people who look different, and thus had struggled to comprehend how I should fit in. But he was mistaken. I'd always found Summer's attitudes towards otherlanders to be far more complex than that—or perhaps much simpler.

Summer hated change, hated strangers, hated accepting anything new. Alice and I had once been strangers with no place in the established rhythm of life in Summer. Every necessary trade was already carried out by an established family, and every family always seemed to have just the right amount of children to carry on the family line as they always had, never expanding nor contracting. No one had liked us hanging about with no purpose; our presence had the whiff of change about it. But now I had a place and a role in the established way of things, and I was no longer a stranger, not to Summer. So I belonged.

But to mainlanders like Tom, I still looked as if I did not fit. To him, I had to justify who I was and why I was what I was. Would I have more such problems when we reached Oxeye? Would I be spending all my time explaining myself and convincing people that I really was Lord Summer? It scarcely seemed like it would be a good start to negotiations.

ADMIRAL ROSTRUM CAME TO the cabin a bit after that, ostensibly to retrieve something he had forgotten there. Yet he lingered to offer up some sort of apology or explanation for his comments the day before. Or rather, that morning. It was still the same day, still the first day of spring. I had little interest in what the admiral had to say.

Here was another who didn't think I looked the part, albeit for different reasons. I was nothing like the big brawny brooding Jack nor the huge hulking hungry Leo before him. And though I had never known a Lady Summer, I had been given to understand that even they tended towards being imposing of stature and stoic of manner. It was no wonder the admiral did not take me seriously or respect me in my role, with my slight form and pretty face.

So how could I expect anyone on the mainland to do so? How was I to have a prayer of intimidating them into treating with us as we deserved? But then again, maybe it didn't have to be that way. As I looked over the admiral's square face, broad shoulders, and solid barrel of a chest, an idea occurred to me. The idea was not truly a new notion of mine, but an old idea of Jack's refitted to new purposes.

When Jack and I traveled the otherlands, we often appeared in different guises or played different roles than what fate had dealt us. It was at Jack's urging, of course, for he did not like to attract attention to himself, did not want to deal with people or talk to anyone most of the time. So I would play the gentleman, and he would play the bodyguard or porter, stoic and silent beside me. After so much time being at the heart of everyone's attention and expectations, I suppose it was freeing for him to be all but invisible.

It had been great fun for me, of course. At the time, it was a revelation to see how easily people accepted me as a gentleman, indeed how readily they accepted anything I claimed to be. I had been so used to Summer, where everyone had known me on sight and known exactly what I was. But in the otherlands, no one knew me, and I could be anything. On the occasional times when we had attempted to reveal some part of the truth to someone, they had often refused to believe it and required some convincing that Jack truly was my superior.

"Admiral," I interrupted him. "Have you ever done any acting?"

He was clearly taken aback, and I idly wondered what point of his I might have cut in on. I did not care. "Acting? You mean like in plays?" the admiral said. "I shouldn't think so, no. Trivial business that, isn't it, Summer?"

Of course. The admiral probably thought actors were about on par with whores. "Hmm, well, it wouldn't be necessary for you to play a different person," I mused. "You'd only have to be yourself, simply in a different role."

"A role?"

I was in no rush to elaborate. I examined the solid

gold signet ring on my hand, impressed with the sigil of Summer—a dragon coiled around a bounteous pile of fruit like a cornucopia. A bit of cord was wrapped around the inner band as a sizer, as I'd never quite been able to bring myself to have it changed from how it had been when Jack wore it, even to resize it for my hand.

I took the ring off, peeled off the cord, and handed it to the admiral. "Put it on," I commanded him.

Warily the admiral took the ring from me. He squinted at my face as if waiting for me to change my mind, to call it back and confess it all to be a joke. But I didn't. I watched him and waited.

So the admiral pushed the signet ring onto his own finger. At once I could see that it was a perfect fit.

A MAN OF INDUSTRY

OXEYE MIGHT ONCE HAVE BEEN A CHARMING SEA-side town. Once. What would have been the old waterfront area had been shouldered aside by several large factories and warehouses, conveniently located right by the docks for maximal eyesore potential. Much of the commerce you might expect to see dockside seemed to have simply vanished. Where were the fish market and the food stalls? Where were the sailors' taverns and brothels? Or the more fashionable, tidy inns? All in all, I counted Oxeye from the sea to be a grim sight.

The docks at least bustled with activity, with ships coming and going, wares loaded on and off with terrific efficiency. A number of armed guards in dark blue uniforms moved among the usual sailors and stevedores. The guards inspected cargo, surveyed the activity, and persuaded disorderly sorts to move along. Each of these blue-clad guards carried a musket across his back and a sword at his hip.

An officious busybody of a harbormaster did not want to allow us to dock, citing some sort of reservation or license that we lacked. But the admiral had no patience with the man and explained in a booming voice that the *Godwit* would be pulling into a slip with his permission or without it—preferably an empty slip, but the admiral assured him that we were not so very particular. The harbormaster relented.

The admiral's authoritative presence on the docks seemed to validate my plan that he ought to impersonate Lord Summer in my place, I rather thought. Admiral Rostrum was now on board with the notion, albeit somewhat reluctantly. He had had some trouble believing that anyone would not immediately conclude that the draconic contractor of the party must be the one in charge, no matter how I'd explained that it would not be seen that way at all. Contractors in the otherlands were more often outcasts or creepy hermits who lived in the mountains with their dragonesses.

One of the sailors went ashore in advance to gather some information. I had wanted to go myself, reasoning that my appearance would excite the least attention in Oxeye, as I looked more like a local than the rest of the Summer natives. But the officers on the *Godwit* clearly regarded the idea as preposterous, and the admiral pointed out that I was likely to turn heads wherever I went. I allowed myself to be placated by the compliment and went along with the consensus.

Our reconnaissance man returned with the most pressing information we sought—that the *Shadowcat* had indeed been in Oxeye, but after some of its passengers had disembarked, the ship had once again departed.

The blue-clad armed guards were apparently patrolling all over town, and it would seem they constituted a private guard under the direct employ of Mr. Light. Our man also learned the location of Mr. Light's house, though that could not be credited as much of a triumph of intelligence gathering. The enormous complex hunkered down just past the edge of the factories, and an unsightly lookout tower was plainly visible from our position on the water.

Before we had long to absorb this information, a runner

hailed us from the docks with a message: Mr. Light invited us to join him in his home for a modest dinner.

A PARTY OF SIX was formed to accept Mr. Light's invitation: the admiral, myself, and four crew members as guards and general help. Brook wanted to join the party, but I would not have it, not at this stage. Tom Hollow was, of course, to be kept belowdecks under close guard while we were in port.

Given the alarming number of armed men that appeared to be at Mr. Light's disposal, we determined that we should play things very carefully in this initial meeting. If Light did not appear inclined to work with us, we agreed not to press things until after the *Avocet* and the *Plover* arrived with reinforcements. They were expected to be only a day behind us, two at the most, so it would be foolish to allow ourselves to be drawn into a conflict sooner if it could at all be avoided.

I gave the admiral precise instructions on how to dress and groom himself, for if he was to be Lord Summer, I scarcely wanted him to show poorly. Nor could he appear to be less well turned out than me on any level, and I did not wish to reduce the quality of my own dress. The admiral made no objection to the interference, but rather seemed simply bewildered at the level of detail I could take an interest in.

Fashion trends in Summer tend to run at least ten years behind the mainland, so I felt uneasy about how our attire might come across. But as we started up the street, I decided I needn't have fretted. The same assembly-line standard style of clothing pervaded all walks of life in Oxeye, it seemed. We certainly stood out—in that our clothes were properly fitted, that they possessed character of any sort—but I could not bring myself to regret it.

Several guards stood at the entrance to Mr. Light's house,

but they waved us in as soon as they saw us. The interior was less adorned than I expected, almost stark in its simple, right-angled lines and clean surfaces. Even though I was well accustomed to living partially underground in the sumptuous cave-palace in the cliffs of Summer, Mr. Light's house felt claustrophobic as we wound through a labyrinth of interchangeable corridors. A cool, lifeless feeling pervaded all; there were not even any cats or dogs around. We arrived at a dining room and at last set eyes on our host.

Mr. Light was a well-fed man; the roundness of his face lent it a sort of softness and gentleness that I had not expected, though his gaze was clear and keen. His gray hair was short and tidy, his clothes the same simple stuff all the people of the town wore. He surveyed our party with a discerning eye and fixed at once on the admiral, though our manner of dress was of a kind. I knew then I had chosen rightly; imagine if I'd had to correct him!

"Welcome! Welcome!" Mr. Light greeted the admiral with a broad, jovial smile. "Never before have we had delegates from the land of Summer here in our little hamlet, and I am beyond honored to be the one to welcome you here. Please, join me!" He gestured towards a table well-laden with meats, breads, pastries, and other elaborately arranged fare.

The admiral returned the pleasantries and expressed an appropriate if restrained degree of gratitude for the generous meal. At first I thought that he underdid the latter, for I suspected that this feast was more sumptuous by Oxeye standards than the admiral realized. But no, it was for the best that the admiral had reacted just as a true-born son of Summer would—unimpressed and underwhelmed by such plenty. This sort of thing was exactly why he was better suited for the role. I was a flatterer and a fawner by nature, while we needed to project power.

The admiral then named himself as Lord Summer, which

Mr. Light accepted without surprise. "And this is Mr. Aloysius Alison," he introduced me with a name I had often utilized during my travels in the otherlands. "My . . . *advisor.*" I little knew whether the admiral intended for the introduction to contain such a tantalizing twist of suggestion, or if that was merely how the novelty of the designation expressed itself. Either way it was perfect. Mr. Light gave me a more apprais-ing glance, but plainly reached no conclusions as to my role.

At a motion from Mr. Light, two more people stepped for-ward: a man and a woman. "This is Lord Thomas Grinhill, who is my guest at the moment while his manor house up on the hill is undergoing renovations." The rail-thin, heavy-lid-ded man looked rather bored with these proceedings, and his greeting to us was strictly correct and nothing more. I wondered if Light had wanted him there as a show of his in-fluence, as if to say, *I'm not intimidated by lords from far off places. I have my own pet lord here at home.*

The woman, on the other hand, was remarkable—a stun-ning beauty possessed of rare poise and elegance. Raven hair reached her waist in glossy waves, and flawlessly applied cos-metics accentuated her high cheekbones and smoky gaze. Her coral-colored taffeta gown certainly had not come off an as-sembly line; it was a work of art sculpted to the curves of her body.

"And this is my wife, Sally," Mr. Light offered.

I could only hope I adequately concealed my double take. I truly had not recognized her as the same woman from the *Shadowcat,* and I flatter myself to think that I am not a man easily fooled by cosmetic illusions. Between the wig, the dress, and the makeup, her transformation was total. Sally must have recognized me as well, perhaps even with her own lesser double take at my improved appearance, but she gave no sign.

We all took our seats to eat. I was placed between the ad-miral and Lord Grinhill, so I was obliged to converse with

Grinhill, all the while attempting to attend to the admiral's talk with Light.

Grinhill did not make conversation easy. Had he any family in town? No. Elsewhere then? No. Was there good sport on his lands? Not so much lately. How were the renovations of his home proceeding? Slowly. Had the town of Oxeye changed quite a bit since his youth? Yes. Did the changes meet with his approval? Not particularly. Why was that? Shrug.

I like to think I have some stamina for lagging conversations, but before too long of talking to Grinhill, I felt I'd rather be dragged behind a team of oxen than endure much more of it. I glanced often towards Sally—I assumed that would not excite much notice, as people must stare at her all the time in that guise—but she only ate quietly, her manner mild and demure. I reminded myself of our determination to proceed with care and tried my best to banish Zinnia from my thoughts.

Mr. Light meanwhile expounded at length upon the operations of his factories in Oxeye, while the admiral listened with apparently genuine engagement. We had no mass production in Summer, and the concept seemed to pique the admiral's interest. He pleased Light with quite thorough and technical questions on the operation of mechanical looms and brass refineries.

As Mr. Light warmed to his subject, he expanded his talk to discuss his broader schemes of reforming the town of Oxeye. Light explained how Oxeye had once been a chaotic place, full of crime, poverty, and vice, but now all was orderly and prosperous, to the benefit of all. He explained how the very ground on which we were sitting was once home to more than one house of ill repute, but that was all gone now.

"What happened to all the whores?"

"I beg your pardon?" Light fixed his gaze on me with a frown.

"The people who worked in the brothels," I clarified pointlessly, as if he might have somehow misunderstood what whores are. "Do they all work in your factories now?"

It was plain that Light thought I was having a go at him; perhaps he had grown so unaccustomed to cheek that he'd forgotten how to react. He stared at me.

"Some of them do," Grinhill spoke up. "Others left town when things changed, along with many others who plied specialized trades." After all my efforts to draw him out, this he took an interest in? Well, at least he had helped me out.

"Oh, I see," I replied as cheerfully as I could. I attempted to convey the sense that my curiosity was now satisfied and we could all move on. I don't believe it worked. To think I had been concerned I might cause problems by airing my unfiltered opinions on machine-made textiles.

The admiral rescued the situation, and once again he surprised me with the nuance of his reaction. "I do apologize, Mr. Light. This one can be a bit eccentric at times." And he lifted his hand to let the backs of his fingers brush across my cheek—intimate and infantilizing at once.

Mr. Light observed the gesture and nodded to himself just slightly. He understood now. It was for the best that he underestimated me, of course. I had told myself that about many people many times before, and I supposed it remained as true as it ever was.

"There was a dragon here too, you know," Mr. Light added, though I couldn't say what inspired this addition to his account of the ills of old Oxeye. "Horrible nuisance for the farmers, or anyone who kept animals, really. It was entrenched on the edges of Grinhill's land, wasn't it, good man?"

Grinhill acknowledged this with a sedate nod. "Technically, yes. Though that part of the grounds was not workable for any purpose."

"Of course, of course," Mr. Light agreed amiably. "It was

my clever lady wife who discovered an opportunity to be rid of the menace for good. Apparently these beasts are quite a bit more vulnerable when they're guarding a clutch of eggs, and they won't simply flee—which only seems to be a victory until the dragon comes back at her convenience. When my Sally figured out that the dragon had eggs and pointed all this out to me, I organized a brigade to confront the beast. Lost three good men in the fight, but we took the beast out, good and done with. Got the chance to destroy the two eggs as well. It's been these ten years now with nary a sight of a dragon anywhere in these parts, let alone in Oxeye proper."

Privately I wondered how many people, if any, had ever been killed by this dragon prior to the brigade to justify the loss of life in eliminating it. Most dragonesses showed a strong wariness of killing humans, knowing full well that exactly that sort of thing might happen if they antagonized their human neighbors too much. That was why they were often left alone, even considered points of local pride. What had the common people of Oxeye really felt about the hunt? Then again, most people have little enough of entertainment and are quick to cheer on anything that breaks up the monotony of their lives.

"I hear these parts have had dragon trouble of another sort lately," the admiral pivoted the conversation. "Cults around dragons rising and gaining power, that sort of thing."

"Not in Oxeye, we don't!" Light insisted. "It's true the so-called Kittevers have gained ground in many other towns on this seaboard, but they're not welcome in Oxeye, and I can promise you won't see a solitary sign of them here."

I thought I caught Grinhill roll an eye at that, though I couldn't be sure I saw right. From Sally, I saw no sign. No one seemed keen to dwell on the topic, however, and the admiral let it lie.

Aside from that, Light showed no other sign of interest in the topic of dragons. Indeed Light's lack of curiosity about

Summer's famous dragon was quite remarkable. When he did allow the conversation to move in the direction of Summer, he chiefly questioned us on practical matters, such as how traditional methods of agricultural production could so reliably support the whole population without fail. Of course such questions were inextricably tied up with the dragon in truth, yet Light did not seem aware of that.

This was quite a contrast to my previous forays into the otherlands. If I ever let on that I was from Summer, I generally found people disappointed by any mundane descriptions of pastoral life, but rather burning with interest in just one thing. The dragon, the dragon, and the dragon normally topped otherlanders' lists of inquiries about Summer. There were other dragons, of course: rare but not unheard-of in the many pockets of rugged terrain throughout the world. But none were so ancient and powerful, none so saturated with romantic notions and flights of fancy, nor so famed for their awesome and terrible beauty. Either Light felt he already knew all there was to know about our dragon, or he was a man of no soul.

Light did not inquire about our purpose in visiting Oxeye, but the admiral found an opportunity to mention almost casually that we sought a young lady who had been taken from our land. Light nodded sympathetically at that but offered up nothing to help and gave little insight into his thoughts. The admiral did not press it, sticking to our agreement to proceed with caution. I thought that was quite right, for Sally Hollow-Light's unexpected presence only encouraged me to think that caution was needed. Something was not right here, but I did not yet understand it.

After dinner, we retired to a reasonably well-appointed sitting room, the first truly agreeable room I'd seen in the complex. Sumptuous wall hangings and upholstered furniture lent it an atmosphere both cozy and elegant. Musical instruments stood about the room in prominent places as if played with regularity. Quite a few guitars were there, but I had only a passing acquaintance with that instrument. I paused by a handsome six-stringed lute and strummed it idly to see if it was in tune. It was.

"Do you play, sir?" Light asked me with an eagerness I would not have anticipated.

"Oh, no, not anymore," I demurred.

"Ah! What I hear is that you *do* play!" Light pressed. "Please, indulge us. My wife is very fond of music, you know."

I glanced in Sally's direction. She smiled sweetly and offered an angelically beseeching look that might have melted many a man's resolve—if he were into that sort of thing. To my dismay, the admiral also took quite an interest in this turn of events and nodded encouragingly. Even Grinhill perked up. It would surely seem strange to refuse.

Even now, my reluctance is hard to account for, seeing as I would not have to contend with obsequious reactions as I did in Summer. Perhaps playing for people simply reminded me of Jack, of his small smile when I played for him, or the way his gravelly voice creaked on the rare occasions when he sang along.

Still, I suppose I relish attention too much to hold out for long. I took up the lute and played a song I recalled as a favorite of Leo's, the Lord Summer of my youth. It was a hunting song, recalling in gruesome detail the chase, the kill, the slaughter, the glee of the hounds, and then all over again with a different hapless beast. I wondered at myself that I remembered all the words, though perhaps the dragon helped me there. She minded the music with keen interest.

It went over well enough with the human audience as well, or at least they were polite. Fortunately, I was not asked for a repeat performance, no doubt a testament to what they really thought. Instead I was relieved by Sally.

She took up a guitar and played a lively piece with great skill, accompanied by her charmingly versatile voice. It was a love song of the type in which the singer purports to tell of their own feelings, rather than recounting the tale of two lovers. It was so much more modern in style than what I had played that I felt some embarrassment for my choice. I had made a poor show of representing Summer, perhaps, revealing it as a backwards and provincial place whose culture perpetually lagged by decades if not centuries.

Sally also then played upon a woodwind instrument, bringing forth a melancholy and evocative melody that nearly brought the room to tears. She was *very* good—far better than me by a long shot, and I don't simply mean her musical talent.

To my satisfaction, Light invited us to stay the night in his home, and the admiral agreed. The room I was allotted in Mr. Light's house was much like the rest of the complex: large, utilitarian, soulless. I waited there alone for the household to fall silent, for the servants to finally go to their beds. I wanted a chance to explore on my own.

While I bided my time, my thoughts swirled in many directions. I suppose I should make something clear at this point. I haven't spoken much of Zinnia in this tale since we arrived in Oxeye, but that is not because she was not on my mind. There simply doesn't seem much to say about the gnawing aching hollow that ate into my heart and mind at all times in those days. I knew she must be alive and more or less well, or I would have received some sense of distress from the dragon. Summer was still linked to Zinnia and would know if something had happened to her. Though Summer felt distant at times, there was no way I could have missed that. Yet her absence tore at me all the same.

I thought back on the evening and tried to draw some sort of advantageous conclusions, something I could use to get me closer to Zinny. But if I were honest with myself, I had no knack for reading people and guessing what would motivate them. Jack had always taken care of that part in our travels, for of course he'd had a contractor's insights into the minds of others and could always tell if people were trying to deceive us. A glance at Jack was all I'd ever needed to know whether to trust someone. Now I was the contractor, but as usual, my own inadequacies prevented me from utilizing such gifts. I had no true insights into Mr. Light, or Lord Grinhill, or least of all Sally Hollow-Light.

Instead I kept coming back to my own choice of song and questioned myself on how a song favored by Leo had come to seem right for the occasion. I had very seldom played for any audience that included Leo, as Jack had quite nearly forbidden it, so I did not learn the song by playing it for him. Perhaps the story of the dragon slaying had brought to mind themes of hunting. Or perhaps Mr. Light had reminded me of Leo in some way. Outwardly he had been quite polite, even gregarious, and yet Leo had taught me not to trust such things.

If I am to speak about Leo, and I suppose I am, I should clarify that I did not actually know him particularly well, not directly. If I were to tally up the times that I came face-to-face with the man and exchanged words with him, it's unlikely I would come to the end of my supply of fingers. Yet Leo loomed large over all the days of my youth: an outsized presence that poisoned all the things I held most precious.

Well can I recall the first time I encountered him, perhaps my very earliest memory. I was quite small, too young to be left alone at home I suppose, and Alice had brought me along to the palace with the intention of leaving me in the kitchens, where the kindly head cook usually kept an eye on me. But something fell through there—I don't recall what—and Alice apparently determined that she'd simply have to leave me sitting quietly in the back hallway to wait for her.

For Alice did not visit Leo by the main corridor, but by way of a back passage that offered more discreet access to his bedchamber. This was my first time seeing these secret back passages of the palace. In later years, I would routinely make good use of them, but at that time I was simply enchanted with the idea of being able to creep about unnoticed through the labyrinthine underground palace.

When we came to the door, she impressed upon me that I must sit still, be quiet, and wait for her return, no matter what I heard or how bored I became.

But at that moment, the door opened, and Leo's enormous bulk filled the space. "What's this kid doing here?"

"I apologize, Lord Summer," Alice said with lowered eyes, in a voice both more submissive and more flustered than I had ever heard from her. "I was just going to leave him here in the hall." She stepped in front of me as if to shield me from view.

Leo was so tall, and Alice so petite, that her efforts to conceal me counted for naught. He looked right over her to stare down at me from what seemed a terrific height. "I'm fairly sure you're not supposed to leave children alone in dark crawlspaces. It's a boy, you say?"

"What? Oh, yes, a boy."

"Pretty for a boy. I suppose they're all the same at that age though, aren't they?" He did not wait for an answer, but turned away into the well-appointed room. "Bring him on over here," he ordered my mother.

Alice's hand shook as she clutched mine and drew me into the room after her, and I could only wonder what she feared.

My attention was called to a tray of cakes and pastries sitting out on a side table. A small tawny cat licked at one of the cheese-topped pastries with unqualified boldness. Lord

Summer noticed my interest and said, "Go ahead, boy. Take one." He scooped up the little cat out of my way. It looked even tinier in his massive arms and yet was more cross than concerned at the interruption of its snack.

I snatched up one of the cakes with more the manner of a furtive animal than a boy and then took a step back to eat it. It was a ginger cake and was perhaps the greatest thing I had ever tasted to that point in my young life. As I gobbled it up, Leo and the tawny cat stared at me with the same unblinking intensity.

Then Leo stood, opened a different door, and called to someone in another room. A valet appeared and took in the situation without surprise. "Take this kid over to Jack's minder," Leo ordered him. "They're about the same age, aren't they? They can . . . play, or whatever kids do."

I heard Alice release a breath that was almost a sob, and I wondered again what worried her so. The valet took me up in his arms and carried me away.

I remember little else of that day, despite what you might think. Although I have many memories of playing with Jack as small children, my first impressions are lost to me. It would not have offered much insight of worth anyway, since we were too young to understand the gulf of differences between us. Jack being kind and loyal towards me can only be counted as notable once he knew that he needn't be.

So I only remember Leo from that day. That first meeting was, I suppose, emblematic of all other times I crossed paths with Leo—all except one. He never did anything to hurt me, and yet the people I loved were so plainly terrified of him that the moments resonated in my mind like an endless chorus. For it was not only Alice who tried to shield me from Leo and inevitably became on edge whenever he was near. Jack did much the same, and he often fretted about his little sister and even his stepmother being too much in Leo's power.

In time I would come to associate Leo with bruises, with nightmares, with sudden silences. But it would take time—more time than I like to admit—to put all the pieces together, even as all the court whispered evil of his name.

But I digress too far, perhaps. I was not in Leo's house anymore, but in Mr. Light's. At length the house became as quiet as I could wish for, and I padded out in my socks to have a look around.

A MIDNIGHT ENCOUNTER

THOUGH MR. LIGHT'S HOUSE WAS VERY MUCH SET along straight lines and right angles, I found it confusing nevertheless. Every corridor and intersection looked too similar to the others, with little to no ornamentation to use as reference points. Unless I counted passageways, it was impossible to intuit where I was. The locks were more challenging to pick than the ancient old iron things around Summer, and I was out of practice at such skills, but I persevered at it. With a couple of hairpins and a generous amount of whispered curses, I found I could open any of the doors.

I peered in a variety of miscellaneous rooms, but found little out of the ordinary. A good deal of the complex was indeed empty and unused, as if it had been built larger than was truly needed. Did Mr. Light anticipate a greater need for space in the future? Or had he simply built on a grand scale to be more impressive?

A large office that must have belonged to Light intrigued me, but it ultimately proved disappointing. A great many papers and logbooks could be found there, all tidily organized on shelves and cubbies by some guiding principle that eluded me, but none of it meant much to me.

After exploring a good bit of the ground floor, I wanted to find my way to the lookout tower in the corner of the complex, as I had some vague notion that it might be a good place to keep a prisoner. Perhaps I'd seen too many plays in which the captured princess is inevitably kept in a tower located stage right. I located a vestibule leading to the tower staircase and headed up.

"You won't find her here," a woman's voice informed me. I spun around.

Sally Hollow-Light sat with calm composure in the vestibule, still fully made up and bewigged, but wearing only a small slip of black silk. After having seen her in such a perfectly tailored turnout earlier, some disappointment twinged in me at the sloppily inelegant fit of the nightgown; it was barely adequate to contain her breasts.

"Then tell me where I will find her," I replied.

"Not in my hands," Sally told me. "Light took her from me almost as soon as I arrived. She might have been sent off somewhere on the *Shadowcat*."

"Why?"

Sally shrugged. "He likes to have control."

"Over what? What does he know of Zinnia? If he wants something in exchange for her, then why did he not mention it?"

"He believes that to speak first is to show desperation and to put one at a disadvantage in negotiations. And what about your lord? Why did he not speak more plainly?"

"I suspect that he wanted to get the measure of your Mr. Light."

"Ah, well, you and I are much more straightforward. As we have already reached an agreement—"

"And I was doing my part before you ran away!"

"From where I stood, I was doing my part when your people ambushed me."

"I could have called them off if you'd only been patient."

"I couldn't know that."

"So you decided it would be best to abandon your brother?"

She did not respond to that at once, but took a sip of something from a wooden cup standing by. "How is Tom?"

It occurred to me that it might be wisest to maintain some mystery on that score, but I found I did not have it in me to make this woman worry needlessly about her brother. "He's fine. Thriving even."

"He would." Sally nodded. "Last I saw your Zinnia, she was fine too. I believe I know where Light would have sent someone he wished to keep safe."

"Then tell me."

"Take me on your ship, and I'll show you. I can't get away from here on my own right now, but I have my own reasons for wanting to go to the same place."

"For your own children, you mean?"

She was taken aback and perhaps a little confused. "How do you know about that?" she asked slowly.

"Tom told me, of course," I said.

"Right. Well, yes, so you understand why it's important to me." She stood up and came closer to me. "If you take me with you, we can all get what we're looking for and get out of here. The place won't be well guarded. The men you have with you on your ship will be more than sufficient."

As far as she knew, I could tell if she was lying. That was almost as good as actually being able to tell, right? Why would she lie if she were certain I could see right through it?

"I will have to talk this over with Lord Summer," I told her.

Her look gave little hint on whether she believed that part of the story. I did not believe she had overheard when I told her brother to call me Summer, but I also had little notion of how much Sally understood of the nature of

Summer as a whole, to know that Summer's contractor and Lord Summer are one and the same.

"Do you? Surely you can persuade him with no trouble." She came even closer, leaning forward in a particular way that made her already tiny nightgown give up its flimsy hold on concealment. She nearly pressed herself against me, but stopped just short. In a husky voice, she breathed, "You can help me, can't you?"

I would rather have liked to tell her that she was only embarrassing herself with this little display, but I did have enough sense to know it would be better to keep some things to myself. If she thought this was working, she was less likely to turn to other, more devious methods of persuasion. She was more likely to drop her guard if she believed me under her sway. I supposed she may have gotten the wrong idea when I'd spent too long admiring the fineness of her gown earlier. Accordingly I now let my gaze fall on her assets. The outline of a knife concealed on her hip drew my attention, but I took no conclusions from it.

I knew it wouldn't take much to convince her she was having an effect. That's the trouble with beautiful women; they always think everyone is obsessed with them and that they can get away with anything. A beautiful man can get away with a great deal, of course, but we at least need some level of discernment about our audience's likely reception before flinging ourselves headlong into such a bald-faced tactic.

"I really need to confer with Lord Summer," I reiterated, though I endeavored to make it seem a struggle.

Sally smiled indulgently. "Very well," she said, and she trailed a fingertip along the edge of my face. "Go back to your fat old lord and convince him for me."

That did not sit well with me at all. The admiral was in

his early fifties and thus only about twelve years my senior. Sally might very well have been under the impression that I myself was younger than I really was, for I flatter myself that my face still betrayed but little marks of the years. A man of thirty might readily scoff at fifty-two as a far-off fate little to be feared, but a man of forty has not that luxury of distance. Nor did I think it fair to call him fat; the admiral had the sort of bulk that can be really quite pleasing, if you prefer a more substantial sort of man.

Sally must have supposed that I had attached myself to the admiral only from sycophantic motives and thus would not mind him being so denigrated. Yet it was rather more unpleasant to hear one's chosen lover maligned for their appearance—all the more so if you cannot defend your choice on grounds of personality. The more I thought about it, however, the more convinced I became that I wouldn't like to hear any lover of mine so insulted, for whatever reason I chose to bed them.

It seemed then a strange misstep from Sally, who had otherwise been so smooth in her dealings with me. Was she intentionally saying something unpleasant to provoke a reaction from me, as her brother Tom sometimes had? Or did this attitude merely reflect her feelings on her own situation? If she thought of her own husband in such terms, perhaps she supposed everyone thought that way. For myself, I've never seen much profit in calling out the deficiencies of other people's physical forms.

I begged off and did indeed go straight to the admiral's room. The admiral was still in his clothes but had dozed off sitting up, with a book fallen by the wayside. He woke at my entry.

"What is it?" he asked, rapidly coming to alertness. "Have you found anything?"

I gave an account of my unsuccessful exploration of the complex, and I told him briefly of my encounter with Sally, though I left out her misguided attempt to seduce me as well as her comment on his person.

He considered it with a frown. "Do you think we can trust her? Woman can be flighty and prone to changing moods, and it sounds as though she won't even give you the details of what she intends for us to make our own judgment. Light may or may not be a good man, but I think we know what we're dealing with there. It may be wiser to proceed with attempting to negotiate with Light, rather than throwing in our lot with his wife."

I shrugged and nodded absently. Having become adept at filtering out his more inane asides, I could see his logic. Could I simply make him decide what to do? I felt reluctant to make any decisions that might come to a bad end, and yet anything I chose at this point might go wrong.

I had never been made for making decisions in these situations. Jack was the leader between us, always. And if one of us were meant to die, surely it ought to have been me—a dramatic end to the first act, giving the hero the motivation he needed to rise to the occasion and fulfill the task he was born to do. But I was not the hero. I was not made to go on without the hero.

"Are you angry with me?"

"Huh?" I looked up in surprise at the admiral. "Why should I be angry?"

"For what I did at the dinner table. I couldn't think of anything else at the moment. This acting business is not as easy as it looks."

"No, no, I'm not angry about that. I thought it was brilliant. You're doing wonderfully."

The admiral looked skeptical, but grudgingly accepted

the compliment with a nod. "I still don't quite follow why this ruse is necessary."

"Don't you think it's going well? You were getting on splendidly with Light. I think that proves it was a good choice," I tried to convince him. "It's really no great matter. Jack and I used to do this sort of thing all the time, you know, just because he didn't like to do the talking with strangers."

"Well, that may be, but Jack was . . ." The admiral trailed off, a thought decidedly unsaid.

"Jack was what?"

He shook his head. "It doesn't matter. The man is dead, and I know you cared for him. But if Jack did this nonsense because he didn't like to talk, that doesn't explain why you're doing it. You can't tell me you have trouble with talking."

"I simply think this is the best way to make the right impression and get what we want out of these people."

"Well, if you say so," the admiral said.

As you might imagine, I wondered what the admiral had stopped himself from saying about Jack. I could speculate endlessly, for there were any number of disturbing things that people tended to believe about Jack.

The most notable, of course, was the notion that Jack murdered his own father. I can assure you with complete certainty that there is no truth to that, though as far as I'm concerned, Jack would have been fully justified in doing so. For some brief time, I did wonder if Jack knew the identity of Leo's killer and kept it secret for reasons of his own, but in time I became convinced that that was not true either.

Ah, but I am getting ahead of myself, forgetting that these days not everyone knows the full details surrounding Leo's death. It was such a tremendous happening at the time that it would have been hard to believe it could so quickly fade out of the general consciousness, but time truly does erase everything, does it not? And more than a few in Summer have been keen to let this one fade away.

Here is what was known. One evening, many witnesses watched as Summer hurled herself out of the sea, climbed up the exterior of the palace, and broke through the window of Leo's bedchamber to shove her enormous head within. She departed again a few moments later carrying Leo's inert body in her jaws. A large pool of blood covered the center of the bed and trailed towards the broken window, but otherwise, there were no signs of what had happened.

This set of circumstances would suggest one of three things. One—a person unknown had murdered Leo, and the dragon had arrived to avenge him. She would have eaten the murderer, of course. Two—Jack had murdered Leo, but the dragon spared him. It was assumed that Jack was the only person who would be so spared. Three—the dragon herself had killed Leo. This last was considered far-fetched to anyone with a passing understanding of draconic contracts, but it had to be allowed as part of the logical proof, which was the name of the game at that time.

As you might imagine, the first possibility was the one that everyone fixated on at first, until it became apparent that no one was missing. If a person unknown *had* killed Leo, the person was so unknown that no one missed them. So it was that the logically minded began to default to the second option and imagine that Jack must have killed his father. It's not as though he wouldn't have had cause.

I spoke to Jack just a few days after Leo's death. When I came to him, he was sitting on his balcony staring out at the sea as the eerie wail of the dragon's lament filled the air. I had always had free access to Jack's room and thus hadn't bothered to knock on the door, but on that day I believe he was startled by my approach, which perhaps put him on the wrong footing.

"Where have you been?" Jack demanded.

I recoiled, taken aback by the hostility of his tone and alarmed by the choice of words.

"I'm sorry," Jack quickly remedied. "It's just that I've needed you, and I didn't know where you were. I was worried. Please, come here."

I went to him and let him draw me into his embrace. He buried his face in my hair and squeezed me tight. We stayed like that for a while, not saying anything, and occasionally I could feel his body racked by a sob that he tried to stifle.

"Where *have* you been?" he repeated, but this time gently and softly.

"I've been with my mother," I told him. "She's been ill."

"Oh, it must be serious. You never call her your mother," Jack noted. "Is she alright?"

"No," I said. "She's dead."

Jack pushed me back to look at my face, to see that I was serious. "Oh, Teddy. What happened?"

"She hit her head, and she got very confused. I took her home, but she didn't get better. She started to have fits, and then . . ." I was unable to go on.

"Why didn't you tell me? I could have sent a doctor there, and—"

"Doctor Kay did come to see her. There was nothing to be done."

"Oh." Jack was silent for a moment. "Do you need help with anything else? With, uh, the arrangements?"

"No, it's all done."

Jack looked at me closely then, but his face was inscrutable.

I learned later that he checked my story. Doctor Kay was questioned, as was the coroner, as were Alice's nearest neighbors. But he would have found it was all exactly as I said, and that his suspicions were impossible. Alice was fully incapacitated well before Leo's murder, and her body was seen by many people. I don't blame Jack for suspecting Alice, nor for not trusting my word on the matter. It was a perfectly reasonable conjecture, especially if one were looking for someone who could go missing without being missed.

I hope you see though that the very fact that he took the trouble to investigate proves that he did not know who Leo's killer was. That was a great relief to me at the time.

But that was all later, as I said. In the moment there was only that brief glance of suspicion, and otherwise he was wholly sympathetic and consoling. Of Leo we spoke but little. I already knew all that there was to know from popular gossip, and I did not press him to give his own account of it.

Nor did I press the admiral to explain his arrested comment about Jack, if I may return to where I was in the story.

My encounter with Sally had indeed placed me in a strangely amorous mood, despite my lack of attraction to her. Perhaps that ought to have seemed notable, for my mind had been far from such matters since Zinnia's capture, and I would scarcely have expected a woman to have woken it in me. But I had often found stirrings of ardor inexplicable in the past, even in the strangest and tensest circumstances. So it was that I climbed further on to the bed and ran my hand up the admiral's leg to touch him through his clothes.

But to my surprise, the admiral pulled back from me. "The walls here seem rather thin," he pointed out.

I could see his dilemma. During our assignations within the solid stone walls of the palace, I could sometimes be loud. I might have told him I was just as capable of being quiet if I wished to, but it occurred to me that he might take it amiss to learn that some of my reactions to him were more voluntary than he might prefer to believe. I suppose it must seem eccentric that I'd be putting on such a show for someone who was in fact my subordinate. But it was still pleasing to please, and nothing pleases a man more than to believe he is pleasing.

I knew how to handle it. "You can gag me," I suggested to him.

The admiral made no further objections.

A CONFLAGRATION

WHEN I AWOKE ENCIRCLED BY STRONG ARMS, FOR A moment I thought I was with Jack, for I had never before fallen asleep in any other man's embrace. To realize that it was the admiral was like getting the wind knocked out of me. But I did not have much time to absorb the devastation, for my attention was called by the clamor that had awoken me.

Startled voices rang throughout the complex. From out on the streets, shouts and shrieks came through the window. I extracted myself from the admiral's hold, pulled on enough clothes to be decent if not respectable, and rushed out. The admiral cursed at me to wait and not go alone, but I ignored him. Now that I was away from Summer, I suppose it was too easy to fall back into my old ways from when I was a nobody. Perhaps some part of me would always feel it most natural that I should be able to go where I would and do what I wished without reference to anyone else.

The guards at the front door watched but did not hinder me as I passed them and moved out onto the street. The smell of smoke tinged the air as soon as I was outside. I followed the direction of it towards the harbor. As I got closer, it appeared that a ship had caught on fire. But it was not just any ship. The *Godwit* was ablaze.

Brook was on that ship. A dragon egg was on that ship. A couple dozen other people who had come at my order were on that ship. I broke into a run to get to the docks. The uneven cobblestones jolted my legs through my thin-soled shoes, and various townspeople stared as I passed by, but I paid little mind.

I scarcely knew what I was expecting that called for such a rush. As you can imagine, by the time I got there, the sailors had evacuated the ship and gathered themselves on the docks. The harbormaster issued orders to get other ships moved further away from the *Godwit,* and other men from the town were beginning to organize a fire brigade. The situation was well in hand, as far as it could be, with little for me to do.

A hodgepodge of random items stood stacked on the docks: no doubt whatever the sailors had deemed worthy of rescuing from the conflagration before it became too dangerous to remain. Among these things was the sealed crate containing the dragon egg, standing off to itself a little and unattended, as if everyone had forgotten it as soon as they'd removed it to safety.

The *Godwit*, I deemed, was beyond saving. It burned quite zestfully with no signs of slowing, and the main mast looked as though it would break soon.

I spotted Brook and was startled to find him more singed and sooted than most of the other sailors. I thought I would have to have a talk with him about taking unnecessary risks and remind him that no possessions were worth imperiling his life. Then I noticed that Brook was bent over Tom Hollow, who sat on the docks with his head bowed. As I approached, I could hear Hollow's breath come in ragged gasps. He must have inhaled quite a lot of smoke.

I spoke first to my stepson. "Are you alright? Your hair . . ." I reached out as if to touch the fine strands of his hair where the ends were blackened, but I stopped short. Surely he would not wish for me to touch him.

"Yes, I'm fine," Brook told me. "I just had to go back for Tom Hollow. Everyone had forgotten him."

"That was well done," I told him. I felt there ought to be more to say, but it did not come to me. Brook only ducked his head and seemed vaguely embarrassed by even the mild praise, so I left it at that and turned away from him.

I dropped to one knee to get a closer look at Hollow. His wheezing breath sounded even more troubling the closer I came to him. My order had kept him restrained belowdecks—an entirely reasonable precaution, of course, under the circumstances. There was no way I could have anticipated this eventuality. Yet it ate at me to think of him trapped there with no recourse, no doubt expecting a horrifying death by fire, and that I had condemned him to such a fate. With a light touch under his chin, I tipped up his face to look closer at him and met his reddened gaze.

For a moment, we only looked at each other. Healing of the body is within the gift of Summer, though I had never managed much in that direction. But looking into Hollow's eyes, I could almost feel the pain in his chest, could sense where the smoke had poisoned his lungs as if it were indeed within my own body. For the first time, the sympathetic magic of healing made some sort of sense to me. I felt I could draw out the poison . . .

Hollow pulled back from me in sudden alarm. "No, none of that," he rasped. "I didn't ask for that." It seemed to me his breath came easier already, and his eyes were less inflamed. Far from being pleased at the improvement, however, he glared at me in horror and mistrust.

"I did not intend . . ." I realized the lack of wisdom in what I was about to say and changed course. "That is, I did not mean to overstep."

Sulkily, Hollow turned away from me and stared at the fire.

THE ADMIRAL ARRIVED AND swiftly took command of the situation. He issued orders to get some of the sailors involved in the fire brigade and others at work moving the salvaged items out of danger. He kept a cool head about him even as he must be devastated by the loss of the *Godwit*, which he'd captained for nigh on twenty years.

Watching him take charge, I admitted to myself that the admiral was growing on me. Perhaps he simply showed to better advantage while on campaign, as it were. I could recollect the way he had so often nattered on about his inane societal opinions back at Summer, but it no longer seemed so important. What had felt such an essential foundation of him was perhaps but a small part. He hadn't ventured into any such topics since we'd been away, except for small asides; he had been focused on the mission at hand. It was easy to admire his competence when it was divorced from his more glaring flaws.

Or perhaps I was simply ill-suited to indulge in physical intimacy without forming an attachment. The better you know someone, the harder it becomes to hate them, and I was beginning to feel I knew the admiral rather well, in some ways. Not in all ways though. Out here it was easy to forget that he had a whole family—a wife and two sons and grandchildren too—with whom I had only the vaguest acquaintance and who were unlikely to look kindly upon our connection if ever they were to learn of it.

I briefly tried to help the sailors with their tasks, but it became clear my involvement caused more distraction and fluster than it aided the efforts. So I simply tried to stay out of the way and watched the flames lick over the masts of the *Godwit*. A black dock cat stopped by to keep me company and to imperiously oversee the activities.

My enforced idleness at least gave me the opportunity to contemplate who or what might have been responsible for the fire. Accidental mishap was always possible, of course, but it would seem a great coincidence. Was someone trying to trap us here? We had not mentioned that more ships from Summer were on their way, so no one would realize that we'd have an escape available quite soon. Or was the point to get easier access to the egg? I found myself less and less inclined to let anyone have the egg, if it could possibly be avoided.

"What a terrible shame."

I turned to find Lord Grinhill watching the fire beside me. Somehow he still seemed vaguely bored. Was it an affectation or did he truly take no interest in anything? He was fully dressed, so he did not seem to have rushed out with any great degree of haste. I was not much pleased to see him, considering how little I had enjoyed attempting to converse with him the night before. But there was nothing for it.

"Does this sort of thing happen often here?" I asked him.

"Can't say I've heard of it happening before," Grinhill said. "Makes it look like foul play, eh?"

I was surprised that he'd bring that up himself. "Why would anyone in Oxeye wish to destroy our ship?"

Grinhill shrugged and changed the subject. "Say, you need someplace to quarter your men, I suppose? Some women too, I see. You all are welcome to the use of my manor house if you like." He gestured inland and uphill towards the outline of the manor house up on the hill, a handsome stone building much more inherently charming than Light's sterile complex.

"Your manor?" I frowned. "I thought it was under renovation."

"The house has been closed for some time, but there are no active repairs underway. The roof and walls are solid enough, and there's more than enough space."

I understood then. Grinhill had closed up his ancestral home because he couldn't afford to maintain it, and now he lived off Mr. Light's beneficence. I would have thought he'd make a bit more effort at charm under those circumstances, but I supposed that men of reduced means handled the humiliation in different ways.

Then something else occurred to me. He oughtn't have been making this offer to me at all. "Your offer is very generous. I will bring the idea to Lord Summer."

Grinhill's expression turned wry, but he only nodded. Did he somehow know we'd been lying about that? Or merely suspect it, perhaps?

I did take the information to the admiral, who naturally wanted to know what I thought of it. I can scarcely say why I kept expecting he would make the decisions, as if he really were in charge.

"As far as I can see, the only other alternative is begging Light for help," I pointed out. "I might be more inclined to take our chances with Grinhill." I also advised him to continue to keep quiet about the approach of the *Avocet* and the *Plover*. If anyone was trying to set us up in some desperate situation, I wanted them to show their hand before we revealed our own.

Before too long, Mr. Light appeared on the docks as well, profuse in expressing dismay that such a thing could happen in his town and solicitous in offering aid to us. When he learned that Grinhill had indeed already offered the use of his manor to shelter us, however, Light seemed put out. "But you mustn't be expected to drag so much all the way up the hill at such a distressing time. Surely my house is much more convenient and fully staffed besides."

"We could not possibly expect you to host so many," the admiral returned.

"No one in Oxeye is better equipped," said Mr. Light. "I wouldn't want your party to be in any way uncomfortable during your stay in our town."

"We can take care of ourselves. We only want for shelter. I think it better if we keep to ourselves, out of the way."

They parried back and forth for a while, but Mr. Light's insistence was off-putting, and the admiral remained firm. To Grinhill Manor we were bound.

The journey up the hill was not so wearisome as Light had warned us. The slope was gentle and the road smooth. The further we got from the docks, the more the old character of the town shone through in the charming wattle-and-daub houses and the winding cobblestone paths. Summer, of course, was more timeless and elegant than any of it, with everything built of the native white stone to our own unique architectural paradigm. But there was a coziness to some other quaint styles that warm the heart and make one feel quite at home. If I were a tree, I'd best like to be planted in Summer. But if I were a migratory bird, I might like to spend half the year in a town like old Oxeye.

No furnishings or adornments remained in the manor house, but it did not carry a desolate air. The stone structure remained graceful and serene in its emptiness, and the stained windows still let in plenty of light. The sailors found themselves places to settle in, and Grinhill showed us where to find what was left of the linens and other supplies that might make us more comfortable to "camp out" in the abandoned house. The stone well in the courtyard remained in good order and offered up clean cool water, the hearth in the kitchen was functional, and the privies were in usable condition. So in many ways it was better accommodations than the ship the sailors had fled.

I took the time to oversee where Tom Hollow was secured, for I feared him being placed in a windowless chamber when I was certain he needed fresh air for his lungs to recover. A storage room with a small barred window was located for the purpose, though it was perhaps slightly too narrow if such a tall man wished to stretch out his full length. Still sulking, Tom settled himself down onto the floor with his knees drawn up before him, and he stared at the wall across from him.

"Do you need anything?" I asked him, finding myself reluctant to turn and walk away. "If you are still unwell, we might see about fetching a doctor."

"I don't reckon there's aught a sawbones can do," Tom grumbled, still with a harsh gravelly tone to his voice. "Needs time is all."

"There are likely herbs that would soothe your throat and eyes . . ."

"You've done enough."

I should have left it there, but his unjust hostility annoyed me. "Truly, I don't see how I did anything so terrible down at the docks. You were ailing, and I relieved some of your distress. Why should you wish to be in pain when it can be helped?"

"There are worse things than pain, I reckon," Tom told me. "I don't want a dragon in my head, not for no reason."

"It was a matter of the body, not the mind."

He scowled at me. "You think I'm stupid? I know well enough that it all starts in the mind. You can't just go and talk to the lungs without talking to the head, now can you?"

I could scarcely admit that he seemed to know more about the principles of draconic healing than I did. "Well, I had no notion you would feel so strongly about it."

"The way I reckon it, a man's not a man if his mind is not his own."

Whether he intended it as a dig towards me or not, his words stung. I have never been terribly invested in the trappings of manliness, but it was clear Hollow did not mean it in that narrow, small-minded sense, such as the admiral might. "What do you 'reckon' that makes me then?"

Tom Hollow shrugged and looked away from me. "That's no business of mine. You have to make your own peace with what you've done, for you and your little girl."

At last I walked away, wishing I had done so sooner. Why

had I even bothered to engage with Tom Hollow and to take such care with him? I could not quite suppress the self-recrimination that my interest in Hollow might not be wholly divorced from the appeal of his striking face and muscular build. Knowing that his sister was not above using her natural charms to manipulate, it would be a mistake to assume that the brother was less dangerous simply because he seemed more straightforward. I needed to be more objective, I chastised myself, to not be swayed by appearances in my judgments of people. I knew better than most that a pretty face spoke little to the true merits of the individual.

The freckled young woman from the *Godwit* crew showed me to the bedchamber that had been selected for my use. The room must have been quite cozy when it was furnished, and the window offered beautiful unobstructed views over the old parts of town and the harbor. I thanked the sailor for her consideration and dismissed her, and finally I was alone. Alone I could be properly miserable.

Until that morning, I had felt that we were making progress towards finding Zinnia and going home. The mission had not seemed so very complicated, and I had expected success in the end. The fire and the destruction of the *Godwit* threw a new cast on things. Someone in Oxeye was very much against us and willing to take extreme measures to get their way. If it was indeed Lowell Light, he had ample resources at his disposal to orchestrate his ends. If it was Sally Hollow-Light, I feared she was far cleverer and more ruthless than me. And I still knew almost nothing of the Kittevers.

What if we didn't prevail?

The very thought sent me into a swirling eddy that threatened to pull me under entirely. More than a black mood—a black flood engulfed me. If Zinnia were truly lost, my whole life was but a cruel farce. Without the promise of an heir who would return Summer to how it was meant to be, I had accomplished nothing. Without my daughter to bring love and joy to my life, I was nothing.

I knew, of course, that moping and allowing myself to languish in such a mood would only serve to make it more likely that I would fail. I had once prided myself on having a certain sort of emotional control, on being able to turn my own mood as I willed it, though I had rather gotten out of the habit of late.

Once I tried to explain my method to Jack, though I do not believe he understood me. This was when we were traveling the otherlands and had but lately arrived in a new town. Some delays on the road brought us in after nightfall, and the only possible accommodation was a squalid little place with cramped dirty rooms and stained sheets. The proprietor was of a recalcitrant disposition and had to be pressed into providing even the most basic of amenities, such as clean towels and wash water. After I had exhausted all my patience battling with the nasty old man, I went up to join Jack in the room.

Jack sat in a chair by the window staring out, though I couldn't imagine what he should wish to contemplate in the dark, stinking alleyway which constituted our view. I told him I had a lead on where we might find more amenable long-term accommodations and that I dared to hope we might be free of this particular hell before tomorrow night. Jack smiled slightly as I spoke, but he did not engage with anything I had to say.

In fact, I was still talking as he caught my hand, pulled me into his lap, and stopped my mouth with a kiss.

His timing left something to be desired. I was exhausted, disgusted by our surroundings, and at least somewhat resentful that Jack's choices had brought us to such a place. But even so, I had no wish to spurn Jack's affections, and I knew well enough that my ardor would rise to the occasion soon enough. So I responded in kind, wrapping myself around Jack and meeting the kiss with gusto.

But Jack pulled away from me and said, "Never mind."

"What? But what did I do wrong?" I objected with a pout, and I settled deeper into his lap, as if daring him to dislodge me.

"I can tell you're in no mood for it, and I would just as soon you didn't pretend," Jack told me. "I never know what you fancy you're accomplishing with all your fakery—you know I can see through it."

Having a lover who could perceive my true mindset even when I tried to disguise it was not always ideal, and this struck me as deeply unfair. To meet his desires, I not only must be ready at any time whatsoever but also must be blissfully happy about it even within my own heart? And did my own decision count for nothing?

"I wasn't pretending for *you*, Jack. I was pretending for me. That's how you *change* your mood—by acting as though you already have. The heart follows where the body leads, if the mind wills it. Haven't you ever convinced yourself of something that way?"

Jack scoffed and shook his head. "That's ridiculous."

"I suppose you've no need to ever change *your* mood to suit others."

"No inclination, I'd say. Why would I ever wish to alter my own feelings, to render my experience of life less genuine?"

Of course it was easy for Jack to remain a rock, steadfast in his mood, if I were always ready to contort myself around him. "Have you considered that perhaps that's why you scarcely get along with anyone but me?" I asked.

Jack smiled, apparently amused at my response.

I tried again to kiss him and moved my hand lower.

But Jack stood, lifting me up as he rose, and he dumped

me on the bed. "No, Teddy." He returned to his chair by the window.

For a moment, I was angered by this treatment and thought to launch a proper quarrel. But I had a better idea. "Very well. You stay over there, and I'll simply get ready for bed."

Jack's eyes narrowed suspiciously, but I could tell he was also intrigued by what I intended. He pretended to turn his attention back out the window, but how could he? I was much nicer to look at than anything out there in the alley.

I started to undress with precise movements, strategically revealing more and more of my body. And when I was naked, I applied oil to my limbs in slow, careful circles. It was nothing unusual for me to give my dry skin some attention after a time on the dusty road, but I took care to turn to just at the right angles for the candlelight to play across my glistening skin. I even did some stretches—casually, as if it were a normal part of my bedtime routine to place my body in picturesque poses, stretching my muscles taut.

Through it all, I felt Jack's eyes on me. I enjoyed his attention, the power I could still exercise over him, and my own ardor warmed within me. At length he rose and came to me, just as I expected.

"You always win in the end, don't you, Teddy?" he murmured against my neck, though of course, I did not see it that way at all. My victory was his, the culmination of his desire rather than my own, though I had certainly met great success in turning my own mind to the purpose.

But that was then. Had I now become like Jack, disinclined to adjust myself to circumstances since I became Lord Summer? No, that did not sound quite right; I often did things I was disinclined to do and did them with a smile. If anything, I was perhaps still too obliging at times, forgetting that I was meant to be a leader rather than a follower and a flatterer.

My current despondency was no small matter of attending

to unpleasant people or tolerating inconvenience. I did not despair over my barren new surroundings but over the life of my child, and my old little tricks of mind seemed pitifully inadequate to the task. How could I even pretend to feel anything but devastation at my failures thus far? I had accomplished nothing and had allowed our party to be pushed about at the whims of others. I might yet lose everything.

Summer's mind nudged at me, but I suppose I wanted neither comfort nor censure from her, whichever it was she offered. I closed the door on her and persisted in my sullen solitude.

WHEN I DID NOT reemerge from the bedroom at Grinhill Manor within the expected timeframe, Admiral Rostrum eventually came to check on me.

"Look, I think it's time to stop playing games," the admiral announced. "We've got to confront Light about all this and see what he says. These otherlanders will only respond to a firm hand."

The admiral's straightforward approach certainly appealed to me at that moment, as I did not feel up to any scheming of my own. I agreed with him.

He looked at me closely then, which I would sooner have avoided. I suspected I had not fully disguised that my eyes were puffy, nor that my breath stank of brandy despite the early hour. Very hesitantly, he said, "Are you sure you should come?"

As he obviously feared another outburst of pride from me, I felt the need to confound his expectations. "I shall get myself in order," I assured him.

"It may be for the best for you to seem dismayed, if we're to confront Light about your missing daughter," the admiral offered.

At that moment, Brook came in. "Apologies for the

interruption, sir," he said to the admiral. He offered no such pleasantry to me before he launched into what brought him. "I've been speaking a bit with Tom Hollow."

"Well, lad, what did he say?" the admiral asked.

"Perhaps I shouldn't have said anything to him of our thoughts," Brook began, and he pushed the singed hair out of his face in a nervous manner. "But I was speaking strictly of my own feelings, so I thought, until I got carried away."

"Hollow has a way of provoking reactions," I acknowledged as a reassurance that it could happen to anyone.

"I told him about how we weren't certain that Zinny was even in this town or if she'd left with the *Shadowcat*, and he said that Lowell Light is fastidious about the movement of goods and assets. He said Light always keeps records of everything—where things go, where they're stored, and that he'd not make an exception even for a living child."

The admiral frowned. "I don't see the point. We've already figured that Light knows where Lady Zinnia is."

"Right, but Tom Hollow reckons that Lowell Light will have *written it down*," Brook explained. "So we needn't get it from his lips."

"I found Light's office last night," I said. "There were certainly a lot of records there, though I couldn't make much of them."

"I might have better luck," said Brook. With a glance at the admiral, he offered the explanation, "I have some experience with sorting out organizational schemes, skimming dense texts quickly . . ."

I nodded at that. "I could tell you precisely where the office is, but the door will be locked."

"How did you get in then?" Brook asked.

"Picked the lock."

The look of surprise on Brook's face was gratifying. The

young do always tend to imagine that we've always been boring. "How do you know how to do that?"

I shrugged. "In my youth, there were often places I wished to be that others did not wish me to be. I flatter myself that I was resourceful in resolving this discrepancy of opinion with the least inconvenience to anyone."

Brook laughed: even more gratifying. "Well, you'll have to teach me then. It must be easier to teach me how to pick a lock than to teach you how to—"

"Indeed," I agreed.

"Then we're not going to confront Light head-on after all?" the admiral asked with a disappointed air.

"Oh, no, we will," I told him. "Brook will need a distraction to do his bit, and I have always had a soft spot for glaringly obvious distractions."

The admiral looked confused, but Brook grinned.

A REUNION

Teaching Brook how to pick locks went smoothly enough. The locks at Grinhill Manor were of the most obliging old sort, much like the locks around Summer, but I warned him that the more modern doors of Light's complex would prove more challenging.

Often the tips of his singed hair caught my attention, and I wanted to offer to fix it for him. I had cut Jack's hair many times, so I knew how to handle fine, straight hair. I had a notion of how to style it to make the best of what remained. But I felt certain Brook would not welcome the interference, nor wish to undergo so intimate a procedure with me. So I kept my peace.

We set out for Mr. Light's complex with a greater show of force than before. The admiral and I took twelve men-at-arms to accompany us, with Brook among them. Not only would this lend a bit of weight to our conversation with Light, but it would perhaps give Brook a chance to slip away unnoticed in such a crowd.

The guards at Light's house let us in with no trouble, though this time we were led to a sort of gymnasium, I can only suppose. Perhaps the room was intended as a ballroom, but it was too severe for me to count it as such. It was hard to imagine anything so cheerful as a dance occurring in so stark a room.

"Gentlemen, I scarcely hoped to see you again so soon!" Light greeted us gregariously upon entry. "Have you re-thought my offer to house you here?"

"We are quite comfortable at Grinhill Manor," the admiral responded with only a slight inclination of his head as greeting. "We've come to discuss the true reason for our visit to this town."

An intrigued look spread across Light's face. "By all means, let us get down to business!" he responded with enthusiasm. "I would be delighted to discuss opening new trade between our lands, new agreements for our mutual benefit."

The admiral paused and glanced at me briefly, but I had no insight. "That's not precisely why we've come," he said. "There's a more specific matter weighing on us. I told you last night of a missing girl, five years old. Lady Zinnia. Perhaps you know more than you let on?"

Light frowned. "A little girl? That's why you're here?"

"My daughter," I added softly. It felt right.

Light looked closely at me, as he had when we first arrived, trying to understand exactly who I was. Perhaps as his gaze roved my features, he mapped my resemblance to Zinnia in his mind. "A moment, gentlemen," Light excused himself and stepped out. We could hear him calling for someone in the hallway and conferring in hushed voices.

Uneasily we waited in the bare, oversized room. Each shuffle of foot or clearing of throat echoed in its pointless vastness. Our party felt very small after all. Brook had indeed slipped away in the corridors, but I had no way of knowing how he was getting on. For all I knew, Light had discovered him in his office already.

When Light's footsteps sounded once more in the hallway,

we all straightened up. He entered accompanied by a housemaid, and the maid led Zinnia by the hand.

I could scarcely believe that Zinnia was there, right before my very eyes. But even more astounding, her appearance left me incredulous. "Zinny! You have braids!"

"Miss Sally did them for me," Zinny replied. "Aren't they pretty?"

"Well, of course they are. But you never let me do anything to your hair!"

She shrugged and started towards me, but the maid's hand held her back. Zinny paused uncertainly. The maid was no dragon, however, and I was scarcely going to stand for having my daughter kept from me when she was right before me. I rushed forward and gathered Zinny up, brushing aside the maid. Zinny readily accepted it. She clung to me, wrapping her arms around my neck and her legs around my waist, and hung on tight. I stepped back with her in my arms.

Could it really be so easy? My treasure was with me once more, and all we had to do was ask for her?

"I apologize if there's been some sort of misunderstanding, gentlemen," Mr. Light said to us in an even tone. "I had no idea this child belonged to you. When my wife brought her back from a trip, well, I thought it was one of her charity cases. She's always picking up strays here and there. And when you mentioned a missing 'young lady' last night, well, I supposed you meant a young *woman*, a runaway-lover situation or some such. And naturally I pictured a girl who looked like your people, not one of ours."

The admiral frowned.

"There must be some reasonable explanation here," Light continued. "When my Sally returns from her outing, I have no doubt we can get to the bottom of it. Yet truly, what does it matter? If the girl is what you came for, then you have her.

Your, uh, advisor is satisfied. But listen, gentlemen, your journey here need not be for so little gain. Stay but a bit longer, let us see what new understandings we can reach between us. I feel certain there are advantages to us both that could emerge from this opportunity."

The admiral cleared his throat. "We have little choice but to remain in this town at present, seeing as our ship has so abruptly been destroyed."

Light clearly comprehended something of the rebuke in the admiral's words and looked briefly abashed but not defeated. "I have already been conferring with my people on what can be done for you in light of the loss of your ship," he said. "The last thing I would desire is for you to leave here feeling that Oxeye is a dangerous or inhospitable place. Wherever the fault lies in the mishap this dawn, I intend to see you made whole and arrange for you to get home safely."

Whatever the admiral might have replied, he was cut short by the entry of a servant in Light's livery accompanied by one of our own sailors. For a moment I was struck with the fear that the sailor was Brook, detained in the act of snooping in Light's office, but I quickly saw it was another man from the *Godwit*, who had not come here with our group. "This man says he has urgent tidings for our guests," the servant said.

"There's been an attack on the manor house!" the sailor announced without further ado. "There are injuries, some dead, I think. And the assailants just disappeared!"

Before the admiral or I could react, Light spoke up with much feeling. "Just as I feared! I knew too well something like this would happen when you decided to stay at that accursed manor!"

After a moment of staring at him, I scarcely knew what to make of the outburst. I gathered Zinny even closer to me. "We have to get back," the admiral growled to me.

"Please," Light went on. "Do not stay in that manor house

any longer. Bring all your men back down the hill and stay here. I can keep you safer."

"With respect, it is not the time for us to decide that," the admiral returned. "Since we came to this town, we seem to be besieged on all sides wherever we go. For now we must see to our fallen men and determine the situation for ourselves."

I had not forgotten about Brook, but I could not see a way around leaving at that moment, and getting Zinnia out of there was my top priority. I whispered briefly to the admiral, reminding him of Brook's predicament. He ordered a couple of our men to stay behind to gather up the things we had left behind from our stay the night before. I could see what he was doing; leaving some of our men in the house would give Brook a chance to blend back in with them before they left, or at any rate to have an excuse for still being in the house.

Light made a few more stabs at offering his assistance to us as we left, but we ignored him with as few polite nothings as we could manage.

Back on the street, I glanced towards the water, hoping for a glimpse of friendly sails on the horizon flying the flag of Summer. But there was no sign of the *Avocet* or the *Plover*. They should have arrived by now. What could be hindering them? Now that I had Zinnia back, I was eager for a chance to be gone from Oxeye, gone from all these dangers that we could not seem to stay ahead of. It was clear enough that the situation was far more complex than I had first realized when negotiating aboard the *Shadowcat*, but I wanted no part in the matter, nor anything to do with the varied troubles of the otherlands. The continued absence of the relief ships agitated me all the more.

The climb up the hill to the manor felt longer this time, and I don't think it was the weight of carrying Zinny on my waist. Anxiety and dread pervaded our party, as we all contemplated the implications of the attack on the manor.

"I can walk, Daddy," Zinny said in my ear as we walked.

I shook my head. "I'm not letting you go until you're safe."

"When will that be?"

"I don't know, but it's not now."

"Where are we going?"

"A big house on top of the hill. The rest of the crew of the *Godwit* is there. They can help protect you."

"Is little brother coming?"

That scarcely seemed to follow, but I was somewhat accustomed to Zinny's non sequiturs. Even so, I struggled to grasp this one. "Do you mean Brook?"

Zinny made a face. "Brook is much, much older than me. He's not a *little* brother."

"You . . . wish to have a little brother?"

"Yes!"

"Perhaps we can discuss that another time, darling. I scarcely even know what your mother would think of the notion."

"What does Mummy have to do with it?"

"Uh, well, the whole topic is one that I rather fancy would be better covered at leisure on another occasion."

One of the sailors walking alongside had apparently been following our exchange and snorted at my expense, in spite of the overall tension of the mood.

"What am I allowed to talk about then?" Zinny whined, clearly a bit put out.

"Tell me how you've fared since I last saw you."

"It was fun when I had a whole ship to play on, but then we got here, and I've just been in a little room, and it was really boring," she said. "I heard you singing last night, but you didn't come to get me."

That smote my heart. "I looked for you," I offered, but she had already moved on.

"Then I saw a ship burning! It looked really pretty, but then they put it out, and now it's a black skeleton."

"So you're alright, my darling?"

"Yeah," she agreed blithely. "Are you, Daddy?"

"Well, of course I am. Now that you're here." I kissed her on the forehead as we approached the manor.

A GRIM MOOD DOMINATED among the sailors gathered in the front courtyard of Grinhill Manor. A moment too late, I realized that a body was being moved past us. Blood veiled the side of the man's face, and part of his head appeared to be crushed. I tried to cover Zinnia's eyes. But she pushed my hand away and stared in fascination.

"What happened to him?" Zinnia asked—too loudly, too brightly.

The sailors turned to look at her with mixed expressions. Whatever they felt about seeing her recovered was clearly muted by the shock at what had recently transpired. The dead man wasn't one of ours, at least. I attempted to shush Zinnia and explained softly that it wasn't polite to stare at the dead like that.

"But *everyone* was looking," she pointed out.

"Please, Zinny."

"I'm not allowed to say *anything* anymore," she sulked.

I pulled her head under my chin and stroked her back. I had no wish to argue with her.

The admiral looked over and suggested, "Maybe you should leave her with one of the girls for now."

I gathered he meant one of the sailors who happened to be women. Reluctant though I was to be parted from her, I considered it.

"Noooo," Zinny objected and tightened her grip on me. "I want to stay with you."

First Mate Caul emerged from the house. A bandage was wrapped around his head, and a makeshift sling supported his left arm. "Thank Summer you got her back, sir," he exclaimed, looking at Zinnia. "At least all this is for something."

"What happened here?" I asked him.

"I wish I could rightly say myself. We were keeping a watch, sir, don't think we weren't, but these assailants seemed to appear out of nowhere in our midst. They attacked and then disappeared again. We don't even know what they wanted."

"What did they look like?"

"Nothing out of the ordinary for this place. Dressed in those same clothes everyone wears around here, though their faces were covered."

"All men?"

Caul frowned and considered. "I had thought so, sir, but I can't say for certain."

"How many casualties?" the admiral asked.

"Perry and Hawthorne are dead. A few injured. We got two of theirs too."

Tom Hollow turned out to be missing as well, though no one had much of a notion whether the attackers had intentionally sprung him from captivity, or if he had escaped opportunistically during the chaos of the fighting and aftermath.

I also inquired after Grinhill, but he seemed not to be about.

I asked to see where the fighting had taken place, though I already had a guess about the purpose of the attack. The bodies had already been moved, but a lot of blood still pooled in patches on the floor. Zinnia's big saucer eyes took it all in with avidity and not the slightest trace of dismay. Though not entirely surprised by her nonchalance, I found myself wishing she would hide it better and try to act more normal. Her outlandish behavior embarrassed me and then made me feel guilty for my embarrassment. Was she not supposed to be a dragon child? Why should I expect her to be anything else?

The crate with the egg was gone, as I had suspected it would be. Most likely someone had been waiting for me to leave the manor before making their play for it. The fire on the ship would have been started specifically to get the egg moved to a less defensible location. No wonder Mr. Light had been willing to give us Zinnia, I thought. No doubt he already knew that he had what he needed; probably he kept us waiting just long enough to make sure the attack could be completed. Had he sent his own people to steal the egg from us? Or had he perhaps tipped off the Kittevers to come get it themselves? Either way, the egg was gone.

Yet there in the manor, no one spoke of the egg. Summer's fog of silence still held sway over all the people from Summer. What was she playing at with that? Would they have done better at defending it if they'd been more aware of it? But they had saved it from the ship in spite of all that. Clearly she was capable of managing the forgetfulness with some nuance.

I kept my thoughts on the egg to myself, though it troubled me. A few days earlier, I had been happy to trade the egg for Zinnia, and now I had Zinnia and no egg. That should have been satisfactory, and yet it wasn't. The egg had been growing in my mind, and my feelings towards it had taken a lighter tone since we had left Summer. Perhaps being further from Summer had eased the strength of whatever strange attitude the dragoness had towards the egg and allowed my own native thoughts on the subject to return to the fore.

Or perhaps it was simply galling to have it taken from me by force and trickery in this manner. Two of our people had been killed. Those men belonged to Summer, belonged to us. The egg belonged to us as well. No one had the right to take any of them from us. Whoever had done this, they did not deserve to get away with it. No one could steal from us so flagrantly and not pay.

I could feel that these thoughts were not entirely my own, tinged as they were with the dragon's fierce possessiveness. That then undercut my initial theory that her influence over me was so much weaker here. If she had been less obviously present in my mind since I left Summer, perhaps that was simply how she wished it. Certainly it was up to me to carry out our will as I saw fit, yet I hardly knew how to go about it.

I EXPECTED TO PRESIDE over the funeral proceedings, but it became apparent that Admiral Rostrum also expected to fulfill that role, and I was wholly unopposed to ceding it to him. He had known the dead men, after all, while I had only a vague recognition of them from my two days aboard the *Godwit*. So I held Zinny and listened as the admiral recited the appropriate sort of words and the bodies were wrapped up. We intended to take them with us when the *Avocet* and *Plover* arrived and give them a burial at sea. If the ships ever arrived.

Zinny remained mercifully quiet throughout the proceedings, taking it in. Afterward though, when I'd taken her back to the bedroom to rest, she asked me, "How long will it take for them to be bones, like the ones in the tunnels?"

"If they are given to the sea as we intend, I suppose it will not be long at all," I responded.

"Because they'll be eaten up," she supplied.

"Yes." After a moment of hesitation, I added, "But you shouldn't mention that around other people. Most people don't like to think about that part, what happens after the body sinks peacefully under the waves."

"What would happen in the ground?"

"The same thing, I suppose, but slower."

"If we put them in the sea near Summer, would Summer eat them?"

"No. She doesn't like to eat dead things."

"Then what does she do with us?"

I didn't follow that at first. "Hmm?"

"Her Lord Summers and Lady Summers, like us," Zinny explained. "What does she do with us when she takes us away when we're dead?"

I was not prepared for such a question, and I found I did not entirely succeed in holding back my reaction as I recalled such an occurrence.

"Or is it not true?" she pressed when I did not answer at once. "Does she not take us away?"

"It is true," I told her. "But I don't know what she does with, um . . .with the bodies."

"I think I'd rather be eaten by Summer than by fishes or worms," Zinny declared. "Since it seems being eaten is the only thing for it."

"I wish you wouldn't speak of that," I said to her. "That will not be for many, many more years, my darling."

"Not so many. Not to Summer."

We lapsed into silence at that point. I wondered briefly if I should revive the "little brother" conversation now that we were alone, but as she seemed to have moved on from it, I felt more inclined to let it lie. The silence inevitably turned into sleep. I had only intended to get Zinny to take a nap, but with her resting on my chest, we both fell asleep.

When I woke up, the afternoon was passing, and the manor house was quiet. An orange cat had also found its way into the room by the window and snuggled in beside us. Gently I eased Zinny off of me and settled her down beside the cat. I made my way out to see what was going on.

A WRONG FRUIT

A SAILOR LET ME KNOW THAT LORD GRINHILL AND Admiral Rostrum were conferring together in the old drawing room. I advised the man of where Zinny was sleeping so that she could be appropriately guarded, and I went to join the conference.

"Ah, there you are, Su—Mr. Alison," the admiral greeted me. "I'm glad to see you got some rest."

I reminded myself that the admiral was not generally inclined towards sarcasm and simply nodded. "Have there been any new developments?" I was hoping to hear of the arrival of the *Avocet* and the *Plover*, or at least the return of Brook, but I did not say so in front of Grinhill.

"Not of note," said the admiral. "Though Grinhill here was offering some speculation on the motives of our assailants."

"I would be very interested in hearing that," I said. I took a seat on a packing crate, which was what currently passed for furniture in the house.

Grinhill looked over at me with his usual disinterested expression, though I was beginning to wonder if I were misreading his face. His heavily lidded eyes perhaps gave the wrong impression.

"There are any number of discontents in Oxeye at the

moment," Grinhill said. "That's inevitable when there's been so much change so rapidly. But whatever someone wants with you lot, I have to assume it has something to do with dragons."

His intonation did not rise, but his pause seemed to indicate a question, so I nodded. "That seems a reasonable supposition, if there is such a faction here."

"There is. The Kittevers have a toehold here as much as anywhere, much as our esteemed Mr. Light refuses to believe it."

"I have heard something about the Kittevers, but we have not encountered them."

"You should count yourself fortunate in that. They have become a formidable force," said Grinhill. "Word is that they completely took over Black Bream Bay last spring, ousted the mayor and installed their own people—a truly alarming development. Before that, their conquests had been numerous but small scale, the sort of places that no one much cared about except the people who lived there. But Black Bream is a manufacturing powerhouse, and they produced weapons—even warships. They'll have a whole fleet at their disposal. They're becoming more ambitious, scaling up their plans."

"What do they want though? What are their ultimate goals?"

Grinhill shrugged. "I don't know that they're quite so harmonious to have one particular goal, except to keep gathering power. Though all the Kittevers share a method and a certain ruthless outlook, the individual enclaves seem to be all in competition with each other as much as they are united in spreading. It's more of a web than a hierarchy. Some nodes in the web are cozier with each other and work closely together, at least for a time, but their alliances are always shifting. I believe the local enclave here is mostly an offshoot of the Black Breams, or a sister faction of some sort—just as keen to seize manufacturing power and turn it to their own ends."

I thought that over. Considering the general instability of

the otherlands and the rapid changes that recent new technologies had brought, I counted it not wholly surprising that a group like the Kittevers could seize on the moment to consolidate power for themselves. The system Grinhill described certainly would seem to have weaknesses that might be exploited, but I had no notion of how to go about that. How could we possibly hope to make the Kittevers turn on one another while still knowing so little about them?

The admiral spoke up to ask, "Well, what would they want with us?"

"The Kittevers derive much of their power from dragons and dragon artifacts. They're not just swaying hearts and minds with their rhetoric, you know—they're swaying minds with draconic influence. Did you bring any such artifacts with you that they might have wanted to steal?"

I remained silent, but the admiral answered. "No, no, we didn't bring anything like that."

"Curious," said Grinhill. "Perhaps they simply thought you did then."

"How do you think they would have gotten past the vigilance of our guards?" the admiral asked.

"As I'm sure I don't need to tell you, one of the powers of the dragon-touched is to have an influence over the mind of others in many small ways—to make them turn aside from noticing something, to fail to question the strength of your assertions, or even to alter the perceptions of their eyes and ears. I think it goes without saying how this could be useful in infiltrating such an encampment. My only surprise is that it came to violence at all, rather than them coming and going without incident."

I could guess what had happened there. Most likely our sailors had allowed the intruders to influence them right up until the moment the strangers had laid hands on the egg. Then Summer would have asserted herself and roused them to defend it.

"If you don't mind me saying so," I began, "you seem far more communicative than you did at dinner last night."

Grinhill made a wry smirk at that. "Mr. Light isn't terribly fond of most of my opinions, and I'm afraid I'm ill-suited to expressing opinions that are not my own," he said. "As I rely on Mr. Light's goodwill more than I would like, I find it expedient to say less rather than more."

I could understand that. While we had such a helpful fount of information, another topic pressed on my mind. "What about Sally Hollow-Light?" I put to him.

"Why do you use her maiden name?" Grinhill inquired with a curious frown.

I shrugged. "That's how she introduced herself when I first met her."

"Interesting," he noted to himself. "Well, to be perfectly frank, she's gutter trash. A nobody who somehow managed to catch the eye of the most powerful man in town. She's a strange woman though—difficult to get a grip on. But why do you want to know about her? Besides the obvious, I suppose, which I would firmly advise against."

"She's involved in all this. I'm sure of that."

"Interesting."

I wanted to press him further on Sally, for it seemed to me he had more thoughts than he shared. But as I contemplated how best to draw him out, I was interrupted.

A high-pitched shriek from Zinnia abruptly pulled all my attention away, and I rushed out of the room to her side.

It turned out that Zinny was upset at being given a piece of fruit that did not meet her expectations. It resembled a type of fruit we had in Summer, but the taste and texture were completely different. This was unacceptable. I spent a great deal of the next hour consoling her as she alternated between sobbing and wailing.

I had hoped that the nap might prevent this sort of

meltdown, but I supposed she was going through a difficult time, and that it was only inevitable that it should come out in her behavior. In some ways, I felt relief that she was acting like a normal child again, even as my patience wore thin.

Brook returned during that time and rushed into the room where Zinny was still quite audibly crying. "What's the matter? Is she hurt?"

"No, no, she's just having a hard time," I told him. "She was perfectly fine a bit earlier." *Perfectly fine looking at corpses, not fine eating fruit*, I thought but did not say.

Brook crouched down beside his sister. "Zinny, what's wrong?"

"The fruit is wrong!" she told him between sobs.

He gave me a quizzical look, and I shook my head and shrugged. There was no explaining it.

"What about you? Are you alright?" I asked Brook over Zinnia's head. "You were gone a long time."

"Yes, I'm fine. I ended up talking to Mr. Light for a while."

I would have very much liked to ask more about that, but as I tried to inquire, Zinny's tantrum picked up again with renewed vigor. That was when I began to suspect that she simply resented my attention drifting from her.

Indeed for the rest of the day Zinny absolutely refused to be parted from me on any account. She would settle down and seem perfectly content—right up to the moment that I attempted to do anything else or speak to anyone else in depth. Then she would become inconsolable once more, shrieking and sobbing, until sufficiently assured that I was not going anywhere. She clung to me more tenaciously than she had since she was two or three years old.

Canna would have told me not to indulge these tantrums, but I could not bring myself to be severe with Zinny just then. Regardless of whether she had been mistreated in any way while held captive, it had no doubt been quite a trial, a lot for her young mind to handle. With her precocious manner, she sometimes gave the impression of being mature and in command of herself. It was easy to forget that she was still quite a small child. I only wanted to comfort her.

I ended up settling us in the central courtyard, where I would at least be aware of what was going on if something important happened. Yet I was obliged to give all my attention to Zinnia. We drew on the paving stones with chalky bits of rock, we played cat's cradle, and we sang little childish songs together. I made her a little doll out of rope. I suppose some men might have found it a bit mortifying to sit on the ground playing with a five-year-old girl for hours on end while other men passed by, busy about their tasks. I did not dwell on it.

Sunset came with still no sign of the *Avocet* or the *Plover*.

At great length Zinnia fell asleep—once again on top of me, as if to prevent me from moving without her knowledge. I reminded myself that I was very, very glad to have her back, and that it was only natural for her to be concerned about being parted again. I reminded myself many times.

Two gray cats sauntered over and piled on, securing my immobility even further. Foot traffic in the courtyard slowed down, but I was trapped.

"You look like you could use a drink," Grinhill observed as he proffered a glass in my direction.

"You certainly won't catch me saying no," I agreed as I accepted the glass.

He sat down cross-legged on the ground beside me and clinked his glass against mine.

On taking a sip, I found it was a rather pleasantly dry red wine, quite well balanced and smooth. "This is good. From this region?"

"From right here, grown up in those hills," Grinhill said with a nod inland. "Of course the vineyards are gone now, so you won't find the like again. But I still have a few cases locked up in the cellars."

"Then I'm honored that you'd share it with me," I said.

"Happy to share it with someone who can appreciate it. There aren't many people left in this valley with any genuine taste." With a sigh, he added, "Though I suppose it's not nearly as good as what you get in Summer."

I took another sip as I considered my answer. "I've never found comparison to be a particularly fruitful way of looking at things. At this moment, this is perfect, and I wouldn't wish for anything else."

"But you do have good wine in Summer, don't you?"

"Of course. In point of fact, my wife's family owns one of the finest vineyards on the island. The best wine comes from the north shore, and they're counted the best of the region—at least if you ask the right people."

"Sounds like you married wisely."

"Very much so."

"Must be nice." Grinhill drained his glass and refilled both of ours.

"Have you never been married?" I asked.

"Me? Oh, what legacy do I have to pass on to children? I'm a dying breed in these parts, and I might as well go extinct with dignity than draw out the decline over a few generations of disappointment."

"That's quite the defeatist attitude."

"I don't see it that way. I can do what I want with my own life, not worrying about what it means for anyone else."

"Well, I hope you enjoy it then."

"Not particularly, no. But that's beside the point, isn't it?"

"What is the point then?"

"Oh, it doesn't matter." He stared into his glass and swirled it around. "I have a lot more good bottles down in the cellars, you know."

I smiled. “Sounds like you have your priorities straight.” It’s not that I didn’t pick up the fact that he was inviting me to come down with him to see his wine collection. But I had my own priorities with Zinnia, and I deemed it best to ignore it. I little knew what he wanted from me, but I wasn’t inclined to give him much at that moment.

“I spoke a bit to Mr. Hollow earlier this morning,” Grinhill said abruptly. “He told me some interesting things about you.”

“Oh, yes, I’ve no doubt he did,” I said. Hollow always seemed to be talking to everyone about everything, damn him. I started to wish that Grinhill would simply leave me alone. I resented being trapped with him.

“Your mother—her name wasn’t Alice Hays, was it?”

I sat up straighter, nearly waking Zinny. I’d never known my mother’s original surname, as it wasn’t used in Summer, but even the use of her given name startled me. I did not speak, but I had no doubt Grinhill picked up on my reaction.

“She would have been about fifteen when she disappeared. That sound about right?”

I nodded.

“She was a . . .sort of a cousin of mine. I have something you might be interested in seeing. Though I guess it could wait until tomorrow, what with you being occupied at the moment.”

Zinny’s clinginess was unlikely to resolve itself in a day, so I’d be in the same predicament tomorrow. I didn’t want to bring her along to see whatever it was he had about Alice, at least not until after I knew what it was. “No, it’s alright. I can put her with her brother for a little while.”

I pushed off the cats that had gathered on me, rose to my feet, and carried Zinny into the room where Brook slept alongside some other sailors. I settled her next to him. Brook stirred only slightly but seemed to understand in his half-stupor. He hooked an arm around Zinnia and went back to sleep.

Grinhill awaited me back in the courtyard, and from there led me to the kitchens. He went over to where several lanterns cluttered the floor near a stairwell, took one up and lit it.

"We're going down to the cellars?" I asked.

"Oh, all the things I keep in storage are locked up down there. Safer from petty thievery, and the cool keeps it all better preserved."

That made sense. I followed him down the chill stone stair. A substantially built locked door stood at the bottom of the stairs, but Grinhill fished the key out of his pocket and opened it for us.

The wine cellar was clearly designed to hold a great quantity of wine, but most of the shelves were empty now. As we passed by the one rack that had a scattering of bottles on it, Grinhill paused and picked up a dusty bottle.

"Oh, you should try this one."

"I'd as soon be getting on," I said.

"We can drink while we go," Grinhill pointed out. "This one is special. You won't regret it."

I don't generally require much arm twisting to convince me to drink, so I consented to the slight delay as he popped out the cork and offered me the bottle.

"Didn't think to bring glasses, sorry. You don't mind, do you?"

I shrugged my nonchalance and took a swig.

I was disappointed. This vintage was not nearly as harmonious as the first one he'd offered me. A very bold fruity overtone intruded on what otherwise promised to be a mellow blend. But Grinhill looked so expectant in awaiting my verdict that I hated to be rude. "An interesting blend. I don't believe I've ever had something quite like this before."

"It's a specialty around here," Grinhill said.

I nodded and smiled, unsurprised. Regional specialties so often are acquired tastes, and often they remain regional for a reason.

As he led on, we passed the open bottle back and forth. I continued to sip on the strangely fruity wine to be polite, and because, well, it still promised to be intoxicating.

"You knew Alice yourself?" I asked him as we walked.

"Hmm, well, not much," Grinhill replied. "Her family lived down in Newall, and mine didn't get over there much. Then she disappeared so young, before I ever had a chance to know her."

How extensive were these cellars? How far were we going? I couldn't seem to focus on the questions, for I began to feel very tired. Initially I attributed the weariness as a natural consequence of a long and stressful day, probably not aided by the wine I'd imbibed. But as the drowsiness continued to settle over me, I yawned and struggled to keep my eyes open. It was not like me to feel so exhausted during what ought to have been an exhilarating excursion. I generally had no trouble staying awake at night and was more prone to drowsiness in the morning.

Black dots swam before my eyes, and I knew I would faint. I tried to sit down, but fell part of the way. A black wave overwhelmed me. I sank away from myself.

I should have known better, of course, from the moment I tasted that wine, the strangely unbalanced fruity blend. The fruit was wrong—either a poison or meant to disguise the taste of a poison, I could not say.

Some part of me fought the descent into oblivion, but I lost ground inch by inch.

"How did you manage it?" Sally Hollow-Light's light soprano voice rang clear through my torpor.

"It didn't take much. I don't understand why you think this one is clever. The only trouble was that he wouldn't leave his daughter. For a while, I was sure I would have to drug him in place and drag him down here." Then Grinhill asked, "What do you want with him anyway? I figured you would have only wanted the egg."

"I adapt to the opportunities that present themselves to me, something that you might learn from, *my lord*." Only cruel mockery resided in the use of the title. "If I am right, and I'm sure I am, this one will be worth a great deal more than an egg, especially just another drake, which I'm afraid is all that egg is."

"Have it out then. What's so special about him?"

"Only that he's broken. Can't even see a bald-faced lie." Sally laughed. "A broken contractor is a door without a lock. Through him, we can govern the silver lady herself. All her power will be ours. That whole island will be laid bare."

"Well, that sounds like something."

"Could you perhaps muster a bit of enthusiasm for once in your life?"

"When I see it, maybe. You Kittevers always have a lot of words and a lot of big promises, but you don't always deliver."

"We always deliver your fee, don't we?" Sally scoffed.

The voices battered on against my senses, but my mind ebbed away. At some point, I believe I heard the piping notes of a flute, playing an alluring melody that drew in what was left of me and led me into the dark.

I submerged deep, deep into slumber, far below where one might even think to reach towards the surface. Yet it was not all silence and stillness down there. Like curious fishes flitting on the edge of oblivion, dreams came to peck at me.

INTERLUDE

A PRACTICAL WOMAN

THE TREMOR FELT STRONGER THAN THE LAST ONE, but the same logic applied. Everything in the apartment was firmly secured against quakes, so there was nothing to do but wait it out, and panic would accomplish nothing. The only thing not secured was a wineglass standing by, so Canna took it up and had a sip.

She could recall the particular year that this vintage had been harvested. Brook had still been little and lovey, and Ash had been away aship almost continually. Her parents had been healthy, strong, and at ease with each other. Good year for the grapes too, of course. Canna sometimes believed that her own family's state of mind had as much influence on the grapes as the weather—a strange thought, perhaps, but not one that she counted as wholly irrational. The blessings of Summer were mysterious, but they were not random.

The shaking slowed and then stopped, and everything was still again. Canna set the wineglass back down with a wistful sigh. In a way, she still had a soft spot for earthquakes. They made her feel that change was in the air, and Canna had never been so content as to wholly rebuff the prospect of change. After all, her first husband had been killed in a quake—killed by an unsecured tea kettle falling on his head, to be precise about it. The blessings of Summer were mysterious indeed.

Her father came in then. "Are you alright?"

"Of course I am," Canna replied. "You're meant to shelter in your own room, you know, not move about during the quakes."

"I waited until the shaking was over. Or almost over." Restlessly his gaze roved the apartment, inspecting the secured items on shelves as if to confirm that nothing had shifted. Dad always needed to be doing something. "Do you think it will keep on like this?"

"It will continue as long as Summer is distressed, I suppose. Which depends on what's making her unhappy."

Dad looked at Canna, but he said nothing on the obvious topic—that her husband and children were in danger, that this could very likely be a sign that something horrible had befallen them. He continued his inspection of the apartment, looking for something to fix.

"Is Mom alright?" Canna asked.

"She got a bit rattled, but she's fine." If Dad said "rattled," that most likely meant she was frantic and out of control. But there was nothing to be done about that; she would have her nurse at her side who was fully competent to deal with these episodes.

He at last found a latch that was apparently not up to standards. A small pocket tool materialized, and he set about tightening it. Canna knew better than to tell him to leave it. She waited for him to finish.

"Won't you sit down? Have some wine with me. There's an open bottle in the sideboard."

"No, I think we'll be going pretty soon."

"Going? You mean going home?" Canna repeated, incredulous and yet not quite surprised. "Dad, you can't travel right now."

"We can stop on the road if the shaking starts up again. Safer out in the open than in this anthill anyway. Your mother isn't doing well being cooped up here."

"You've only just arrived, only a few days ago."

"People at home will be worried. We should get back and tell them what's going on. You could come with us, if you want."

It ought to have been tempting, should it not? The alternative was staying here alone. "I don't think it would be wise to do anything that would make it seem like I expect Teddy and Zinnia to be gone for a long time. I should be here when they return," she said quite carefully. "But I suppose I ought to say goodbye to Mom before you leave."

"Maybe it's better you didn't. It'll just get her more worked up."

Canna sighed. "I wish I could do more to help you with her. When Zinnia's a bit older, maybe I can start spending more time up north with you. Zinnia too. I'd love for her to get to know the north country."

"That would be good," Dad nodded. "We could use you up there. I can manage most of it, the tenants and the house and all. But when it comes to the home vineyard, your mom was the one who really knew the grapes. I don't have the palate for it, not like you and she do."

"I'll bet Zinnia will be good with wine too," Canna said. "She gets it from both sides, you know."

"Her father certainly *drinks* wine well enough."

Canna laughed. She hugged her father goodbye, and he left. Did she regret that she couldn't go with him? The rugged wilds of the north shore certainly called to her, but it was hard to be there when nothing was right at home. Even in Summer, decay and rot could not be avoided forever. Having the excuse that she couldn't leave the palace cut through whatever agonizing about the matter she might otherwise have done. At least that was one benefit of locking oneself into marriage—it reduced the available options, which made life simpler.

Then again, she might be a widow again already. No, she ought not to think that. Teddy was not dead. She could still remember the dragon's lamentations when the last Lord Summer had died. All the way on the north shore they could be heard, reverberating through the land itself and bringing a pall of melancholy over everything, like a bank of cloud rolling in. Here in the palace, right above Summer's lair, it would surely be deafening. Teddy and Zinnia must both still be alive.

With that in mind, it might be comforting to see Summer herself as she left her sea caves, and sunset approached. Canna took her wine and shifted herself to the balcony to look out over the sea and await the passage of the dragon.

Perhaps after sunset she might go find that man who'd been flirting with her at the ball. Sex would be an easy way to forget about things for awhile. Would it be too forward for her to seek him out? Beneath her station or some such? Sigh. As if she cared about such things.

It was a mystery to her why she'd ever thought it would be a good idea to raise her station in life. Her position only ever seemed to bring tiresome social obligations and bizarre restrictions on her behavior, with little benefit to make up for the inconvenience. People in Summer could be so casual about rank, but that only made it more bewildering to navigate. There were no rules to follow, only unspoken expectations. Canna wondered at how she had never noticed it until she had stepped ever so slightly beyond the expectations of her birth; she had been far more content in her previous position of more provincial prominence. The novelty of going to balls on Lord Summer's arm had quickly eroded.

That was the funny thing. Nearly everything she had counted in advance as a benefit of marrying Teddy had turned out to be disappointing or irrelevant. And everything she had counted as a disadvantage had also turned out to be quite different from what she expected. Then there were aspects that she had not anticipated at all.

Perhaps marriage was always like that. Life with Ash had certainly been nothing like what she'd thought. Strange to think that she had been little more than Brook's age when she'd first agreed to matrimony, naive and smitten with a charming officer. One would think Ash might have been grateful to marry into an old and noble northern family, that the honor might have humbled him into restraining his worst impulses. But instead he resented her for it. He always had this idea that she looked down on him, that she didn't respect him, and thus that he needed to force that respect on her.

At least he'd given her Brook, and at least he'd had the decency to die. That was about all she could say for Ash.

Teddy could hardly be more different from Ash, and he had done his level best to give her no surprises. He had laid out his deficiencies as a husband from the outset, with particular attention to detail—not only his preference for men, but also his habit of drinking too much, his tendency towards unpredictable "black moods," and his unresolved devastation over his lost love.

Canna had considered it all carefully. It had seemed the right thing to do for Summer, and she already knew what it was like to be married to someone she did not love. She had known she could handle it, so long as it did not come yoked to other horrors. But she hadn't known what it would be like to be married to someone she *did* love, who could never love her back. She had not foreseen that at all.

On reflection, she supposed both her husbands had chosen her for the same reasons—her connection with a prominent noble family, her respectability, her ability to bear a child for them. Nothing to do with Canna herself, not really. For once it might be nice if someone saw her for who she truly was and loved her for it. No doubt it was too late for that.

Certainly there was little hope for one's children to ever see their mother for who she was. But then in her case, the feeling was perhaps mutual, at least where her youngest was concerned.

Among the many things she had not foreseen, the most disconcerting was Zinnia—the dragon child, the uncanny creature come to live with her. She loved Zinnia, and yet she did not know her, not like she knew Brook. The child was a perpetual stranger. Teddy never seemed to have any trouble with it, never seemed to show anything but pure love and devotion for the girl. Thank Summer for that. At least Zinnia had one parent who loved her without reserve.

Canna was certain she had never actually done anything wrong by the girl, nothing that could be brought to her door as an accusation. And yet there was a distance that could not be breached. Zinnia deserved more effusive motherly affection. Perhaps if Canna had been able to give it to her, she wouldn't have needed to run off to her dragon-mother that night.

A fat waning gibbous moon began to rise over the horizon, and Canna became aware that it was fully dark. The dragon Summer's comings and goings had always been as reliable as the tides, as the rising and setting of the sun, an unwavering sign of hope and promise brighter than the evening star. Canna was quite sure her attention had never wandered from the view of the sea before the palace, and yet she had seen nothing.

Summer had never emerged.

A CONCERTED EFFORT

"COME ON, ZINNY. STOP DRAGGING YOUR FEET." Brook had always thought that was just an expression, but it turned out it was real. Zinnia was finding every possible way to move as slowly as possible towards the sea, down to letting her feet drag behind her with each step. Brook sighed. When did he become the designated baby-minder? "Come on. It's all decided."

"I didn't decide anything," Zinny whined.

"That's because you're five, sprout," he reminded her. "Admiral Rostrum and Captain Grace decided we're going back to Summer. Grown-ups make decisions, and we listen." Brook wasn't fully sold on the idea of returning to Summer himself, but that hardly signified.

"But Daddy is *here*."

A stab of guilt obliged Brook to regret his impatience with her. He had more or less already given up on the idea that Teddy would be recovered alive. The more days that passed, the more unlikely it seemed, much as one might like to pretend otherwise. But of course Zinny would not be thinking like that, and she would not forget about it for a moment. She was missing her father, after all, and the two of them were so close. If Teddy never came back, would Zinny forget all about him, as Brook had nearly forgotten his own father?

"You'll be safer in Summer, and if you're safe, everyone who stays behind will be able to focus more on finding your dad," he offered.

Zinny showed no signs of relenting in her obstructionist attitude, so Brook stooped down to pick her up. It was hard to manage her squirming weight along with the big bag he was carrying on his shoulder, but he didn't want to ask any of the other sailors for help. At least they started making better progress towards the docks.

What would happen if Zinnia had to become Lady Summer sooner rather than later? Would a regent be appointed until she came of age? Who would it be? Mom? When would Zinnia be deemed old enough to enter her contract under such circumstances? Surely no one would expect her to wait until she was twenty-one, but there must be some limit. The one thing that Brook looked forward to about being back in Summer was the opportunity to look up the historical precedents for such matters. There would be a lot to consider.

Whatever happened, it would make for an altogether different direction for his book than he had ever anticipated. For years, Brook had perceived that Teddy's tenure as Lord Summer was likely to be of significant historical import, and since Teddy himself was unlikely to record it in memoir, Brook had decided that he was the best positioned for the task. After all, he had been able to observe Teddy from an impersonal perspective and reflect on his significance to Summer as a whole. But now it seemed that all that material he had gathered would only be fit for a chapter or two before moving on to Zinnia's reign.

The black husk of the *Godwit* still hulked over the harbor, a stark reminder of the failures and disappointments of the mission so far. Even the long-awaited arrival of the *Avocet* hadn't raised spirits as much as expected, coming as she did accompanied by a tale of woe. The *Avocet* and the *Plover* had been ambushed en route—fired upon at night without warning—and the enemy ships had slipped away just as fast as they'd appeared. The *Plover* had taken severe damage, leaving it barely seaworthy enough to limp back to Summer. Captain Grace had been forced to make the difficult call to escort the *Plover* to ensure the safety of its crew, delaying her arrival in Oxeye.

Now that the full picture of these events could be seen, it was apparent that a concerted effort had been under way to strand the *Godwit* party in Oxeye while preventing aid from arriving. Clearly their enemies were more numerous and organized than they had at first believed, and they all kept making the wrong calls. If only the *Avocet* had remained on schedule, there would have been no opportunity for Lord Summer to be lost. Now even with the relief ship arrived, the *Godwit* crew was obliged to stay behind to search for him, and who knew what else might go wrong before they gave up the search.

By the time Brook made it to the *Avocet*, his shoulder ached where the bag's strap cut into it, and he was exhausted from walking unevenly with the unwieldy weight on his hip.

"You need some help with that bag, Brook?" Poppy spoke down to him from the gangplank. She looked so pretty, even with sweat gleaming on her brow and a flush in her cheeks from exertion. Especially so. Brook felt he could stare at the pattern of freckles across her nose for hours.

"Oh, no, it's nothing," he insisted with a cavalier shrug. "Just a little tricky with Zinny too, but it's fun to carry her."

Poppy nodded and smiled. "It's so cute how close you two are."

"Right, I mean, she's my little sister. I love her so much," Brook hastened to say. He hoped Poppy didn't notice the way

Zinny rolled her eyes at him. He started up the ramp, and Poppy fell in beside him.

"I'm a little jealous," Poppy said. "I always wanted a little brother or sister."

"I have a little brother!" Zinny piped up.

"No, you don't," Brook shushed her. To Poppy, he asked, "You're an only child then?"

"Nah, I have an older sister too," Poppy said. "The standard Summer family, you know? Except maybe I should have been a boy, but I make up for it by acting like it anyway."

Brook laughed, since he could only imagine she was making some sort of joke, even if he couldn't follow it. "I'm glad you're a girl," he told her. "Are you coming back to Summer on the *Avocet* too? I thought most of the *Godwit* crew was staying here."

"But I'm on the crew of the *Avocet* now!" Poppy enthused. "Captain Grace has agreed to take me on."

"Oh." Brook took that in with a bit of confusion. "But why? Surely the *Godwit* will be replaced and everyone brought back on. Even before all this, I know there's been talk of expanding the military, adding more ships, so there should be plenty of jobs for everyone. Lord Summer and Admiral Rostrum have been discussing it."

"Is *that* what they've been discussing?" There was a note of amusement in her voice that Brook did not understand. He wanted to follow up on it, but she moved on too quickly. "It doesn't matter. I wanted to get on a different crew anyway, and Grace had a few spots. I moved fast and impressed her, so I'm in. I think this will be a much better fit for me."

Brook wondered uneasily what exactly had been a "bad fit" about the *Godwit*. Was it something about the way the women were treated? It's not as though anything really bad had been going on. In some ways, the girls were given an easier time and lighter duties. Poppy seemed so happy about her new situation though that he didn't like to press her on it. "Well, it'll be nice to have you as company on the way home."

"Yeah! Maybe we can get to know each other better."

The way she said it—the way she looked at him sideways with a sly smile—made his heart beat faster. Despite what seemed like clear signals, it was still hard for Brook to believe that a girl like Poppy might actually like him. She was practically a grown woman—so confident and cool and . . . curvy. He knew he had filled out a lot himself in the past year, but sometimes he still felt like a little kid.

He was so absorbed in Poppy that he hardly noticed where they were going, but at some point he found himself in a cozy little stateroom. "Will you two be comfortable enough in here?" Poppy asked.

"Of course. It looks great," Brook said. "But we're not displacing someone, are we?"

"Don't worry about it. Obviously Lady Zinnia needs a private room—it would hardly do to have her with the sailors, even us girls, and it's not as if we're giving you the captain's quarters. The second mate is just going to bunk with the first for a few days is all," Poppy explained in a rapid tone. "Anyway, I'd better get back to work, but let me know if you need anything, yeah?"

Brook barely had a chance to thank her before she was gone. At least he could put down his burdens though. Everything was so heavy. He sank down onto the lower bunk with a grunt.

Zinny stood still and straight and stared at him with her strangely dark eyes. She seemed judgmental, or maybe that was his own thoughts clouding it. He shouldn't have ignored her so much to flirt with Poppy.

"We should probably stay down here until they're ready to make way," he suggested to Zinny. "We'll just get in the way otherwise."

"Always in the way," Zinny agreed. She climbed up onto the top bunk and started bouncing on it. Brook wanted to tell her to cut it out but feared what she might do instead.

It might have been nice to stay in Oxeye a little longer, with more time to explore and talk to people. It was so different from home—so many different types of people living all kinds of lives, and everything was changing all the time. He could already see that they had far more problems than Summer, and that some of the solutions were nearly as bad as the disease, but it was all so *interesting.*

Mr. Lowell Light certainly seemed to understand quite a lot about how societies fit together and the challenges of trying to improve them. He hadn't even been angry when he'd discovered Brook looking through his library, not when Brook explained that he was simply interested in history. Mr. Light was delighted to talk it all over with an eager listener, and everything he had to say had been absolutely fascinating. When he'd expounded on all the ways history and economics went hand in hand, it put a completely new cast on the way Summer never seemed to change. Why had Teddy been so dead set against Mr. Light from the first?

From the deck above, the sounds of some sort of commotion filtered down to them, and Brook itched to check it out. Zinny would be fine on her own for a few minutes, right? Now that they were on the ship, it was not as though she could just wander off. Someone would notice if she started down the gangplank. Brook made some vague excuse about needing to use the head, which Zinny may or may not have seen right through, and he started up.

No one was working. Everyone seemed to have paused in their tasks to gather and murmur to each other in an anxious manner that made the hair on the back of his neck stand up. Without the usual rowdy clamor of people at work, the uncanny stillness was broken only by coughing and sneezing.

Odd to see how many of the crew seemed to have come down with colds all of a sudden. Usually Summer folk were quite hardy and resilient to such maladies.

Brook went over to the group Poppy was in and asked what was going on.

The first mate answered him. "We've heard reports from a merchant ship that a large fleet of warships has been spotted heading south. Their bearing would suggest they're headed straight for Summer."

"Flying the mark of the Kittevers," another sailor chimed in.

Brook still did not have a firm grip on what the Kittevers were supposed to be, but it didn't seem good. "What does this mean then? Does it change our plans?"

"That's for Admiral Rostrum and Captain Grace to decide," the first mate reminded him.

"Surely Summer is still the safest place for Lady Zinnia though?" another sailor asked. "As long as we can avoid tangling with this fleet en route, once we're within Summer's range, surely she will protect us and bring us into the harbor safely."

"We'll wait for orders," the first mate said. Then she raised her voice across the deck. "That goes for all of you. Get back to work and wait for orders."

Brook had no obligation to work aboard the *Avocet*, but he joined the other sailors in whatever ways he could help. He didn't want to go back down below while there was so much to think about. Something about the situation was very strange and disquieting. No one in their right mind would launch a fleet to attack Summer unless they fully believed that the dragon had somehow been neutralized. Of all the things that might befall Summer, nothing more disastrous could be imagined.

Everyone had been hoping to find Lord Summer alive, but of course every adult had been fully aware they were as likely to find him dead, perished in an accident or altercation in the dark. Perhaps even Zinny knew that. What if something far worse were possible? Something that would threaten all of Summer?

The bark of a cough sounded near his ear, swiftly echoed by several other coughs and sniffles around the deck.

A TREE

THE MAST ROSE UP LIKE A GREAT TREE SPREADING ITS branches over the ship. Did it remember being a tree? Did it like to travel around now, as most trees never got to do? Or did it think it was all a lot of bother, when one spot in the world was all a tree really needed to be happy? Were trees happy?

It was so easy to climb, and no one was paying any mind at the moment. Up, up, up, until the sea unfurled like the underside of the sky. Like hiding under the bed covers, all the same above and below. Sea and sky, sea and sky.

Wind skipped over the surface of the water and tugged playfully at the sails. Where did wind come from? Where did it go? Did the birds know? Birds always seemed to know an awful lot about the stranger magics of the world, even though they had very small heads. Maybe that's why they often had such wild eyes.

Birds were also good to eat, but they didn't seem to impart any of their wisdom when you ate them. In that way, they differed from humans. Or did you have to eat them while they were still alive, like Summer ate her food? That did not sound so good. Would a cat know? Perhaps. Cats had very strange ideas though.

The world was so bright and bouncy and boundless. All filled up with magic that was almost too much to hold inside without bursting.

But there was something else too, a stowaway that didn't belong. Like a praying mantis you find still clinging on after coming in from the forest; it belonged to another world entirely and seemed silly in the inside world. This stowaway was no stranger though.

Stop being so silly, Daddy. Wake up.

So I did.

PART THREE

A CHANGE OF CLOTHES

I FOUND MYSELF LAID OUT ON A STONE SLAB IN A chapel, like the guest of honor at a funeral. I wore only a loose, filmy garment of soft white muslin. Although I felt certain I had been asleep for some time, no crust had gathered around my eyes, nor was there any other such bodily detritus to give testimony to the passage of time. My face was shaven and my fingernails trimmed. My hair had been washed and combed back into its natural shape and texture.

So I had been kept clean. That disturbed me nearly as much as anything else, the thought of someone moving and touching me so intimately while I slept, without having my best interests at heart. It seemed to me as if someone had been rather taken up with the aesthetics of having me laid out here in a picturesque way, quite in excess of whatever purpose they sought with it. Otherwise they might have just as easily put me in a bed or in a closet for all the practical difference it would make. But what did they seek?

Shivering shook me. The chapel was cold, and I had been there long enough for it to seep into my bones. Could they not have at least put a blanket on me? But I did not normally get cold, not since I'd contracted with Summer. I'd forgotten how miserable it was, how utterly impossible it was to focus on anything else while the cold so mercilessly insisted on my attention. Why was I so cold now?

The only light came from narrow slits in the ceiling, bringing me to the conclusion the chapel was mostly underground. The chamber was an oval, and it was empty but for the table or altar that I rested on and a ring of stone benches built in to the curved walls. A place for rituals? For sacrifices? Grooves in the floor seemed to speak of blood running down from the altar.

I had to get out of there. My stiff legs protested the movement, but I tottered off the altar and found the stone floor even colder under my bare feet. The only obvious way out of the room was a heavy door made from a single enormous piece of densely grained wood. A tree must have grown in the sun for five hundred years at least to furnish such a door, now idling alone in this desolate place.

The lock looked simple enough, but there was one little problem. I had absolutely nothing on hand to pick it with. I felt all over my hair, knowing that pins could occasionally lose themselves in there, but whoever had washed it had done a thorough job. My kingdom for a hairpin! My shirt contained no haberdashery whatsoever. I scoured the floor of the chapel, but whoever cleaned the floors was also infuriatingly scrupulous. Not a nail, not a pin, not a toothpick. The door itself was sanded so smooth that I had no hope of getting so much as a splinter off of it.

"Summer. Please. Give me strength," I whispered into the still air. I tried to force the handle with brute strength. It didn't budge.

I had known that wouldn't work. Lord Summers were often renowned for their feats of strength, and certainly I had seen Jack do amazing things on our travels. But in the end, that strength was fueled by muscles, grown over a course of years and fed by the bounty of Summer. The small increase in muscular development that Summer had recently granted me was scarcely enough to shift that massive door. Whatever she had expected of me, I was not doing it.

I sat on the floor and drew my legs up close to my body, hugging myself for warmth. I thought of the dreams. I had very little doubt that they were real. It had become apparent that I was far too self-absorbed to even imagine such details about Canna and Brook, and so much of their inner lives had been completely unknown to me. Foreign countries, the lot of them.

But whence came the dreams? Had the dragon pushed me on them, or had I wandered the dreamworld myself, seeking them out? A niggle of guilt wormed at me for the intrusion of privacy in these dabblings into the minds of others, but on another level, I felt fully justified. Anyone who was part of Summer was part of Summer, were they not? Surely that was the dragon's thought, not mine.

Footfalls echoed on the other side of the door, growing closer. I scarcely wanted to be found out as I was, and I saw only one other option. I returned to the altar, laid myself down, and pretended to sleep.

The iron hinges creaked to declare the door opened. The rustling of fabrics and the gentle slap of footfalls told me that at least two people were moving about the chamber. I focused on keeping my breathing slow and even.

Hands brushed against my face, smoothed down the edges where my hair met my face.

"What are you doing? Just leave him be." Sally Hollow-Light.

"I don't reckon he needs to look a mess for your spell to work."

"It's already working. I only need to seal it in iron," said Sally. "But didn't I tell you to just shave all that hair off anyway?"

Tom Hollow did not respond. I ought to have been repulsed by his hands on my face, but somehow the touch did not feel wholly ungentlemanly. Was he the one who had washed me and cared for me while I slept? How could he be so tender in manner and yet be willing to do this to me?

At this point, I considered jumping up and trying to rush past them out the door. However, I knew Tom Hollow was stronger than me, and Sally was no fainting damsel either. I remembered how she'd sported a knife on her hip even while wearing only a tiny nightgown; she and her brother were most likely both armed. They might very well have other allies close at hand. Thus even if I broke free of them, I'd be running around barefoot and half naked in unfamiliar surroundings with my enemies hot on my heels. I suspected they could catch me with little effort.

All in all, the potential benefits were too uncertain a return for the risks and drawbacks involved. My only advantage in this situation was that they did not know I was awake. I would not give it up for a few minutes of inconveniencing them. Then they'd surely be able to put me back to sleep and continue on with their plans.

"Didn't you close the door all the way? That cat is in here again. Get it out."

A fair cacophony of hissing, yowling, cursing, and stumbling proceeded from there.

"I don't reckon that cat is going anywhere."

"For pity's sake. Fine, just leave it."

Tom Hollow chuckled slightly to himself. "Hey, you remember that mean old black cat Aunt Rose used to have?" He spoke with the unmistakable tone of one trying to cheer up someone in a bad mood.

"How could I ever forget?" Sally replied, her annoyance unabated. "I still have the scars."

"I ever tell you about the time Uncle E. got so fed up with

that cat he had a mind to drown it in the lagoon?" Tom persevered. "Somehow he got it into a bag. He roped me along to help, and down we went to the banks. But when he opened the bag just a pinch to add some stones for weight, that old cat somehow launched itself out and threw such a fiery fit that Uncle E. went head over heels into the lagoon—came up cursing and sputtering, covered in muck from head to toe. And that cat just sat in a tree and watched, not a hair of it come to harm."

Sally laughed—a true, genuine laugh that echoed strangely in the cool stillness of the stone chapel. "I wish I could have seen it. Why did you never tell me about that before?"

"Oh, ah, I reckon I was a bit ashamed—for going along to help, you know."

"It doesn't sound as if you were of much help at all."

"No, I don't reckon I was. But all the same, you wouldn't have approved, not back then. You liked that cat, claws and all."

Sally sighed, but I had no sense of whether it was wistful or rueful or some other color altogether.

"It will only be a few more hours now," she said. "Let's go."

Footsteps shuffled out, the door closed, and the lock turned. I opened my eyes.

Tall white tapers now stood in sconces along the wall, herbs were strewn over the floor, and a variety of impenetrable symbols had been painted on the walls. I supposed these were preparations for the ritual they had discussed, but none of it looked to be any use in my predicament.

A black cat with a silvery undercoat stared unblinkingly at me from where he had settled on a bench. He was a scrappy creature, missing a chunk from one of his ears and a few patches of fur from the scars on his face. I judged him to be quite old by feline standards. He had that hollowed-out look about the cheeks and the sides, and his mouth didn't quite close right.

As I approached, a low growl rose in his throat, and his back arched. The hostility took me by surprise, as cats had normally been enraptured with me since I entered my contract, just as they always had been for Jack and now were for Zinny. But something was clearly off there. So I was obliged to go through the usual rigamarole—getting down on the floor, avoiding eye contact, slowing approaching and offering a hand to sniff. It took ages for him to let me near him.

I felt his fur, hoping for some sort of stick to be caught in it, but there was nothing. He looked at me contemptuously, as if to say, *What did you expect? I groom myself.*

Claws were surely not long enough to pick that lock. I'd try anyway if I thought I could, but I wasn't getting any part of that cat into the lock while he still lived. The alternative certainly occurred to me. I knew he wouldn't be easy to kill, but with the dragon's ruthlessness, I felt I could do it. There would be bones in there that would certainly get the job done, if I could extract them with bare hands and teeth. As unappealing as that prospect appeared, it would not perhaps be the most disgusting thing I'd done in my life.

As I pondered these imponderables, the cat started heaving and straining. I pulled back as it hacked up a truly monstrous hairball in my face.

"How kind of you," I told the cat. "It's just what I always wanted."

He gave me another reproachful look before beginning to clean himself up, and I felt a stab of guilt. Here was the only friend I had, and all I could do was contemplate killing him and make sarcastic remarks.

"I'm sorry," I said. "I hope you feel better after getting that up. I'd give you a treat if I had anything."

That reminded me of my own stomach as it protested its emptiness. I must have been given something while I slept—broth poured down my throat, I supposed—for I didn't feel very thirsty or particularly weak. Whatever it was didn't fill my stomach, though. The smell of the cat vomit added an edge of queasiness to my hunger. I may have started to cry at this point.

But as I let misery overtake me, I realized there was one more place to look. A scrappy cat like that wouldn't be eating dainties from a lord's table. It would be eating all sorts of things. Coughing up all sorts of things. Grimacing, I picked through the hairball until I found what I sought.

A fish bone.

It was so delicate that I scarcely thought it would be adequate to the job, but it was all I had. As I knelt in front of the door, the cat stalked over to keep an eye on my efforts. I had to be very careful, as the slightest wrong move or excessive force would snap the fish bone. But it was ultimately a simple enough lock of the old style, and I had plenty of experience with such pieces. I got it open.

I tucked the fish bone into my hair and proceeded through the door. I looked back to see if my feline friend was coming, but he had settled himself on the altar and resumed grooming.

On the other side of the door was a rough passageway that appeared to be underground. I say "appeared" in a general sense. The absence of light sources in the passage spoke to it being subterranean, but ultimately that meant not much of anything was visible at all. I went back to grab a couple of the tapers from the chapel. Of course I had no means of lighting them, but nevertheless it seemed prudent to have them on hand in case they became useful. Yet since I had no pockets or even a waistband in which to tuck them, it was an annoyance to carry the candles with me.

I set out into the darkness, feeling my way against the wall. It was tempting to go slowly and cautiously, but I knew that carried its own risks. I could not be caught out in this passage—blind, unarmed, and vulnerable. The faster I made my way through it, the sooner I could reach a safer situation.

Sharp fragments of rock bit at my bare feet and had me longing for the calluses of my boyhood. It had been a very long time since I'd gone barefoot with any regularity, and I could feel every pebble beneath my feet. I could scarcely even tell if anything had broken the skin, and I cringed to think I might be leaving a trail of bloody footprints wherever I went. But there was nothing I could do about that.

At length a dim strip of light appeared near the floor, foretelling a chamber of some sort. This represented a dilemma for me. Any illuminated chamber might very well be occupied, yet I could hear no sign of anyone moving around in there. The light too was of a feeble sort; someone might have left a lantern burning low for ease of having it on hand later. I decided I would have to take some sort of risk sometime if I was to find any clothes or supplies to help me escape.

I tried the door, found it unlocked, and then threw it open as violently as I could. Easing it open would serve no purpose except to give someone more time to prepare. But there was no one within.

A stack of crates and a trunk with a lantern on it was all that filled the little room—more of a closet than anything. That suited me fine, since all those boxes promised to have something of use in them. At the very least, I'd be leaving with a lantern. I went first to the trunk, as it looked the sort of thing that might have clothing in it.

When I opened the trunk, it became apparent that it belonged to a woman, for it was full of dresses, corsets, soft slippers, and cosmetics. In fact, I thought I recognized Sally Hollow-Light's style in the items. My initial disappointment gave way to a more amenable mindset. Sally and I were alike in size, if not in shape, so these clothes would most likely fit passably enough. Anything would be warmer and more protective than the flimsy nightshirt I was wearing.

If I did make it out of this underground lair, I would need

clothes that would allow me to blend into a crowd in town well enough to get back to my own people. I knew that with the right stylings I could quite tolerably pass for a woman, or at any rate I could at one time. I considered the options anew.

A striking chiffon number in mint green caught my eye, but I reminded myself that the purpose was *not* to draw attention to myself. I settled for a much more modest dark blue dress with a square neckline. The bodice offered a lot of room for storage, thanks to Sally's generous assets, so I considered what to put in there. I couldn't find a proper weapon, but a pair of sewing scissors might serve in a pinch. A few of the tapers went in, along with a bit of rope, and I padded it all out with a silk scarf.

The slippers were the most disappointing, since it turned out that my feet at least were much larger than Sally's. I ended up having to slice open the seams to let a couple of toes stick out the front, and it was still a tight fit. At least I wouldn't be barefoot.

Though time felt scarce, I nevertheless took a few moments to apply some cosmetics to complete the effect—to smooth out the angles of my face into a more feminine shape and to draw focus to my eyes and lips, which had always been on the softer side. There was no time to do anything with my hair, but then there was nothing particularly masculine about it to begin with. I stuck a few pins behind my ear though.

As I considered the effect in a small hand mirror, I was reminded with a sharp pang of Alice. I fancied I was seeing how she might have looked if she had lived to forty.

I set out back into the dark corridor with a new sense of confidence in my purpose. Perhaps that feeling came merely from the presence of the lantern shedding a bit of light on the rough corridor, or perhaps it was the clothes indeed. It might seem strange that wearing a dress would lend assurance, but

I think I was brought back to the mindset of another time when I did something similar.

The first time I ever donned women's clothes was not long after Alice had died, before anyone else was aware of her death. I dressed myself in one of my mother's outfits, put on her cosmetics, and styled my hair in her fashion. I was still barely more than a lad then, even more slender and soft featured than I am now, and the resemblance between Alice and me had always been strong. In the mirror, I might scarcely have been able to recognize myself, so much did I look like her.

I went to Lord Summer's chamber by the back entrance, the same way Alice had taken me there as a child. When I entered, Leo glanced over from his chair by the hearth where he sipped a glass of brandy.

"Where the hell have you been?" he growled.

"My apologies, Lord Summer," I said in a soft voice. "I've been ill."

"Ill? You've been ill for two weeks then?"

"You may recall last time, I hit my head . . ."

Leo grabbed me by the hair and yanked my head back, exposing my throat to him. I swallowed nervously, thinking of the masculine shape of my voice box, but he did not take any notice of it. "Is that some kind of joke?"

He shoved me up against the wall and pinned me with all his weight. I remember the moment so clearly—his breath in my ear, his teeth on my neck. He still had a firm grip on my hair, and his other hand grabbed my arm and twisted it back. My fear and pain must have been naked on my face, and his obvious arousal rose in proportion to it.

"I really must have hurt you last time. Look how scared you are." He was delighted.

The violence of his passions was no surprise, and I had thought I was prepared for it. I'd attracted perhaps more than my share of beatings in my young life and knew what it was to be hurt, but this was different than I expected. I feared I might give myself away in a far more definitive manner than the apple in my throat.

Then he swung me around by my hair and threw me onto the bed. I almost wanted to back out at that moment, to jump up and run away. But on some level, I knew it was already too late. His reflexes were that of a dragon. I'd never make it out of the room without him catching me, and what would he do to me if he discovered the ruse? I knew I did not have much time before he would discover that I was not Alice.

When he came closer, I pulled a knife from under the corset and brought the tip of the blade up just as he brought his own weight down upon it.

His face, when he understood what had happened, is imprinted in my memory. Not angry, no—more surprised and baffled, as if he never could have imagined that anyone would dare to hurt him. I believe he still failed to recognize that I was not Alice, and I had no desire to enlighten him. I would let Alice have her revenge.

I pulled the knife out and stuck it back in at a sharper angle, being sure to get under the breastbone to puncture the heart. His blood spilled out all over me, soaking Alice's dress. I scrambled out from under him and jumped to my feet.

At that moment the bedroom window shattered, and Summer's sensationally oversized silver head burst into the room. Her head alone dwarfed all the furniture, filled the space with her power and presence. Her eyes were as dark as I have ever seen them, a deep, churning cobalt blue. At the time, I did not know how unusual that was, for it was the very first time I ever looked into her eyes.

She caught me in her gaze, and I froze, utterly unable to move or assert myself in any way. I said earlier that I am no longer afraid of Summer, and that of course is rubbish. I am still quite terrified of Summer, every time, just as I was then. I had no doubt that I would die. I had not come to Leo's chamber intending to live. This was to be my dramatic exit, my bold, foolish sacrifice. I waited for her to kill me.

I was certain that she knew exactly who I was, that she knew *everything* I was. As she held me in that trance, she could perceive all that was inside me—the fear, the pain, the grief, the triumph, the exhilaration, the arousal, the anger, the horror, the sorrow, the despair. Had I ever felt so much all at once? Not regret though. I felt no contrition for what I'd done.

The dragon's breath bore down on me like a hot summer breeze—bitter like dandelion, sweet like death. But she pushed past me, actually brushed me aside and left me stumbling as I fell out of her trance.

Gently, so gently, she picked up Leo in her jaws and bore him away.

Footsteps sounded in the corridor outside, and I recovered my wits just in time to slip out of the room by the back way. I was careful not to leave blood smears leading to that hidden door.

At that time, I always kept some basic supplies and clothes stashed away in the back passages, in case I should ever have a sudden need for them. So I was able to change back into a boy and return to my own modest quarters in the palace before the corridors filled with guards and gawkers. I went back later for the bloody dress and burned it.

And I completely got away with it. Although it was clear enough that Leo had been violently killed, no one even looked for the murderer. It was assumed either that the murderer had been eaten by the dragon, or that it had been Jack, or that the dragon herself had killed Leo. Jack was the only one who might have any information, and he never said a word. The idea that the dragon might have spared a murderous intruder did not occur to anyone.

As for that, I was as baffled as anyone. I had no notion why Summer chose to spare me.

Did any contrition come later, you might wonder? Not much for ending Leo, but perhaps for the consequences of that action. I did not do it for my own benefit—that much should be obvious. Even if I'd nurtured some hope of surviving the ordeal, I would have anticipated that such an act could only serve to increase the demands on Jack's time and push him towards fulfilling his responsibility to procreate, and thus hasten his inevitable withdrawal from me. So it was certainly not for me. It was for Alice, and maybe for Jack.

But it did not turn out as I anticipated. A great many things might have been different if Leo had gone on being Summer until Jack had fully come of age, and perhaps Jack might still be alive today.

AN IRON COLLAR

THE UNDERGROUND CORRIDOR EVENTUALLY brought me to a fork in the passage. To the left it slanted slightly upward towards the surface, while to the right was a staircase that headed precipitously downward into the earth. Naturally my first inclination was to head up and out, but something about the other way gave me pause. Something was down there.

My own notion was that it might be the egg. I had sometimes felt something from it, a reaching out from within. That was perhaps what had made me start to feel defensive about the egg, reluctant to trade it and determined to follow after it when it was taken. If there was a chance I could still recover it, I did not want to leave it. Clearly these people would not treat it well.

I headed down the stairs, which soon became hard to navigate. The height of the steps was variable, and the way zig-zagged at random as it descended. I had the impression that the staircase had been built around the natural shape of the rock veins, carving its way through soft parts of the soil and avoiding the hard bones of the earth. I deemed it to be much older than all the other portions of this underground complex—built when the options for cutting through solid rock were more limited, or when people were more patient to find the natural ways.

The stairs opened out into a natural cavern. Despite not being able to see very far by the light of my one little lantern, the echoes of my footfalls told me that the cavern was immense. I took the precaution of lighting one of the tapers and sticking it at the base of the stairs before I continued on my way. I knew how difficult it would be to find the entrance of the stair without a guide light.

Then I almost tripped over a cat. It was small and dark colored, and it completely blended in with the darkness aside from the reflective glow of its eyes. The cat's presence so far down in the cavern interested me immensely. Was it down there hunting? Perhaps these caverns were used to store grain and thus attracted mice. Perhaps it had a taste for bats and blind fish. Or perhaps there was a dragon down there.

I already knew there was, if I admitted it. The presence I had felt at the top of the stair was stronger here, and it was no egg. It was too . . . angry. What would an egg have to be angry about?

The smart thing, of course, would be to turn around and leave as quickly as possible. Being a contractor for a different dragon would scarcely guarantee my safety, especially not as a "broken contractor" as Sally had called me. Jack and I had sometimes encountered dragons in our travels, sometimes even by design, but he at least was adept at communicating with them and making our purposes clear. I could barely communicate with my own dragon.

Dragons do not *often* eat people on sight, but that's a bit like a rabbit saying that about humans. It's not that humans are unwilling to go there; we're simply not always hungry or in the mood for rabbit meat. Rabbits generally have the good sense not to hang around and find out. It would seem I had less sense, because I pressed on.

When I finally set eyes on the dragon, it broke my heart. I had been fearing an enormous, ancient creature like Summer, but this dragon was much smaller, perhaps about twice the size of an elephant, if you gathered her all up. She would be quite young: if I understood dragoness growth correctly, less than a decade old.

In that decade, she had never left the cavern; that much was plain. Iron manacles, affixed to chains bound to rings set deep in the stone floor, enclosed her legs and her neck. Around the edges of the manacles, her flesh bulged and her scales had warped. The manacles must have been put in place when she was much smaller and not replaced as she continued to grow. Perhaps it had become impossible for anyone to approach her. Certainly the waves of rage I felt emanating from her were not inviting.

Her eyes opened. They were light green like polished aventurine, and her scales were emerald. I wondered if she were related to Crispin, the green male that had been with Sally Hollow-Light on the *Shadowcat*. I hadn't thought about that drake in a while, which now seemed a strange oversight on my own part.

As I started to approach her, a growl rose in her throat, deep and menacing. I halted, but I still wanted to help her. It was not right for a dragon to be kept in such degradation, and I little cared if that was my own thought or Summer's. Nevertheless, if I were to have any hope of helping her, I'd need to get closer, and I scarcely thought the standard cat strategies would work.

Most of my experience with dragons was with Summer, but I knew what she liked. So I started to sing. I went for one of Summer's favorites, a tragic ballad about lovers who are kept apart by war and jealous family members. It might have been better if I'd had a lute or something to keep me better in tune, but the acoustic properties of the cavern were at least quite amenable. My voice bounced back at me from a hundred different angles.

I saw little change in the dragon's demeanor at first, but the epic had many verses, so I kept at it. Eventually she seemed to harken to my voice, listening and weighing the words as they came. I edged closer to her, and her eyes followed me.

I continued to sing as I got close to the manacle on her foreleg and investigated it. Not so complicated. Now that I had a hairpin, it was easy enough to pop the manacle open. The raw, naked flesh under the iron made me wince. The dragon watched me now with keen interest as I opened the other three leg manacles, and she stretched her legs in satisfaction as they were released.

The iron collar around her neck proved a greater hurdle. No hinge nor lock interrupted the band like the other manacles; it formed a solid ring. Had it been pulled over her head when she was much smaller? If so, there was no chance of getting it off that way again. Moreover, the collar was carved all over with symbols that I could make nothing of. It must have been enchanted, binding her with more than merely the strength of the iron. Whatever the dragoness was being used for, this collar held her to that purpose. No possible means of getting it off were on hand.

"I'm sorry, love. I can't do it," I told her. "If I get out of here, perhaps I can come back with more men and help you. Right now, it's only me."

The dragon looked dolorous but unsurprised by my failure. I couldn't bear to go away and leave her alone again quite so quickly, so I sat down with her and finished the song. The tragic finale of the piece, when the lady throws herself off a cliff after learning that her lover is dead, seemed to suit the mood. Then I fell silent.

The horror of being confined, trapped, hemmed in began

to creep over me. Naturally I assumed this feeling was somehow emanating from the green dragon before me, and yet it grew stronger and stronger. Surely I could not be feeling her pain so vividly without any sort of bond to her? Yet it became overpowering, this feeling of being pressed in on all sides.

I felt I might scream, throw my weight against the cavern wall, do anything to get out. I had to get out, get out, get out. It was the only thing that mattered. Yet I didn't even know what enclosure I felt such a need to escape from. Though I was trapped in a sense, the cavern was a wide-open space that ought not to induce such a feeling of claustrophobia. But the sensation did not subside, and I pulled at my hair as if to split my very skull open to free my brain from its hold.

Something gave way, and all at once I had double vision. I don't mean like what happens when I've drunk too much and the eyes start to gain a sense of independence from one another. No, I could see an entirely different view of another chamber altogether, overlaid on my sight of the cavern around me.

I looked upon a sort of makeshift office, perhaps, still in the underground tunnels, though a few bands of natural light came from slits near the ceiling. I could see Sally Hollow-Light from behind, seated at a table, though oddly I seemed to be looking up at her, as if I were seated on the floor. Sally was dressed more like I had seen her on the *Shadowcat*: in practical trousers and her close-shaven head laid bare.

A young man spoke tentatively to Sally. "I don't suppose it might be possible, um, under the right circumstances, for one of these contractors to, um . . . turn into a cat?"

"What are you on about?" Sally's tone was not amused.

"I went to the chapel to check on things as you asked, but there was no one there! No one but a black cat sleeping on the pedestal. I thought maybe . . ." He trailed off, presumably at the expression on Sally's face.

I have to confess myself a bit insulted at the thought. If I were to transform into a cat, surely I would be a sleek, handsome feline in the prime of life, not that gaunt, scar-bitten old-timer I'd left in the chapel. How could anyone confuse us? But that was perhaps a less important detail than the revelation that my departure from the chapel had been detected, the significance of which did not escape my notice.

"The cat is not the conduit," Sally said in a flat voice. "If the conduit has escaped, then we have to find him. At once." She stood and left the room with the man.

I still did not understand how I was seeing this scene, but it continued even once the people had departed from the room. Now that the singular focus of the conversation was gone, the gaze began to rove the room more curiously, fixating on the most minute details to no clear end. Then I caught a glimpse of a shimmery fragment of eggshell before me, and I understood.

The egg had hatched, apparently without anyone noticing, and I was looking through the hatchling's eyes. But why? How could I see out of this new creature's eyes as if they were my own? Why had I felt its frustration as it yearned to break free of the shell?

The answer sat within me already, perhaps knowledge from Summer or something I recalled from when I had bonded to her, though that process had been too overwhelming to consciously recall the details. The contract had always gone both ways. Just as my firstborn child belonged to Summer, her first child belonged to me. That was why she had given the egg into my keeping in the first place. He was mine.

Be careful, little brother. Those people might come back, and they are not your friends. I thought as stridently as I could, and the hatchling cocked his head as if unsure where the thoughts were coming from. His confusion swelled.

Get out of the egg, if you can, but try to keep it in one piece and not make a mess.

Daintily the hatchling slithered and stepped out of the egg. Dutifully he gathered up the pieces of shell that had fallen, put them back inside the egg, and turned the whole shell over so that an intact side faced up. It would appear that he perfectly understood the overall intent of my directive as well as the letter. His relief at having a clear purpose was palpable.

Then he fanned out his wings and started licking himself clean.

There's no time for that right now, little brother. Do you think you can open the door?

He looked over at the door and examined it. Considering how dexterously he had managed the eggshell, I was certain he could handle a knob, but he was cautious. The sound of footsteps approaching the door made me reverse course.

Never mind! Just hide! Hide now!

He scrambled behind his crate as the door opened.

"Someone is creeping around the passages here." I recognized Grinhill's voice.

"Yes, I am aware," Sally responded. "The conduit has gotten out of the chapel, but I know he's still around here somewhere. The exits are all being watched."

"No, not him, another of the Summerlanders. He must have followed me in here from the entrance at the manor house, picked the lock to the cellar door. A big fellow—his hair's all messed up from that fire you set on the ship."

"You mean the stepson?" I hadn't realized Tom Hollow had come in with them until he spoke.

"Stepson? Whose stepson?"

"The contractor's. The kid's name is Brook."

"Well, we'll find him soon enough, just like the conduit, and then we'll deal with him."

"Hmm." Hollow seemed somewhat uncomfortable with that, and I wondered if he were thinking of the fact that

Brook had saved his life in the fire on the ship—the fire that his sister had apparently set with flagrant disregard for his safety.

"Don't just stand there like a fool. Join the search, why don't you?"

Tom Hollow left the room again, and Sally picked up a book from the table. She muttered phrases to herself that sounded like part of a spell. Practicing for the rite?

I could scarcely believe this news that Brook had come here on his own to find me. He didn't even like me. I rather wished he wouldn't have, for now he was another factor I had to worry about and get to safety, but I did appreciate the thought.

At that point, I decided I'd been in one place long enough. If Brook and Little Brother were both in danger, I needed to get back up into the upper passageways, join up with them, and escape. I whispered goodbye to the unfortunate captive dragon and headed back the way I had come.

A PUPPET

NAVIGATING MY WAY UP THE STEEP STAIRS IN THE dark proved more challenging than the way down, for my senses were overwhelmed. I still saw double with the hatchling's eyes. Gradually I learned to focus more on what was before me and less on Little Brother, though I did not wish to abandon him completely to his own devices either. He might very well misstep without my guidance, and I knew that no good fate awaited him if Sally discovered him.

At some point, Sally once more left the room where Little Brother was hiding, but I advised him to stay put for the present. There was too much going on in and around that room.

When I reached the fork where I'd originally taken the steep staircase downward, I headed up at a slight angle instead. In very little time, some shafts of natural light were introduced into the corridor, so I could see without the lantern. I closed the cover so that it would draw less attention if I had to hide. I did not have much idea where I was going, and as more side passages opened out, the whole place became a confusing maze.

I heard someone coming the opposite way, so I ducked into a small recess and tried to be still. I gripped the lantern with the idea that it might be used as a bludgeon in a pinch.

But to my immense relief, I recognized the man coming the other way.

"Brook!" I called to him in a low hiss.

He turned and looked at me with an impassive air. As we had never been close, I did not take it much amiss that he showed so little excitement at encountering me, though I would have thought a sense of triumph might prevail if not elation. But when I reflected on it, the odder thing was that he gave no reaction at all to the way I looked. Of course I'd more or less forgotten that I was dressed as a woman, as I had other things on my mind, but it ought to have been a surprising double-take for him.

When Brook wrapped me in a big bear hug, I was further confused. We scarcely ever touched for any reason, let alone so effusively. Then I realized that he was not expressing affection, but attempting to immobilize me.

A second figure appeared in the corridor; he had the look of an Oxeye man about him. He swiftly joined in the struggle on Brook's side, trying to get me pinned down.

From a young age, it was impressed upon me by rather memorable means that I had no chance of prevailing against larger boys or men in a clean fight. That is why I never fight cleanly. I bite, I scratch, I pull hair, I go straight for the eyes and testicles, I latch on to whatever my teeth can sink into and don't let go. One might call it the feral-cat method, and it usually works well enough to get people to leave me alone. All I generally want out of a physical altercation is for it to end.

It did not work in this case however. Brook and the Oxeye man did not react at all to my wild assaults. When at last I got a good angle, I jabbed a finger towards the Oxeye man's left eye. To my horror, he did not loosen his grip to flinch back as any sane man would. He held his position as if keeping me in place was the only thing in the world that mattered. My finger went straight in, and the eye actually popped out of the socket. Never before had such a thing happened to me—people always, *always* pulled back when their eyes were threatened. Yet this man still did not react. The half-squished eye bulged out grotesquely far beyond its usual place.

I stopped struggling then, since it was clearly pointless. Both men were larger and stronger than me, and if they could not be cowed with pain or self-protection, I had no chance of overwhelming them with strength. Moreover, I scarcely wanted to hurt Brook in such a manner. He was clearly not himself.

More men appeared in the corridor then, sealing my defeat. The men all had the same empty expressions on their faces, chilling my heart and further sinking any hopes of escape. I was half-marched, half-carried to the same makeshift office I had seen earlier.

Little Brother was still there, still hiding. He peeked out from behind the crate, and I had the unsettling experience of seeing myself through other eyes. I felt self-conscious of the smallest movements, seeing them reflected in his eyes, and the fact that I was in disguise did not help with the uncanniness of the sensation. I would very much have liked to see Little Brother for myself, but I did not dare look in his direction.

Instead I looked to Sally, who was seated behind the desk once more. From her posture and manner, she might have been on a golden throne amidst a lavish court, surveying me with disdain from a dais high above. A vision of her as a queen-empress, magnificent and merciless, rose in my mind. And yet if such a thing came to pass, would it be so different from the arrangement in Summer, where our dragon-empress ruled us by the lights of her alien whims? *Yes*, my heart screamed. *No*, my mind whispered.

But Tom Hollow spoke first, from where he stood in the dark corner behind Sally. "You look different again," he said, looking me over with an appraising frown. "I reckon I like you better as a man."

"We're in accord there," I responded. "Though I should note that I could have made a much better job of the cosmetics if given adequate time."

"You're wearing my clothes," Sally cut in with an annoyed tone.

"Now there's no need to be jealous, just because I wear it better than you," I returned. "We all have our own strengths."

"I'd say you look better when you're asleep. And silent."

"And I've no doubt your husband would say the same about you."

Her mouth twisted. "My husband is an idiot who has almost outlived his usefulness." She spat the word *husband* with total disdain.

"Hmm. You know, I was taught you should *never* insult a client—if you'll consider some advice, from one aging whore to another."

"I do hope you're enjoying this," Sally said with a strained smirk. "Your last meal, as it were, if wit is the food of life."

"Well, I wouldn't say no to a slice of mutton and a whiskey either, if you're offering."

"I'm not," Sally said. "You've caused me some trouble today, but it will soon be at an end. It is regrettable that you will have to be sacrificed for the cause. But you do understand, don't you? All that power, and always just out of reach for you. It needs to be wielded by someone who understands these things, someone who truly deserves it.

"And don't imagine that block you put in place will stop me," she continued. "It posed some challenges, I will admit, but in the end I got around it. In case you haven't noticed, I've already seized control of your power. All these little puppets would never be possible without a truly ancient and powerful dragon behind them. And they are only the beginning, a little foray into what I will soon be capable of."

She looked at me and smiled. "Perhaps you do deserve that

drink after all." Sally brought out a bottle from under the desk and poured two glasses.

I looked at the glass. "On second thought, I'd rather not."

"As you will. It matters little to me." Sally shrugged. With a glance at her brother, she said, "Take him back to the chapel, Tom."

Four of the other men, including Brook, moved in unison without any direct order from Sally; they took my arms and manhandled me out of the room. Tom Hollow followed behind with a musket at my back.

I knew I was running out of time to change the direction things were going, but it occurred to me that Tom Hollow might be a chink in Sally's armor. Certainly I had no chance of reasoning with or manipulating the other men in their current state, with their wits stripped away from them, so Hollow was my only possible chance.

"Do you not feel ashamed of yourself, Mr. Hollow?" I asked him over my shoulder. I nodded towards my stepson, striding blank-faced beside me. "After Brook saved your life in that fire, you can watch your sister do this to him? Did you not tell me you disapprove of draconic power over men's minds? How is it you can be so repulsed by a bit of healing, but all is well when your precious Sally does such heinous things?"

Tom Hollow frowned and fidgeted with his gun. "I reckon Sal knows what she's doing."

I scoffed. "You really just do whatever she says, do you? What sort of a man are you?"

"You don't know what you're talking of. Sal and I have been through more together than you could ever know, and she's done more for me than can ever be repaid."

"She has some hold over you then? Is she forcing you to help her?"

"It's not like that . . ." Tom said, but I thought his

discomfiture grew. There was something odd about him that I couldn't quite grasp.

"Then you must be in love with her. No man is so devoted to his mere sister."

Tom snarled and lifted the butt of the musket as if to strike me with it, and for a moment, I really thought he would. "*It is NOT like that!*" he shouted at me, and his lips pulled back to show his teeth. It was the first time I saw him truly angry, and I must confess it frightened me. He was a large and physically powerful man, and I had been foolish to provoke him.

"No, no, of course not, I didn't mean that," I spoke softly in as soothing a manner as I could. "I don't know why I said it. I know it's not true. You're not even inclined towards women, are you? I could see that from the first."

That seemed to calm him a little, so I continued in the same soothing tone. "I have you to thank for tending me while I slept, do I not? You must have taken a great deal of care with me, and you didn't cut off my hair, even though your sister told you to, and it surely would have been easier to manage that way. Why put so much effort into me, if only to let me sleep forever?"

I glanced over my shoulder to see how he was taking it, but Tom's face was impossible to read. Perhaps it had been the wrong angle, for it must have been too obvious that my supposed gratitude was feigned. Reminding him of how he'd handled my unconscious form without my leave could only arouse his guilt. Guilty men swiftly became defensive men, and defensive men could not be reasoned with. He did not reply to me.

We arrived at the little chapel with the stone altar. The cat was still there, but only lifted his head briefly to observe our entrance. Strong arms enclosed me, and I was aware that Brook had taken hold of me again to hold me in place.

The other men started to file out without a word, and Tom Hollow moved to follow them.

Frustrated and increasingly desperate, I at last unleashed my temper on Hollow and snarled after him, "I do hope you enjoyed all that touching me in my sleep, Tom Hollow, for you'd never have a chance with me awake. I only go to bed with *men*."

Tom Hollow did not look back.

Brook held me in place while the other men exited. The door shut, and I heard the lock turn. Most of the men must have remained there guarding the door, as only one set of footsteps sounded down the corridor.

A SECRET

ONCE THE DOOR WAS FULLY SECURED, BROOK abruptly came back to himself. He swore quite creatively and moved his limbs around in wild circles, as if to confirm that he had control of them again.

I moved away from him, which he noticed at once.

"Oh, fuck. I'm sorry," Brook said. "I didn't mean to—It wasn't me. I'm sorry."

"I know that," I acknowledged.

He sank down on one of the stone benches and buried his head in his hands. "I was just trying to help."

"I know that, Brook. This isn't your fault. None of it." It was mine entirely. "Come, let me see your face. You have blood on it."

Brook reluctantly lifted his head, and I used the edge of my skirt to clean the scratch along the side of his face.

"That was you. The scratch, I mean," he told me. "You hit me really hard in the balls too."

"I am sorry about that."

"No, no, I wasn't complaining," Brook insisted. "It was impressive. You really fought hard."

I said nothing to that.

He looked around at the chapel. "Why did she even put me in here with you?"

"Probably to keep an eye on me. Make sure I don't escape again."

Brook's eyes widened in horror. "You mean you think she can take me over again whenever she wants?"

I might have been tempted to lie to spare him, but I knew he wasn't truly asking. He already knew. "Yes."

Stricken, he looked away from me. To my dismay, he started to cry. "I don't want that to happen again. It was awful. I could see everything, think about everything that was happening, but I couldn't do anything to change it. I don't want it." He seemed to be trying to hold back the tears and to turn away to hide them from me, but neither effort was particularly effective.

I knew what I should do, but it was strangely difficult to bring myself to it. Though I'd never much thought about it, I was sure I had never before embraced a man who wasn't a lover of mine. I'd had no father or other male relations for such things, and I felt awkward at the thought of attempting it. I reminded myself that Brook was really only a child, even if he had recently gained the shape of a man. And in this situation, surely he could not misinterpret or impute perverse motivations to it. I hugged him.

To my relief and yet some degree of alarm, he accepted the embrace readily and leaned into me. I supposed I wasn't the only one who was missing a father. Perhaps I ought to have tried to do better by Brook all this time. I had always assumed he wouldn't want it.

"How is it even possible that she can do this?" Brook asked me at length, sitting up and wiping his eyes on his sleeve. "She just looked at me, and then she had me. I couldn't do anything about it."

"She's siphoning off Summer's power," I explained. "It's my fault. I'm not a good enough contractor to stop her."

Brook frowned and seemed thoughtful at that, but what he said was not what I expected. "Does that mean Summer could do that to any of us, at any time, if she wanted to? Take us over like that?"

"Oh," I said. I hesitated, for the temptation to lie was much stronger. I didn't though. "Well, yes, of course she could. She does it all the time."

Brook stared in horror. "What do you mean? *She does it all the time*?" His voice turned almost frantic as he repeated my assertion.

"Have you ever felt like you wanted to leave Summer, but when you start thinking about the particulars of how you would go about it, the thoughts sort of fizzle out?"

His dismay only grew. "How did you know that?"

"Because it used to happen to me, when I was a lad."

"But you did leave. With Jacaranda."

I did a double-take at hearing Jack's full name, which I'd heard more at his funeral than ever in his life. To hear it from Brook's mouth made Jack sound like a historical figure, which I suppose he was. "Yes, I could leave with Jack, but even Jack couldn't leave until after he became Summer, even though he wanted to. Then when he did become Summer, he left almost at once, which is quite the opposite of what you'd expect, is it not? Most men would feel some sense of obligation to such a position. And I always felt the pull to go back. It was I who convinced Jack to return, you know, which is not at all what you'd expect of me either. There was no good reason for me to want to go back to Summer and the way I was treated there—though you wouldn't know much about that."

It was strange to think of that, how often I had hounded Jack to return to Summer at the flimsiest excuse. If we ran out of money, I was always quick to encourage Jack to think of the material comforts of Summer. If the weather turned particularly cold and inclement, I proposed it might be time we returned to the mild climes of Summer. If any situation we had gotten ourselves embroiled in began to seem too heavy and complicated, I was ready with the suggestion that we could always simply go home. How obnoxious that constant refrain must have been for Jack, who surely would have known its source even when I did not.

"But why?" Brook pressed me. "Why would the dragon want to keep us from leaving?"

I shrugged. "You've perhaps heard that some dragons have hoards of gold and jewels that they guard jealously and refuse to let a single piece out of their sight? Summer prefers to collect people, I suppose. She takes good care of us, keeps us well fed and happy, makes sure we don't overbreed for the size of our range. But we belong to her, and she holds on to her own."

Brook was silent for a while, and I thought he might let the subject drop. But eventually he asked, "How long have you known all this?"

"I can't say precisely. Certainly since I became Summer." That was the truth. There were many things that I simply knew, without quite knowing how I knew them, which perhaps came from the dragon or my own conclusions or some marriage of the two. In this case, I scarcely thought I was the only one in Summer who knew these things. Plenty of smart people would have pieced it together. It simply wasn't polite to speak of it.

"And as Lord Summer, you're not as subject to all of this? You said Jacaranda could leave at that point. Why would Summer accept that? Why would she give up some of her power over the one she's most attached to?"

"A contract must always have give and take, and Summer

has no use for any of us without a contractor. What good are pets without being able to see them and interact with them? No one would have an ant farm or an aquarium without glass sides, would they? I'm the glass, I suppose. I allow her to walk among us and experience the passions of our lives." Not that I'd been giving her much to sink her teeth into of late. She must have been disappointed at what a humdrum middle age I'd sunk into, after all the reckless passions of my youth.

Brook made a face as I spoke. But then he sighed. "Are you telling me all this because we're going to die?"

It was at that moment I became aware that Little Brother was on the move. He slipped out the door right behind Sally and flattened himself against the darkened angle between the ceiling and wall of the corridor. He knew on an instinctual level that he blended in with his surroundings, that his silver scales reflected back the colors around him, and sure enough, no one noticed him.

He scuttled along the ceiling quiet as a mouse, though he wondered what a mouse was as the thought came to us. *Where are you going, Little Brother?* I asked, but he did not respond. He did not quite understand the connection between us, though the image of me standing in Sally's office rose in his mind as I pressed on him. He knew who I was in some sense.

I wondered if he were coming towards me, following the way I had been led from the office towards the chapel, but he took a different turn. Rather he was retracing the footsteps I had taken up from the chained green dragon. Swiftly Little Brother found the steep winding stone stair and started down it.

I became aware of Brook crying beside me. Oops. I'd never responded to his question about if we were going to die.

"Brook, I'm sorry, I got distracted."

"Distracted? By what?" he demanded. He looked about the tiny bare chapel with an incredulous air.

"There's a dragon near here."

That got his attention. Hope kindled in his eyes, and I wished I hadn't said anything, but it was too late for that.

I couldn't tell Brook about Little Brother. Sally might very well be listening in on everything we were saying. I hadn't minded her hearing all that other business, for none of it was particularly a secret, merely a bit unpleasant to contemplate. But she absolutely could not learn that the egg had hatched and that the hatchling was on the loose in her domain.

But I did tell Brook about the young dragoness chained in a cavern below us. I told him that I thought Sally had been using her to draw power for some time—perhaps not very much power, not from a dragoness so young, but enough to sway people to her point of view, tell if people were lying, that sort of thing. It made sense to me now that Sally would have a dragoness, for on reflection there had been times when she had been more compelling or soothing than I could quite account for, and she couldn't have been drawing such power from a drake. The drake was mere muscle for her. Yet the limitations on the young dragoness's strength would necessitate replacing her with a more formidable power if Sally wished to continue on her ambitious road.

Brook became very focused. His expression reminded me a bit of when Zinny had contemplated the problem of concealing the egg not so long ago. Sometimes I almost forgot that they really were siblings. Zinny looked so much like me, but she was Canna's as well.

He asked more questions about the dragon, and he drilled down on my description of the iron collar around her neck. He wanted to know all about it and was undeterred that it had no visible latch. It seemed he had heard of such relics before and had some notion of how they worked. Brook explained that the collars could force a bond, allowing one to draw power and assert control over the dragon without giving anything up as in a traditional contract. Such magic had not been seen in centuries, and the knowledge was believed to have been lost to time.

Apparently the Kittevers had discovered the secret once more, and in the spirit of the changing times, they were putting it to work on an industrial scale. The implications chilled my heart; with such powerful magic married to the ruthless tactics of the Kittevers, they posed a threat more horrifying and insidious than I could have imagined.

When I mentioned there were symbols on the band of the iron collar, Brook's interest reached a crescendo.

"Symbols? What symbols?"

Little Brother had encountered a guard on the staircase. As the stair was quite narrow, it would be tricky to get around the guard, but I thought he might be able to manage it with a small distraction—perhaps something falling to the floor that would cause the guard to bend down to investigate. After all, it was quite dark, and bats in the caverns could explain a slight rush of movement overhead.

But Little Brother had different ideas. Dragons usually eat as soon as they hatch, and he had been out of the shell for hours now. He was very hungry. He dropped from the ceiling directly onto the guard.

"What? What is it? What's wrong?" Brook asked frantically.

"Oh, um, nothing. Nothing's wrong. Everything is perfectly alright." I tried squeezing my eyes shut, but of course that only made it worse. I had to focus on my own surroundings. The cat blinked slowly at me, and that steadied me a bit.

"Hardly anything is alright," Brook noted with a sardonic air. "And you're a terrible liar. It's something to do with that dragon?"

"Yes, the dragon." I was breathing very hard and having trouble focusing. The triumph of the kill, the glut of eating to satiation. The blood was hot and rich. Life was glorious after all. And I was going to be sick, or at least I would have been if there had been aught in my stomach to heave up.

"What were the symbols?"

"What?"

"The symbols on the iron collar of the green dragoness. You mentioned them just a moment ago. You didn't recognize any of the characters?"

I shook my head in frustration. "I don't know." There had been one that seemed familiar. A version of it often appeared on the top of official documents I was meant to put my seal to. I thought it meant "contract," or something like it, but the one on the collar was a different variation—a verb, maybe?

Little Brother had found the taper I had left at the bottom of the stair still burning, though shrinking down to a stub. Dragons could mostly see in the dark, like the dark of a starlit night, but not in the total darkness of the cavern. He took up the candle stub and stuck it to his own head. It didn't stay put at first, but he carefully scrutinized how the wax melted from the top, dripped a little on his forehead, and stuck it down. He continued on.

The green dragon lifted her head and looked at Little Brother with a curious air. Had she ever seen another dragon before?

Little Brother chirped at her with strange squeaking sounds, which surprised me, as I'd never heard a dragon make such noises before. I presumed it must be something that only very young hatchlings did, though it still struck me as odd. Dragons didn't raise their young like mammals, so there would be no need for mewling as little kittens do to get their mother's attention. Even Little Brother seemed a bit frustrated with how squeaky the sounds were coming out, but he persevered at it.

The chirps took on rounder tones, the intervals between the notes grew steadier, and I realized it was an attempt at music—not the alien-sounding mating song that mature males employed, however. Little Brother was singing the very same song I had sung to the green dragoness.

She recognized it as well, and her manner softened; she acknowledged it as the shibboleth of an ally. She even lowered her neck to him, as if inviting him to investigate the iron collar. Little Brother readily accepted the invitation and hopped up onto her neck.

I could see the symbols clearly now through the hatchling's eyes. They meant no more to Little Brother than they meant to me, but for that he could scarcely be blamed. After all, he'd only been alive for a few hours, while I'd had forty years to learn them. Revealing them to Brook would be more humiliating than anything I've ever done in my life, which is . . . well, it's really saying something.

But then Brook must have already suspected what the symbols were, or he wouldn't have been pressing me on them. Despite all my careful workarounds and playacting, he had somehow figured out my most shameful secret. I supposed he must have known for a good while, since before he encountered me in the library and questioned my presence there with such acute suspicion. Certainly he had known when we talked about making sense of the papers in Light's office. There was a great deal one could learn about being a gentleman by watching people, by listening to their talk, by studying their dress, but one couldn't learn everything that way. Some things required true instruction from learned tutors.

I looked around the chapel. There was nothing to write with, but there were herbs strewn on the floor. I lowered myself to the stone floor and started arranging the plant stems to match the symbols on the collar. The black cat jumped down to help by playfully batting at the herbs, but I pushed him away. Brook noticed what I was doing and watched closely.

"You're doing that from memory?" he questioned as the symbols started to take shape.

"Yes, from memory," I muttered. That was scarcely believable, but I still could not tell him about Little Brother. Perhaps he'd think it was a contractor talent. Dragons had good memories, after all.

"Are you sure there wasn't a tail on that character there?" he asked, pointing out the mistake.

I had thought that was merely a flourish. I added it to my character, and after that, I was careful to reproduce all the little fiddly bits.

"Yeah, that makes more sense," Brook said to himself.

I finished and said, "That was it." I didn't look at Brook.

"*One soul must be sacrificed. Blood binds. Bile breaks.*" He read it out so confidently, effortlessly.

I considered the words, but I had only a moment.

Brook grabbed me by the shoulders and shoved me down to the floor, scattering all the careful work. The guards outside burst in, and more footfalls came running down the corridor. Of course. We'd managed to tip off Sally that we were up to something.

A FLIGHT

SALLY WAS IN NO MOOD TO TAKE CHANCES THIS time, it would seem. She arrived with the green drake I'd first seen her with, the one called Crispin. Tom Hollow still carried his musket, and over a dozen other men—about half of whom had that same blank "puppet" expression that Brook wore—flanked them. They crowded into the little chapel to surround me.

One man carried an open presentation box, displaying an iron collar not so different from the one I'd seen the dragon sporting. But this one was fitted for my neck.

"All this for little old me?" I said to Sally, while I was still held immobile in Brook's arms. "You shouldn't have." Glancing at the iron collar, I added, "You know, that's really not my color."

"I don't know what you've been up to, but it doesn't matter anymore. We're starting the ritual now, and there's nothing you can do to stop it." Sally turned to her brother. "Tom, get that potion down his throat. Put him back to sleep once and for all."

Tom Hollow started forward, but there was something off in the way he approached. I had the distinct impression that he didn't want to be doing this, but he felt he had to.

Or he did have no choice? Twice he glanced over my shoulder at Brook's face, which only seemed to increase the lag in his step.

Was it possible that Sally was controlling him as well? If so, it was of a different nature, more nuanced and malleable than her control over the rest of her puppets. I recalled the many contradictions in his behavior, how strange it seemed that he would help Sally in such matters despite showing every sign of having a good heart and being wholly opposed to draconic influence. I recalled how often he had found ways to suggest that I was a bad person, perhaps as if attempting to convince himself—to rationalize his own actions that he could not otherwise account for?

Tom Hollow forced my head back, and I knew I couldn't keep my mouth shut for long.

When I had inadvertently started to heal his injuries, I had found a way in, and I could almost remember the path. Could I infiltrate him again? Perhaps release Sally's hold on him, if indeed it existed?

"What is the holdup?" Sally snapped. "Just get out of the way. Crispin can do it."

The green drake shouldered Tom Hollow out of the way and his claws closed on my face. Truly there was no point in trying to keep my mouth shut when his foreclaw forced its way between my teeth and levered open my jaw.

Little Brother nagged at my mind. He stared into the open torso of the man he had killed and half-eaten, pondering the guts that were strewn over the stair. Where to find the bile?

I did know my sweetbreads; quite a few hunting songs offer excruciating details on the innards, and I'd done enough butchering myself to know the truth of it. *There, there—the stomach, the gallbladder!*

The poison started down my throat, though with the images in my head, it was easier than usual to gag at it and bring it back up. But the green male was patient.

I was already slipping away.

Little Brother spat out a chunk of flesh. A chunk of metal clanged to the floor of the cavern. The green dragoness reared up in triumph. The green drake faltered and fell back. Brook's grip on me loosened. My grip on consciousness loosened.

The ground shook. The ceiling shook. We were all shaking. We were all screaming. The sky was falling.

I floated out of the chapel. No, that wasn't right. Someone carried me. I could not see a face, for it was too dark. All the lights had fled.

To my right, I felt a strange updraft of air and knew somehow that it was the entrance to the steep staircase. I was being carried past it. "Wait! Wait!" I struggled against the arms that held me.

"What is it?" Brook asked me. "Can you stand?" He set me down on my feet, but quickly grabbed me about the waist as I tilted sideways. He took my arm and put it over his shoulders to support me.

The ground was still bucking under my feet, and everything was spinning quite a lot, and I had little notion how much of it was in my head or truly occurring. The tunnels were completely dark, but a soft spray of rock dust and pebbles fell on us.

I knew there was something important I had to say. "We have to go down that stair."

"The left is the way out," Brook told me. "We've got to get out of these tunnels before they collapse entirely."

"Did the dragoness break through to the chapel?"

"What? Oh, uh, no. I think she was right under the floor,

but she didn't break through, not before we left. The ceiling of the chapel collapsed though, and it's all blocked that way. Some of the people got buried in the rockslide."

"There's a friend down there who helped me. We have to go get him."

"Who?" Brook demanded.

It was still too dangerous to tell Brook about Little Brother. Though the release of the green dragoness had clearly posed a challenge for Sally and disrupted her power, I had not dislodged her from the hold she had on Summer, through me. Of course Brook would find out about Little Brother soon enough, but by then I'd have another ally by my side—an ally with large claws and teeth. I ignored Brook's question and said instead, "There's a lantern halfway down the stair." As if that explained my obsession with wanting to descend it.

I staggered towards the stairs, obliging him to keep up with me if he wanted to prevent me from continually falling on my face.

Navigating the steep stairs in total darkness—while the ground shook, while I was under the influence of half the sleeping draught—certainly *sounds* challenging. It probably was. But in truth, I scarcely remember it. It was like running an obstacle course while drunk. I didn't have enough sense to worry about anything going wrong and simply barreled ahead. I think I did fall a few times, but the pain didn't register much, and Brook dragged me back up.

At the very least, not much rock debris fell on our heads. As the stair was most likely the oldest part of the underground labyrinth and built around the natural structure of the rock, it was more stable than the other corridors.

A faint glow of light became visible up ahead, and I recognized a particular narrow curve in the stair. I stopped dead before we rounded it, and Brook collided with me. "You should close your eyes," I told him.

"Don't be ridiculous," Brook snorted. "Just when there's some light, you're telling me to close my eyes? You're not thinking straight. It's that potion."

"Please, Brook. Trust me on this."

"What could it possibly be that I can't see anyway? I'm not a child."

It was a losing argument, and I could not gather enough wits about me to launch a more persuasive case. Perhaps I ought to have reminded him that Sally might still have access to his eyes, as that likely would have sufficed to gain Brook's compliance. But my thoughts were hazy and lingered elsewhere, and my motivations for wishing to conceal Little Brother's handiwork had little to do with Sally. I gave up and continued on. I picked my steps very carefully as I edged around the corner. If I needed any further evidence that the things I had seen through Little Brother's eyes had been real, I got it.

The fallen man lay face up—what was left of his face anyway—with his head lower on the stair than his feet. His torso was torn open and ravaged, with the guts strewn around him. Most of the meat from his left thigh had been gnawed down to the bone.

A string of curses broke from Brook and showed no signs of stopping. I continued to edge along the wall, quite aware that my thin slippers would not keep the blood from my skin. I stooped to pick up the lantern where it had fallen a few steps below the man, and I waited for Brook to be ready to follow.

When at last he tore his eyes from the corpse, there was accusation in them. "How did you know this was here?"

I'd had plenty of experience with people angrily shouting

questions at me that not-so-subtly hinted at something unsavory, and I typically ignored it and walked away. So that's what I did.

"What the hell is wrong with you?" Brook shouted at my back. "You expect me to just keep following you around without telling me what's going on? I know you're not quite yourself, but maybe that's all the more reason not to follow you blindly into a dragon's den."

I knew he would keep following me though. I had the lantern.

Brook trudged down after me with a sulkily heavy tread, muttering to himself as he came behind, but follow me he did. We came to the bottom of the stair, and I paused to get my bearings in the vast natural cavern. As before, I set a lit taper at the base of the stair, in case we needed to find it again.

The double vision began to return to me, and soon I was aware of why it had ceased—Little Brother had been left in total darkness when the first taper went out, and so he hadn't been seeing anything. Now he had spotted the glow of my lantern and approached eagerly. I turned, and for the first time, I laid eyes upon Little Brother.

He was stunning. His folded wings and the curve of his spine were more elegant than I ever could have dreamed. I already knew his scales were silver white, like Summer, but his eyes were an alarming violet. He moved with a fluid grace that left me speechless.

Between us there was no need for words. We knew each other at once, and I could feel his admiration and regard for me mirror mine for him. From that moment I loved him fully, fiercely, forever, and I knew nothing would ever change that. The fog on my mind from the sleeping draught lifted entirely, and I felt myself again. More myself than I had in years.

I knelt to put my arms around Little Brother's neck, and

he happily climbed into my lap and wrapped his long tail around my waist. I laughed as I plucked the stub of wax off his head where he'd stuck the candle earlier. He chirruped a few notes of song at me, and I hummed them back. It was so lovely to know him.

"Is that the thing that killed the man on the stairs?" Brook's voice had a hard edge—an unwelcome introduction of hostility into the pure moment Little Brother and I had been sharing.

I stood, bringing Little Brother up with me. Though he was heavy, it felt manageable with his weight distributed around my waist and his claws clinging to my shoulders. Not like when he was an egg. Little Brother squinted warily at Brook.

"This is the son of Summer, hatched this day," I said to Brook. To Little Brother, I thought, *Be easy. This is the child of my mate.* He could understand that, somewhat, and understood too my meaning in calling Brook a child. *But he also may be Sally's creature at times,* I warned.

"Is that what mauled that man?" Brook repeated his stubborn demand.

"He's a dragon," I snapped. I had little patience with Brook's mistrust of Little Brother. If he was only now coming to the realization that dragons weren't cuddly and harmless, I scarcely knew what to do for him.

I did feel some contrition for my sharp tone, of course, what with how Brook had risked his life to come here to rescue me. To be honest, that still seemed rather too improbable to be fully believed, for all that the evidence could not be denied. It didn't quite follow that Brook would have any particular desire to save me, though I supposed he must have been motivated by more general heroic principles than specific affection. As I could scarcely claim more than a passing acquaintance with heroic impulses, I simply could not relate.

The rumblings and shakings had been continuing through all this, and I was thinking it was about time for us to find the green dragoness and persuade her to stop slamming her body against the ceiling of the cavern in an attempt to get out. I was about to say so, but—

A terrific CRACK resounded through the cavern, followed by the rumble of rock shifting and falling and scraping, and everything around us seemed to be in motion. I pulled Brook with me back into the stairwell, which was protected against falling debris by a substantial bulkhead of solid granite. The three of us all crouched there until it settled down. Little Brother clung closely to me, and I stroked his little scaled head.

"I suppose the green lady made it out after all," I said when the movement stopped. "Maybe we can get out that way."

We started over towards where the green dragoness had been, but found the whole cavern collapsed in that direction. So we headed up the stairs, but quickly found that falling rocks had filled in the stairs as well. That left only one other direction, so we started to explore the cavern where it tended slightly downhill.

The floor of the cavern was quite treacherous to navigate, and it quickly became a strenuous exercise to climb over rock formations and loose gravel. But what else was there to do? Little Brother at least did not have much trouble clambering over the stones, and he enjoyed himself. Brook did not complain, which was all I could hope for there.

My cat friend from earlier showed up at some point in our explorations. He also had no trouble navigating the uneven terrain and watched our slow progress with typical feline impassiveness. He did not appear particularly alarmed at the current situation, which gave me some hope. If he knew a way out, was there a chance it was big enough for two humans and a dragon hatchling? I watched him closely as we went.

When I saw the cat flounce off down a side tunnel, I called our party to a stop, and I suggested we follow him.

Brook frowned down the narrow tunnel. "There's no way that's going to stay wide enough for us for long."

"There's little to lose from trying it."

Little Brother was eager to give it a go. Of course, with his sinuous body shape, he'd fit nearly anywhere the cat would. Something else enticed him though, a scent on the air that he did not know but that excited him greatly. It was salty, like fresh blood, and also a bit foul, like the pile of bones near where the dragoness had been chained, and yet somehow wholesome even for all that. I knew what it was, of course, though I could not yet smell it with my inferior human nose. *The sea.*

"This tunnel does have an outlet," I told Brook. "Little Brother can smell sea air coming from it." Brook gave me a quizzical look, and I realized that was the first time I'd used the name "little brother" with him. With a vague sense of embarrassment, I clarified, "That's what I call the hatchling." And I started down the tunnel.

I had to stoop quite a bit, and the sides often brushed against my shoulders, so I knew Brook must be suffering to squeeze his way through. But we pressed on. Eventually we were almost crawling. The skirts hampered my progress, and holding the lantern while I scrambled became a burden as well. But the scent of the ocean became stronger as we went, encouraging us to press towards it. We even began to hear the sound of waves, which felt like being back home at the palace in Summer, where you could always hear the ocean resonating through the stone walls every moment of the day and night.

At last the tunnel deposited us into a wider grotto, where

the sound of the sea crashing echoed and multiplied in an overwhelming raucousness. Little Brother gleefully skipped ahead while Brook wrested his broad shoulders out of the last bit of narrow tunnel. The floor of this cave was smooth and easy to traverse—no surprise there, as the whole of the grotto was no doubt sculpted by the ocean with every tide. We walked on down to the sea.

Little Brother splashed happily in the surf, but Brook and I were grim as we considered the situation. The mouth of the cave was not visible from our standpoint, making it hard to tell exactly how far away the open ocean was. Nevertheless, the water was clearly far too high into the cave for us to walk out, and swimming out of sea caves was frightfully dangerous.

"Do you know if the tide is going out or coming in?" I asked Brook.

"Unless more time has passed than I'm aware of, I should think it's coming in," he said.

I swore. That's what I was afraid of. There was a good chance the whole cave could flood.

Why don't you go on ahead, Little Brother? See if you can see where we are, and how rough the waves are as they come in the cave opening?

Little Brother shot off into the water with such alacrity that it was a jolt to my system. Like his mother, he was incredibly swift and sure in the water, and it was disorienting to see it all streak by. I had to steady myself against Brook.

Brook gave me a flat look from the side of his eyes. "Did that thing just abandon us or what?"

"Hmm?" I was still getting re-oriented to my own senses. "No, no, I told him to go on ahead and do some reconnaissance. I can communicate with him without talking."

Brook sat down on a rock and rubbed his shoulders. "When we get out of here, what are you going to do about Sally Hollow-Light?"

"I can scarcely say," I replied. "I'm trying to take things one at a time."

"But she's still tied to you, isn't she? Still drawing power from Summer?"

"I suppose she must be. I don't seem to feel Summer's presence like I normally do, and I do feel the cold, which I ought not to. But I have no sense of how that connection is working. I don't . . . sense anything of Sally in me."

"She's still there," he said.

"You mean with you?"

"Yeah. But that means she's in both of us. Without the green dragoness, she wouldn't have any source of power if not for you. And she said herself that the 'puppet' thing wouldn't be possible without an ancient dragon."

"That all seems sound enough logic," I nodded. "Do you feel like she's still controlling you then?"

"No, not really. Only if I think about doing something she really doesn't want me to do. Then it just squashes out. Like you talked about with thoughts of leaving Summer."

The natural follow-up question came to my lips but died there. There were only so many things Brook might have wanted to do that Sally would be so firmly against, and I abruptly knew what it must be. Did it get colder all of a sudden? I should really have waited for Little Brother to come back to acknowledge that I followed Brook's drift, but I suppose I've never been a cautious man. Besides, he'd already said that Sally wouldn't let him do it. And I couldn't help it.

I laughed.

"What could possibly be funny?" Brook asked, annoyed.

"Nothing. Truly it's not funny at all." But I was still laughing. I couldn't seem to stop; the laughter kept coming. Little Brother, climbing the bluff outside, noticed my unusual mindset and felt concern. "It's only that I finally figured out why you're here."

Brook looked deeply uncomfortable, which confirmed my suspicions.

"It seemed a bit odd from the first, you know? That you'd risk your life coming here to save me. You don't even like me! But you didn't come here for that, did you? You came to save Summer—even if you had to kill me."

He turned away from me, and his response was a mumble. "That's not exactly true. It's not as though that was my main plan, or like I wanted it to come to that."

I just kept laughing.

"Well, you don't have to mock me for it!" Brook abruptly snapped back, his chagrin overtaken by anger. "I can see now that it was stupid to even *think* of the idea, that I never could have gone through with it, but from the beginning, I only wanted to do what was right for Summer."

"I'm not laughing at you, Brook." I can scarcely say what I was laughing about. At the sheer absurdity of the situation? At myself for not seeing it sooner? That I'd simply accepted that he'd come to rescue me like a damsel in a romance? It made little difference.

A peal of terror from Little Brother pulled my attention away from the conversation. Crispin was closing on him. Of course. Sally would know where we were, and it was only natural she should send her dragon to deal with our dragon. Crispin was a fully grown male, bigger than a horse, while Little Brother was only around the size of a large dog and had no experience with combat.

Clinging to the bluff, Little Brother knew he was a sitting duck. He launched himself off the bluff and for the first time, he spread his wings. He soared, and it was glorious—but only for a moment before Crispin collided with him and sent him tumbling. Little Brother struggled to correct and glide again.

You don't want to fight that one in the air either, I warned him. *Dive! Dive!*

He took my advice, folded his wings, and plunged into the sea. I was betting that Little Brother would be faster in the water than Crispin, and so it turned out to be. He could easily stay ahead of the larger drake in the water, but that could only ever be a stalling tactic. At some point, we had to deal with the threat.

"It's not true, what you said, you know—that I don't like you," Brook said. "You're the one who always ignored me."

Wonderful. We were going to have *that* conversation right then. I could not reveal to Brook what was distracting me, for that would be giving away to Sally the depth of connection between Little Brother and me. She most likely had no idea that I could see exactly what was going on with the drakes right then, and I wanted to keep it that way.

"Brook, I had always been under the impression that you didn't want my interference in your life."

Little Brother artfully darted around underwater rock formations with dizzying speed, but Crispin was getting wise to the tricks. At one point, he cut a corner and nearly nabbed Little Brother's tail. *Dredge up sand from the bottom. It will obscure his vision,* I suggested.

"But you used to pay attention to me a bit in the beginning, when I was little," Brook reminded. "Then I started to grow up, and you just stopped."

Throwing up sediment from the ocean floor was working to confuse Crispin, but I knew Little Brother ultimately needed help.

I had no weapons at all on my person, but I surreptitiously surveyed Brook for weapons. A musket and a bayonet would have been lovely, but of course Brook hadn't come so well armed. All he had was a long knife on his belt, the blade about the length of a forearm from elbow to fingertip. And of course there were various rocks about the cave.

Lead him into the cave and go straight for that narrow tunnel we came out of.

"You can't think that was all me," I spoke. "You cooled towards me first, and I was only respecting your wishes. And I didn't take it personally. There's no question I am ill-equipped to teach anyone anything about manhood."

"I don't even know what that's supposed to mean. I didn't need someone to teach me how to grunt and burp or whatever you're thinking."

A blur of silver shot past us, followed by a streak of emerald green. Brook stared blankly, too stunned to react, and while he was distracted, I seized the knife out of his belt sheath and leapt after the dragons.

Little Brother vanished into the tunnel so fast it was as if he was never there. Crispin could fit in the tunnel, due to the long serpentine shape of dragons, but it was a tight fit for him. After shoving his head in, there was a moment's delay for him to fold his wings tight to his body and squeeze in his shoulders. For that brief moment, his head was in the tunnel while his rear end stuck out.

Eyes, ears, mouth, and vent—those were the options if you wanted to hurt a dragon, as you couldn't hope to so much as dent a scale with anything shy of a ship's cannon. Many tended to overlook the last, either because it was hard to spot when closed or because it seemed vulgar and unheroic. But as I might have mentioned, I'm not much for heroism, and I *always* fight dirty.

I slammed the knife into the vent.

The howl of pain and rage chilled to the bone. I found myself very grateful that the drake could not turn around swiftly in the tunnel. Indeed as he tried to turn around, he got stuck and found himself unable to move in either direction. Little Brother advanced and lashed out at the other drake's eyes, and all he could do in defense was thrash his head. It wasn't long before Little Brother got in a good strike and sank his longest claw into an eye and through to the brain.

The drake's thrashing stilled.

A SOLUTION

BROOK HELPED ME DRAG THE EMERALD-COLORED drake out of the mouth of the tunnel so that Little Brother could emerge. Through the process, Brook was subdued, perhaps in shock, and he forewent the many questions that must have been on his mind. Perhaps he was sorting it out in his own head. Perhaps he realized that there was only so much I could tell him.

"You're a strong swimmer, Brook," I said to him as he washed his knife in the sea. "From what Little Brother saw, I think you could make it out of here. The only tricky part is a big submerged rock right at the mouth of the cave. Bear left to avoid it. Once you're out of the cave, turn north, and it's not far at all to a sandy beach. Then you should be able to walk back to Oxeye with no trouble."

"Why are you talking as if it's just going to be me?" Brook asked.

"I'm not much of a swimmer. Never learned properly," I explained. "I have another notion for myself, but it will be easier with only Little Brother and me."

"You mean because as long as I'm here, Sally Hollow-Light knows everything you're doing."

"That's a part of it," I agreed. "It can also be distracting to have heart-to-heart talks about my failings as a stepparent."

"I didn't know you were busy!" he objected.

"I'm aware. But that's neither here nor there. This plan only works for me," I said. "By the way, have you any notion how long it's been since the *Avocet* set sail?"

"Can't have been more than a few hours. They weren't ready yet when I slipped away."

I nodded at that, as it agreed with my own understanding. My dream of Zinnia had left the impression they had only just gotten under way.

Brook gave me a look I couldn't read. I feared he guessed my purpose, but in the end, I don't believe he had any idea. "Are you sure about this?"

"I am." I wanted to say more, to give him a message for Zinny, for Canna. But I knew I couldn't. He was too smart.

So Brook removed his shoes, his jacket, and his knife belt. He left them in a neat little stack on a rock, as if he would be coming back for them. He waded out until he was up to his chest, then started to swim. I nudged Little Brother to follow and make sure he made it out alright. Though Little Brother was too small to be of much help, if Brook got into serious trouble, he might be able to render some assistance. I watched through Little Brother's eyes until Brook made it up onto the beach, exhausted but very much intact. It couldn't be more than a mile to Oxeye proper, which would be nothing to him even barefoot.

One less thing to worry about then.

Little brother, you should catch up to the Avocet. *Go find my daughter Zinnia. She will love you and take care of you.*

The hatchling was confused by that, but he did not perceive my purpose either. It was very important that he didn't, and so I was careful to avoid dwelling on it. I still had little notion how much he could read from my thoughts without my will behind it. Very likely my purpose would never have occurred to him. As clever as he was at so many things, he did not have the experience or context to begin to understand it.

I pictured for him the *Avocet* and Zinnia and even Captain Grace and Poppy and others I knew from the crew. I pictured the path they would have taken, the currents that moved swiftly towards Summer. I felt sure that Little Brother would be able to find them. I tried to convey how amazing and beautiful and kind Zinnia was, to convince him to seek her out.

When you get there, she will know what to do next. Hurry to her.

Little Brother did not understand, but he did trust me. He set off through the water, determined to find Zinnia.

I turned to the pile of possessions that Brook had left behind. I had no true need of any of it, but I was cold, and a habit of caution urged me to have all possible tools close at hand. I belted on the knife, pulled the jacket over my clothes, and changed into the boots, which fit surprisingly well.

Then I sat down beside the corpse of the drake, looked out at the waves bumping their way into the cave, and I waited. I couldn't do anything until I was sure that Little Brother was too far away to turn back in time to interfere.

It may seem that up to this point I hadn't completely grasped the full extent of the threat before us. Believe me, I was very much aware. If my dreams were to be believed, and I knew they could be, a Kittever fleet was headed for Summer, and the dragoness Summer was incapacitated, unable to defend the island. All her immense power was yoked to Sally Hollow-Light, who could wield it in a way that would make her nigh unstoppable. I did not for a moment underestimate how much raw power was at stake here. If I returned to town, I might find that everyone there was a puppet in Sally's service. Not only was all of Summer in danger, but possibly a great many other lands and peoples. Sally might set herself up as a queen-empress of whole swathes of the world.

And it was completely, utterly my fault. I should never have become Lord Summer. What had ever made me think I was in any way fit for such colossal responsibility? I had lied to myself that it was merely a ceremonial position, that there was nothing really for me to do in so prosperous and peaceful a land as Summer. I had allowed myself to be entrusted with the greatest power in the known world, and I'd proved myself a completely incapable steward of it. What had I expected? An illiterate middle-aged whore who'd played at being a gentleman so long he had forgotten he wasn't? Who'd never accomplished anything but to trail after greater men? That I had ever risen so far was but an accident of dragons, not known for the extravagant sanity of their schemes. Of course I had failed. But it was not too late to correct my error.

The fact was that Brook had the right idea about the situation. He was a smart lad and had figured it out even before he fully knew what was going on. He simply hadn't been able to carry it out.

Without me as a link in the chain, Sally would have no grip on Summer. The dragon could freely swat away the enemy fleet. Brook would be free of the heinous mind control she had placed on him, along with all other such slaves. Zinnia could rise to become Lady Summer. It would be hard for her, of course, but she would be well equipped to fill the role in time. In the end, she'd probably be better off without me anyway. I'd thoroughly ruined the lives of everyone else I'd loved, after all. More importantly though, all of Summer would be much more secure with her as Summer.

For it was not merely this current crisis that necessitated a solution. As long as I remained Summer, I was a weakness that could be exploited. Even if Sally Hollow-Light were killed, it was clear that she had already spread word of me to her Kittever allies—in Black Bream Bay and perhaps beyond. Others would come for me.

No, I could not remain Summer, and, well, there's only one way out of the contract.

I was inclined to walk into the sea rather than use the knife, but I considered that the latter might be more proof against second thoughts. I didn't want to fuck this up. Ah, but thinking about it triggered Little Brother's attention. He was confused. I reassured him and cleared my mind.

As I always tend to do when I am idle, I thought of Jack. Most days I did not allow myself to think of Jack's death and the stupid, pointless circumstances that led to it. But it befitted the occasion.

It was my fault that we returned to Summer at all. I pressed him on it, urged him to remember his responsibilities and to think of all the people he'd left behind without leadership, and in the end, I wore him down. Otherwise I suppose Jack might have been content to live out the whole of his natural life in the otherlands, having our small adventures and enjoying our small pleasures. But I knew Jack was meant for more than that. I couldn't watch him waste his potential on frivolities.

His stepmother, who had been acting as regent in his absence, was ecstatic to have him back. But she found it prudent to separate us, which she accomplished by the rather crude means of accommodating me in a locked cell. Thus I can't speak to the details of what transpired over the next week, though I know that Jack was pressed in all possible ways to do the one thing he had determined not to do—to father a child. As if everyone had given up on Jack himself ever doing anything of worth and had already turned their hopes to the next generation. If they had only been more patient and let Jack come into his role on his own time, I'm sure he would have eventually accepted it all.

Luring in dozens of drakes to sing Summer into some kind of mood that might spread to Jack was probably not one of his stepmother's shrewdest moves. When it all went horribly wrong, Jack fell defending his stepmother and little half sister from the drakes. So they say, at any rate.

I knew that was not precisely the truth.

I did not make it out of my cell in time to have any impact on events. Jack's stepmother had known of my tricks too well to place me somewhere unguarded with a pickable lock. Only when the guards were called away by the mass chaos did I finally have a chance to free myself, and then only to witness the end result with no opportunity to change it.

Summer arrived too late as well. Quite a lot of singing drakes had been needed to lull her into a mating stupor, but it had worked in the end, and only Jack's death managed to rouse her. Much too late. Or rather, I suppose I must acknowledge that she did save the rest of us—me and countless other denizens of the palace—from the horde of drakes who had broken free of all restraint and run roughshod over the lower halls. Summer killed all the remaining drakes with no trouble. But I scarcely cared on my own account. Once again I met Summer's eyes over the lifeless body of a Lord Summer, but this time, I felt nothing. All feelings had been gutted from me.

I later learned that many nobles witnessed our wordless communion, and they saw too that Summer took me away with her, alongside Jack's body. I spent the night in her cave, too sick at heart to be frightened. Her lament filled the air and vibrated through her scales as I nestled in the warmth of her coils.

When I emerged again the next morning unscathed, general amazement prevailed throughout the palace, and I suppose all the nobles knew at that point that Summer would accept me as a contractor if I sought it. But it would be weeks before anyone broached the idea to me—no doubt after they had already tried advancing Jack's sister and other young nobles for Summer's consideration. Their politicking held no interest for me in those weeks, however. I spared little thought for why I was suddenly treated with deferential respect, or why I had been accommodated in one of the most lavish suites of the palace.

My mind in those weeks was filled with only one thing—the image of Jack's face in his final moments. I'd seen Jack fight countless times against all sorts of wild odds, and when the mood was on him, he was unstoppable. Truly a force of nature. But on that occasion, it was different. I saw the defeat in his face. He gave up. He didn't wish to do it anymore, so he didn't. He stopped fighting. He let himself be killed by the rampaging drakes.

I don't believe he knew I was there at that time, that I saw him at the last. Would it have made a difference if he had? If he had known that I had never abandoned him? I don't know what he thought had happened to me. I'm told he made no particular effort to find me in that week before his death, but perhaps he'd been given a convincing story to explain my whereabouts. Perhaps he thought I'd simply fallen into a black mood and wished to be left alone.

But then, why should it have made a difference? Was I not yet another source of pressure on him? Jack might once have thought I was the one person in the world who was reliably safe from pushing him to marry, but in the end, even I became impatient with him putting it off. If a thing is to be done, I'd as soon have it done with. I suppose I never took seriously his *philosophical* objections to the Summer scheme, no more than anyone else.

Instead, I had always imagined that Jack's disinclination to perpetuate the system had more to do with his broken relationship with his father Leo. Something had been wrong between them from the start, and it had poisoned Jack's life in ways I did not fully understand. Somehow the contract made him feel yoked to his father in a strange and intimate way, and his feelings did not resolve when I eliminated Leo. At least such had always been my belief. For all that I'd been so obsessed with and devoted to Jack, a great deal of his motivations had ever remained a mystery to me.

Maybe Jack simply hated Summer? The scheme as a whole, I mean, not the lizard or the land. Brook's recent reactions when confronted with the realities of life in Summer drove me to give this prospect more credence than I had before. It had always seemed impossible to me that anyone could truly consider Summer to be a bad bet on the balance. There was so much to recommend it, and the objections were all, well, philosophical. Perhaps whores simply don't have as much use for philosophy as princelings do.

Thus I had casually reversed Jack's lifelong determination to end the line of Summer. Did I feel guilty about it? Was that perhaps at the heart of my troubles to bond with Summer? No, I did not, and it wasn't. I had disagreed with Jack about Summer, and though sometimes I thought I ought to feel bad about it, I didn't.

Had I not deserved to take something for myself for once, without reference to Jack's opinion? Then again, when had I not? I had certainly not sought Jack's opinion before I took my revenge on his father Leo, after all.

So often I had tried to convince myself that all of this just happened to me, as if it were pure coincidence that I went from nothing to the highest station of my land. I admitted that I had wanted to be a gentleman, of course; it could scarcely be denied that I had obsessively studied the ways of the nobility and taken them as my own. But ever I had insisted to myself that I was not truly ambitious or grasping, that I had not orchestrated any of the circumstances that had led to my rise. I did not consider myself to be like Sally

Hollow-Light, but I knew that the comparisons could be made on almost every level (except perhaps that she was better than me at everything).

Yet the distinction—and I do believe it's a crucial difference—is that I hadn't forced my way into stealing a dragon's power. My dragon had chosen me. But why? Why had Summer wanted me? The traditional explanation about Jack's love had never truly satisfied me. Summer had been angry at Jack, furious at his abandonment, not at all inclined to take his preferences as her own. And if that were the explanation, it would have to date back all the way to the time I had killed Leo and she had spared me. Most damning for the theory was the truth I had always known in my heart—that Jack had never loved me. I knew he hadn't, and no loremaster could ever convince me otherwise.

Thus one must conclude that Summer wanted me for mysterious reasons of her own. Yet if she had wanted me so particularly, why had she always shut me out?

As I sat there in the sea cave pondering these things, I watched a hermit crab make its ponderous way over the rocky terrain. The cat, eyes gleaming, stalked over to watch the creature's progress alongside me. I had little notion whether the cat would enjoy making a meal of the hermit crab, but I supposed it a moot point. The crab was secure in its shell, shielded from all the world that wished it well or ill.

Something Sally Hollow-Light had said came back to me abruptly just then. She had mentioned a "block" that had made it more difficult for her to access Summer through my mind. Sally seemed to think *I* had put it in place. Was it possible she was right?

Other moments began to come back to me, times when I had shut down Summer's thoughts and interference—most often when she had thoughts on Jack that I did not wish to face. At once, I knew the block was indeed something I had done, but not as a measure against Sally's intrusion. It was something I had done from almost the moment I entered my contract, an instinctive defensive posture that had colored everything since then. Summer had not been holding herself aloof and distant from me. I had been the one barricading myself against her. I had been shutting her out.

Incredible as it may seem that I should even be capable of thwarting Summer if she wished to access my mind, it was so. To realize it sent a thrill of exhilaration through me. I was not the lesser partner in our bond, some puny plaything that she could do whatever she wished with. In some ways, I was the equal of the dragon. I could hold her at bay if I wished to. I could set terms and boundaries on our partnership, and I need not fear that she would run roughshod over me if I let her in.

It may sound strange, but I had never known such a thing before. My early life had been dominated by Alice, my mother, who had been my whole world and firmly the sovereign of our strange little family. Then there had been Jack. I had poured all of my love and devotion into Jack, with no thought for anyone else, least of all myself. So of course I had thought that letting the dragon in would mean giving myself over to her, losing myself in her entirely as she took control. I had never known any other sort of love but to let myself be overwhelmed by another.

As this notion seeped through me, I found its poison clinging at the roots of much of my life. Had I not held myself apart from everyone who might have made my life more tolerable? If I could not be a whole husband to Canna, I would be nothing to her. If I could not be a father to Brook, then nothing. If I could not have a lover who I would adore with all my heart and soul, I would give none of my heart to anyone.

Perhaps the most frustrating part of this revelation was the realization that Admiral Rostrum had been right about me.

All his inane advice was absolutely spot-on in its way. Fuck, I hated that man.

I might have gone further down the road these reflections took me on, but I became aware of something new in the cave—a gentle splashing among the waves, a glow of light bobbing along from the mouth of the cave. A rowboat was approaching with a lantern fastened to its bow.

I was scarcely surprised that Sally would come for me, as soon as she could marshal the resources to do so. I drew the knife, stepped back into a darker recess of the cave, and considered.

Though I had perhaps elucidated some corners of my mind, I still did not know how to remove the block on Summer, nor if that would at once solve my problem with Sally. I had always been more likely to feel Summer's presence whenever Zinny was around. Or when I was angry. Or during my assignations with the admiral. My feelings on such occasions could scarcely be more different from one another. What mindset should I be summoning up to clear the barricade from my mind?

If I was to carry out my original purpose, now was the time. Let Sally find my lovely corpse and see all her ambitions dead on the floor of the cave. I gripped the knife.

A KISS

About a dozen men were packed into the little boat. Each of them sported the blank faces I had come to associate with Sally's "puppets." One also wore an eye patch, and I recognized him as the man I had scrapped with earlier to alarming effect. The only people with their own wits about them in the boat were Sally Hollow-Light and her brother Tom—or half his wits, anyway.

Sally jumped out of the boat and rushed over to the body of the fallen drake. Of course he was quite dead and there was nothing she could do, but it was interesting to see that she cared. The rest of the party trundled out more slowly behind her.

"That's far enough," I said, and I emerged just enough from the shadows that they'd be able to see me by the lights of their lanterns. I held the knife to my own throat.

Sally saw what I was doing and halted. But she smirked. "Would you really do it?"

"My dear Sally, that whole business about you having children—that was a lie, wasn't it?"

"Of everything, that's the lie you choose to harp on at this moment?" Sally asked with a quizzical quirk of the brow.

"It's only that it becomes obvious in a moment like this,"

I explained. "If you had children of your own, you wouldn't question that I'd do this for my daughter's sake." I let the knife bite and draw a ribbon of blood from my neck.

"Fair enough," said Sally. She held up her hands in a universal gesture of concession, but not surrender. "I believe you."

"Your plan is flawed, you know," I told her. "If you put that collar on me, put me to sleep, pour broth down my throat twice a day, how long do you think I'll last? Ten years? Is that all you need for your purposes? I am older than you think."

Sally crossed her arms and smiled in a lazy way, staying in control. "And what do you suggest instead?"

"That there's no need for us to be at odds. We are two of a kind, you and I. Do you never get lonely, having no one to share your triumphs with? I know you do, or you wouldn't drag your brother around after you, half subsumed as he is."

At that Tom Hollow stirred in confusion, but the dismay faded from his features as quickly as it appeared.

I raised a brow at Sally, but her face remained steady.

"Such a terrible pity, that a person as clever and talented as you should have no one around who truly appreciates your gifts. Think of it. Wouldn't we make a handsome team?"

I had a suspicion that underneath all her schemes Sally might actually like me a bit. I had thought perhaps she did, that time in Light's house when she'd tried to seduce me. I know, I know, you'd think a whore would know better than to be deluded about the sensibilities of someone like her. But I did not underrate my own charms either.

I might have wished I weren't still dressed like a woman, but after all, Sally herself sported men's trousers and a shaven head. She well knew all the ways in which clothing is vitally important—and also all the ways in which it is not. Surfaces and illusions are the stock and trade of our sort.

"You're only trying to save yourself," Sally noted, though I thought I detected a tone of temptation in her voice.

"Your first plan for me is certainly unappealing, but you mistake me if you think my ideal outcome in all this is simply to return to the life I had before. You have awoken in me the hunger for more, for the hungers I've tried to forget. In the passion of my youth, I had so many desires—for power, for admiration, for love. I still want it all." I spoke no lie, for I knew that Sally would be able to detect it if I did not speak true to my heart. "You can unlock so much more of the dragon's power than she would ever grant to me of her own will. And if I were by your side, you need never fear to lose it." I moved closer to her as I spoke and met her eyes. I knew very well how pretty and alluring my eyes were.

I was taking a great risk in getting close to her. If in fact she wasn't going for this idea at all, if she got the knife away from me, then I would be lost. Everything would be lost. I was risking all of Summer for this.

"You need someone by your side, my dear," I continued. "We all do. A person cannot thrive all on their own, doing everything for themselves. Sooner or later the loneliness wears too deep, and it will erode all else you build."

I reached out and put my hand at the base of her neck, pulled her in, and I kissed her. I kissed her with everything in me and allowed myself to feel for her everything that I truly felt—admiration, envy, anger, loathing, fear, respect, sympathy. Empathy. Sally Hollow-Light was everything I hated and loved in myself, heightened and honed into a perfect monster. I felt no arousal for her, but nevertheless I had a deep, powerful need for her. I accepted everything she was, and I loved her.

Summer's rage and ardor thundered into me, surging like the sea into a cave, and I accepted that too. I had always been so afraid of Summer, afraid of the way that my feelings resonated so faithfully in tune with hers. From that moment she had looked at me in Leo's bedchamber, soaked in the fury of bloody revenge, she had seen me and loved me. And I loved her too, Summer my soul sister. I stopped fleeing from her and embraced her completely, let her in without reserve. Like the summer sun baking into my skin or a summer rain soaking me through, she spared no part of me and yet left me more myself than ever. The blissful feeling of contentment that sighs through life's finest moments distilled into a pure acceptance of myself and my place in the world, with all its love and fury, its beauty and ugliness.

When I pulled back from Sally, she was smiling. Because she had wrested the knife from my hand. But I smiled too.

Sally did not at once become aware that the men around us were shifting restlessly and muttering to themselves. I can't say I blame her for being distracted. She must have been quite focused on getting that knife from my hand, and well, I'm a very good kisser.

Clear as glass on her face, I could see the precise moment Sally realized that the men surrounding us were no longer under her control. I felt for her. Truly, it isn't much fun being physically weak when everyone around you is naturally stronger, especially when they despise you. From the tension in her stance, I could tell it wasn't Sally's first time in such a position. What had made Sally who she was? What had made her so determined to find ways to use mind and magic to bend others to her will? I didn't like to dwell on it.

I could see her differently now—I mean that in a literal sense, for something had shifted in my perception of living beings. It was as though she were overlaid with a "true" version of herself in which I could perceive her mindset and her feelings as they developed. I understood that this must be what people meant when they said that contractors can "tell when someone is lying," though that now felt like an oversimplification bordering on the absurd. I could tell who she truly was, at least in that moment.

The collective grumbling of the men increased, and Sally

took several rapid steps backwards, until her heels hit the waterline. She gripped the knife before her in a desperate sort of way.

One particular voice cut through the confused chatter, though not for its volume. Tom Hollow spoke quite softly, and he spoke only one word. "Sal?"

Sally looked to her brother as though she'd been struck.

"What have you been doing to me, Sal?" Tom Hollow asked, more a plea than a demand.

"Tom, I didn't mean to . . ."

"Didn't mean to what? How long has this been going on?"

"It started with small things—just a nudge here and there to ease your worrying. I was always right in the end, wasn't I? But then I couldn't stop without it all coming apart."

"Without me realizing what you were up to, you mean to say?"

Tom and Sally continued talking, but it became harder to follow as the other men broke in with angry shouts. Unlike Tom, they were still piecing together what was going on, but they knew well enough that they had been used ill. Weapons appeared out of sheaths and holsters, and the scene might soon have turned ugly.

I turned away from them all and walked over to where the boat had been pulled up out of the water.

"Wait! What do you reckon you're doing?" Tom had noticed my departure from the crowd. When he called attention to it, the whole group stopped their grumblings to look at me. I had no notion whether the men had any idea who I was.

"I should like to return to Oxeye, and I am taking this boat," I announced. "If anyone else is not burning with curiosity to find out the extent to which the high tide will fill this cavern, they will be welcome to join me. Especially good rowers."

The voice of a draconic contractor can be quite persuasive.

There's famously a sort of glamour to it that sways people to see things in a suggestive way. I could see them wanting to follow, yet also hesitating in confusion.

A streak of movement passed before us, and the boat rocked with a new addition. It was the little dark cat who had first led me to the cave, having apparently materialized from concealment and hurtled itself into the boat. Cats have a rather keen instinct for survival, and I suppose everyone there knew it. They all stirred themselves to follow the cat and filed on to the boat.

Except Sally. It was plain she was afraid to get on the boat with those men, and I did not blame her one bit.

"I'll take my chances here," she said in response to my glance.

"As you will," I said with a shrug. "Is there any message you should like conveyed to anyone, in case?" There was no need to specify in case of what.

"No."

Tom gave her another look, and the pain he felt was palpable to me. He truly did love Sally, truly wanted to stay with her and protect her. He hated to leave her behind in this way. But he got in the boat.

Sally stood very straight and very still in the cavern, not quite watching the boat as it rowed away. She looked small and quite alone. That was how I last saw her.

A DEPARTURE

"HEY, YOU WITH THE HAIR," SOMEONE ADDRESSED me as the boat emerged from the cave.

I turned to find the man with the eye patch leaning over in my direction. I dreaded whatever he was to say, but I looked up obligingly.

"Are you a man?"

Not what I expected, but a fair question, I suppose. "Yes, I'm a man," I responded. "These clothes are only a disguise."

"Ah, good. At least that's something." A sense of relief suffused him that I did not begin to understand.

"I beg your pardon, sir, but what does it matter to you? I am merely curious."

"Well, I wouldn't want to have had my eye gouged out by a woman, would I?" He expressed the sentiment as if he held it to be self-evident. "That's just wrong."

I suppose I ought to have simply let him have his odd victory, but I was too puzzled. "The person who caused all of this was a woman," I pointed out. "That woman we left in the cave was controlling your mind during that fight between us."

"You think I don't know that? But that's just the sort of thing women do, ain't it? They mess with your mind, drive you crazy. Nothing strange about that. But they don't go around gouging your eyes out, do they?"

"Not in my experience," I acknowledged.

"Now, when someone asks how this happened," he continued. "I'll say, well, the fellow who did this—he slayed a dragon, he defeated an evil witch. And he plucked my eye right out of its socket. Not so bad, eh?"

Yet another strangely mythologized account of my deeds, but I didn't let it make me feel uncomfortable this time. "And I never even mussed my eyeliner!" I added cheerfully.

The eye-patched fellow frowned at that but did not deign to continue the conversation. Just as well. Remembering Brook's tears and confusion at being controlled by Sally, I supposed I got off lightly if that was the whole of this man's take on the ordeal. I could tell that he was quite earnest in all he said, and I was glad for him to have made peace with it in his own way.

I can't claim to have managed much rowing to get to Oxeye. To be honest, in spite of the new sort of strength that suffused me, I started to feel quite weak and lightheaded. I needed to eat. Fortunately, no one seemed to expect much of me—a privilege of dressing as a lady, I suppose—and the others did plenty of rowing.

I looked often to Tom Hollow, but he kept his head down, seemingly focused on the physical act of propelling the boat forward. My sense of him was confused and conflicted, a wild tangle of discordant feelings surging for dominance. How would he reconcile the idea that someone he loved had controlled him and subverted his will for years without his knowledge? How could he ever hope to recover from such an ordeal? To trust anyone, to love anyone, ever again? I wanted to speak to him, but nothing I could think to say sufficiently encompassed the matter. Platitudes and empty words would serve no purpose. I let the moment pass.

When we arrived at the docks at Oxeye, Lowell Light was arguing with the harbormaster. I could only catch bits and bobs of the conversation, but I gathered Mr. Light was dismayed by his wife's unexplained absence. The harbormaster acknowledged that Sally Hollow-Light had indeed departed with a group of men whom she had never before been known to consort with, and he had indeed allowed them to take a boat that belonged to the harbor authority without a proper explanation of their errand. Yet the harbormaster could not quite account for *why* he had allowed this to transpire or why he had not questioned the matter. Mr. Light became increasingly incensed at the circular conversation.

"But there they are now!" the harbormaster declared with some relief. He pointed out our little boat. "Look! They're back."

Mr. Light looked directly at me, and he squinted in con fusion for a moment before satisfying himself. "That is *not* my wife," he stated in a flat tone.

The boat pulled up to the dock, and I stepped out. "No, I'm certainly not," I agreed. "Mrs. Hollow-Light is in a sea cave a bit down the coast."

"You all left her there?" Mr. Light demanded. "The tide is coming in!"

"It was her choice. I'm afraid I can only refer you to Mrs. Hollow-Light to account for her actions."

"Wait now—aren't you the fellow who was with Lord Summer?"

"That was me, yes," I acknowledged. "But I must confess that we deceived you somewhat in our representation of ourselves. I am, in fact, Lord Summer."

Mr. Light's eyes widened; he looked me up and down to take in my current appearance. I suppose I could scarcely have less matched expectations of what Lord Summer is supposed to look like. "Is that so?" Mr. Light asked with a noncommittal air. I couldn't blame him for his caution. Imagine what a fool he'd look if he simply took my word for it and was proved wrong.

I smiled, and Light seemed to see something in my eyes that shifted his mind about the matter. "Of course . . ." he muttered almost to himself. "How did I not see that before?"

Then Light saw something behind me that dismayed him further, and he jumped back from me in a hurry. I knew what it was, for I could see Mr. Light in double.

I turned right at the moment that Little Brother swooped in on me. He barreled into me and wrapped himself around my waist, and I laughed. I stroked Little Brother's head and held him close. So strange to think how recently I thought I'd never see him again. He was practically a part of me.

When I looked back at Mr. Light, I found he was engaged in earnest conversation with Tom Hollow, who was providing him with precise information on which sea cave Sally could be found in. I supposed it was just as well for the two of them to figure out what to do about Sally. I also caught a mention of Grinhill in the same breath as the Kittevers, so it seemed Hollow was not inclined to hold back what he knew now that he was free of Sally's hold.

I couldn't help but wonder what Tom Hollow would do with his life now that he would no longer be working with his sister, and again I wished to speak to him. But when I attempted to meet his eyes, he turned away from me. Perhaps I was not the right person to reach out to him—far from it, I suppose.

The *Avocet* glided into the harbor, and Zinny's little face looked out over the bow. I waved cheerfully to her, but her big dark eyes merely stared at me. She must have been the one to convince Captain Grace to turn back somehow or other, for no one else would have understood the meaning of Little Brother's appearance. But Zinny gave no sign of what she was thinking.

As other people on the *Avocet* caught sight of me, my appearance naturally caused something of a stir. Much jocularity at my expense arose, but I knew that the way to play off this sort of thing was to be in on the joke. I bowed to the crew with a broad flourish of my skirts and grinned at their applause.

Little Brother could not understand what was humorous about my appearance. Nothing I attempted could convey to him the concept of gender-dependent modes of dress, nor of why it was funnier for me to dress as a woman than for Sally Hollow-Light to dress as a man. He was indignant on my behalf that the crew laughed at me, but I assured him I did not mind. To be a source of entertainment to my people pleased me well enough, and I still counted myself more or less immune to embarrassment of that nature. And the crew did indeed seem happy to see me.

The harbormaster sighed in resignation as he allowed the *Avocet* to dock without the proper protocol.

I wanted to ask for something to eat the moment I stepped aboard, but I knew I should present a more dignified front and greet Captain Grace properly. And even more importantly, I wanted to know what was bothering Zinny. As soon as I could reasonably extract myself from the officers with promises to render a more complete explanation of my recent whereabouts soon, I drew Zinny to the side.

"My darling, my love, what is the matter?" I asked Zinnia. "Aren't you happy to see me?"

Zinny's dark eyes drank me in, but her face did not soften. "Are you Summer now?"

"I already was, you know. But I suppose I am more so now," I acknowledged. "But what is wrong with that? You're not afraid of Summer!"

She said nothing.

"Or rather, it's alright if you are. Summer is very scary,

after all," I hastened to correct myself. "It's just that I never thought you were, darling."

Zinny cocked her head to the side and kept looking at me. "But are you still Daddy?"

I picked her up and tossed her in the air, at which she couldn't help but giggle. Once I caught her and hugged her against me, I whispered in her ear, "What do you think?"

Zinny hugged my neck and pressed her head against me. "Don't go to sleep again," she instructed me quite severely. I assured her that I would not.

Little Brother, who had been much occupied in climbing the mast, swooped down on us and butted into our embrace. He was jealous of any of my attention going to someone else, even though he was already fond of Zinnia as well. I let him nose his way in, and Zinny laughed.

Though Zinny was now smiling and seemed at ease, I knew that it was only on the surface. Something still troubled her; I could see a disturbance in her true self. But I did not deem it the time to press her further.

NOT MUCH TIME WAS required for things in Oxeye to wrap up. Sailors are efficient at packing up when given the order, and everyone was heartily sick of the mission and ready to get home. Brook had already rendezvoused with the former *Godwit* crew who had been left behind as a search party. With his news already in hand, it was not entirely a surprise to anyone when word was sent to them that I had been recovered. They all arrived at the docks in short order, packed and ready to depart.

Brook must have left some details out of his report though, for when Admiral Rostrum caught sight of me, his eyes went wide with surprise. He took in the dress and feminine cosmetics with clear confusion and dismay.

"You don't like my dress, Admiral?" I laughed with another twirl of the skirts.

"You're a sight for sore eyes whatever you wear, Teddy—I mean, Lord Summer." He hastily corrected his address with a guilty look.

"It's quite alright, Ros," I assured him and smiled upon him, for I was no longer concerned with what others thought of his familiarity with me. "My friends call me Teddy, and I do think we are friends indeed after all of this." The vague dismay I read in him convinced me he comprehended some part of my meaning, though perhaps not fully. It was no matter though; I would have plenty of time on the journey to make clear to him that our time as lovers had ended.

It would be tight quarters on the *Avocet* to get the whole crew of the *Godwit* home, but fortunately it was not a long trip. Once again I was offered the captain's cabin for the journey, but this time I declined and insisted I would be fine in the small cabin that had already been set up for Zinnia. I imagined that Brook, relieved from the responsibility of keeping an eye on Zinny, would elect to join the ordinary sailors in their standard sleeping arrangements.

However, as it turned out, Brook did not choose to join the journey home at all. In a matter-of-fact tone, he informed me that he would be remaining in Oxeye.

"Mr. Light invited me to stay earlier. Said he could use a secretary with my skills," Brook explained. "I think it would be a good opportunity."

"I would not wish to keep you against your will," I said. "But are you sure that you wish to work for someone like him?"

"Someone like what? As far as I can tell, Mr. Light is trying to do the same thing that Summer does, to bring about an orderly and prosperous society. I want to know if it could be done that way, with human ingenuity rather than magic."

His answer startled for me, for I had not considered it in

that light at all. "And you are certain you aren't perhaps a bit afraid to return to Summer? Considering some of the things we talked about."

Brook shook his head emphatically. "It's not like that. Summer is my home, and I want to *help* Summer by living apart for a while. I want to understand what we're facing. The world is changing so fast, and even Summer will eventually have to reckon with it." He spoke truly, and I knew that he was determined on this course of action.

"I suppose that is true," I acknowledged. "Changes are coming even to Summer. Little Brother will make sure of that. And I deem that these Kittevers will have to be dealt with soon, down to the root. We cannot allow people to be imprisoning dragons and abusing their power."

Brook nodded. "I may be able to learn more about them too."

"What about Poppy though?"

"Poppy?"

"I rather thought you liked her."

"Oh! I hadn't known I was so obvious about that. I mean, yeah, Poppy is a really great girl. But I'm not about to base my life around that."

"Of course not. I don't know what I was thinking." I'd forgotten that my stepson was a great deal smarter than myself.

"You'll explain to Mom though, won't you?" he said earnestly. He pulled a crumpled paper out of his pocket and proffered it to me. "I tried to write to her, but I didn't have much time . . ."

"I will try," I agreed, taking the letter. I had little notion of how Canna would take the news, or whether she would blame me if she were dismayed by it. But I would simply have to take that as it came.

Brook wanted his boots back then, which was unfortunate, as they were quite a bit more comfortable than any of my shoes—I still had never learned my lesson about selecting footwear for function over form. With some reluctance, I handed over the boots and the jacket, and I apologized for losing his knife, which had remained with Sally.

People were watching us, so I was certain Brook would not wish me to embrace him even if I had felt so inclined. I clapped him on the shoulder awkwardly. "Promise me you'll get your hair fixed though, won't you? It pains me every time I look at you."

Brook laughed, and we parted. I hoped he would be alright, and I felt he had as good a chance as anyone.

AT LAST I WAS able to sit down and eat. The rolls were rather stale and the meat rather tough, but it seemed a glorious repast to me. Well did I know that there was a risk of overdoing it, but I was so hungry and so entranced with the prospect of eating real food that I abandoned all caution.

Summer was hungry too. Dragons don't need to eat in the same way that humans need to, of course, or at least fully grown females do not. They have been known to lay themselves down and sleep for years, decades even, before rousing themselves and wreaking havoc in their ravenous flurry to make up for lost time. But Summer had never been prone to long sleeps of that nature, and though it had only been a handful of days since her last hunt, she was well ready to resume feeding.

Fortunately, there was plenty of meat for her at hand—brought to her on fine wooden platters, one might say.

The Kittever fleet out of Black Bream Bay had reached Summer expecting to find it all but undefended. Even among those who perhaps feared the dragon might rouse herself, they would have no true notion of what they were facing. Most dragons could be defeated by a determined group of well-armed men. Most dragons, though large, were of a comprehensible size that could reasonably be compared to familiar things, such as a house. Summer was not most dragons. Summer was an ancient and colossal creature without peer.

The splinter of wood, the crack of bones, the screams of horror—I perceived much of it, and I did not try to block it out. Nor did I allow it to impede my meal. It was time that I accepted Summer for what she was. For other people in Summer, it may be best not to think too hard on it, but it was my role to know the dragon.

She gloried in the battle, for it had been some time since she had exerted herself, and she had forgotten how satisfying destruction could be. The fleet's attempts to counter her attack merely amused or irritated her in turn, for not even a cannon could mar her scales, and she was too astonishingly fast for them to even think of getting a direct hit to her eyes or mouth.

To the men aboard the ships, Summer must have seemed a silver storm swirling all around them—flashes of silver above, below, all around—bringing death and desolation wherever she struck. But I cannot say that for certain, for not one of them would ever tell the tale.

PART FOUR

A HOMECOMING

WRECKED SHIPS LITTERED THE WATERS NEAR Summer, and fishing boats prowled the debris field for salvage. Yet Captain Grace directed the crew with cool confidence in their ability to navigate the hazards, so I did not worry as the *Avocet* crept its way through. The docks too were abuzz with salvage activities. Large pieces of ships were hauled out, and various flotsam was sorted and bartered. Yet they'd plainly spotted us and given way for us to dock. Most of the crowd paused in their efforts to watch the *Avocet's* approach.

Little Brother became impatient and glided down from the mast to the docks ahead of us. The onlookers gasped as he wheeled overhead, and they shrank back when he stopped to investigate miscellaneous things on the docks. Despite all of Summer's close connection to a dragon, most of the people never had the opportunity to see a dragon up close. Even such a tiny one as Little Brother could be startling, for he was well capable of tearing the arm off a man if he so chose. But they'd simply have to get used to it. Little Brother would not be inclined to stay cooped up in the palace, and he was already becoming notably larger.

All at once Little Brother spun away from the docks and returned to the ship. He alighted on the rail by my shoulder and pushed up against me. I put one arm around him to scratch under his horns, and with the other, I waved to the curious onlookers. I counted it important for them to see from the outset that Little Brother was with me.

When it came time to descend from the ship, neither Zinny nor Little Brother were keen to be separated from me. I ended up carrying them both down the gangplank, each wrapped around me as their limbs allowed—perhaps the most strenuous test yet of that extra strength I'd been granted. With awe in their eyes, the people stepped back to allow my passage. I spoke a few of the right sort of words—announcing that Lady Zinnia had been recovered and introducing Little Brother as the newly hatched son of Summer. But the applause was more muted than I might have expected.

As I scanned the faces around me, I knew that the people were a bit afraid of me, and not merely for the fact that I had a dragon wrapped around my waist. They could see the change in me. They could see that I truly was Summer now, and they didn't know what to make of that. Come to think of it, it had been a good while since a true Summer had resided in Summer, and Leo had not left the people with many fond memories.

Canna was there, standing so still and unassuming amidst the hubbub that I had not noticed her at first. She looked so lovely and so solid that my heart broke a little. Despite all the new realizations I had come to, some things had not changed at all. I knew I could never give her what she deserved. My best hope could only ever be to slightly improve our relationship, not to cure it. But perhaps that is simply the nature of getting by in a family. The particulars of my situation may have felt terribly unique, but the distances that prevented me from connecting to others were not.

I went directly to join Canna and passed Zinnia over to her mother, freeing myself of one burden at least. Canna readily accepted her with a squishy hug, and Zinnia laughed.

"Did you two switch hair?" Puzzled, Canna looked from me to Zinny, whose hair had only recently come out of her braids and thus fell in smooth waves instead of her usual frizzy halo.

"Oh! I've been wearing mine natural for the time being," I explained with a self-conscious touch to my own hair. Had Canna truly never seen my natural hair? No, of course she wouldn't have. "There's been so much to do, what with keeping Zinny and Little Brother occupied and out of trouble on the ship. I simply haven't had the time to work on it."

"I like it," said Canna. She looked to Little Brother, who squeezed my waist almost uncomfortably tight. He could sense my unease with Canna but did not understand the cause of it. "And this is 'little brother'?"

"He needs a better name, I know. It's only what I've been calling him."

"Amazing," Canna remarked, though she did not mean the name, but Little Brother himself. Certainly he was astonishingly beautiful, I must say, sparkling silver in the afternoon sun. He shook out his wings and stretched his neck in an arc, the little show-off. His eyes that day were pale lavender.

"And Brook?" Canna asked.

"He's very well," I hastened to say. "But I will have to talk to you about that later."

Her brows rose, but she accepted my evasion.

With Zinny on her hip and Little Brother on mine, we could scarcely have embraced closely. I settled for leaning in and kissing her on the cheek. She gave me a quizzical little look at that, but she accepted my arm to lead her back to the palace.

I thought we would have to fight off well-wishers the whole way, but the nobles we encountered around the palace had the same air of hushed awe as the common folk down at the docks. They made their courtesies, of course, as their good breeding demanded, but there were no forays at detaining us for further conversation.

Once we reached Canna's rooms, Zinny immediately enlisted Little Brother to go out to the balcony and investigate a litter of kittens that had been born during our absence.

"Is that alright?" Canna asked in some concern as she watched the girl and the little dragon scamper off together.

"Hmm? Oh, yes, they're fine," I assured her. "They've been playing together constantly on the ship. Peas in a pod."

"And he won't hurt the kittens?"

"I shouldn't think so. He's not hungry."

That answer perhaps did not offer perfect reassurance, but Canna had more pressing matters on her mind. She asked me again about Brook, and I explained his decision to stay behind in Oxeye as well as I could. She perused the letter without sharing its contents with me. In the end, I suppose she took it alright. At any rate she was not angry at me for allowing it, though she may have been annoyed with Brook.

I gave only a brief account of the rest of the excursion, emphasizing that Zinnia's ordeal in captivity had been mild and of short duration. I was sure that I would soon be called upon to explain my own adventures, which even the party aboard the *Avocet* was not privy to. But I was not yet ready for that.

"I shall have to take some time to visit Summer this afternoon," I told her once I had said about as much as I was willing to say. "But I was thinking I could come back here later and perhaps even stay the night? Now that we're all back together again, I rather think we should stay that way for a time."

Canna frowned. "Are you concerned that Zinnia will have a difficult time with being apart from one of us?"

"Well, yes, that is part of it. She has been very clingy since I recovered her, and she's still having a rough time in some ways," I acknowledged. "But that's not all I meant." I paused and cleared my throat. I confess I was embarrassed to continue, but I was determined to at least try. "Do you ever think it might be nice to live more as a family? I've always assumed that you preferred for me to keep my distance, but it was never my own inclination, you know."

Canna looked away from me. It was not that she was hostile to the idea so much as that she did not trust it. "What's happened to you?" she asked. "You're so different."

"It's difficult to explain," I said.

"If I had to guess, I'd say you seem like you've fallen in love," Canna said. "But I know it's not with me."

"Fallen in love?" I repeated, startled. It had been a long time since I had even thought myself capable of such a thing. I considered it, and then I laughed. "Perhaps I've fallen in love with myself."

Canna laughed along with me, and she gave me a teasing smile. "I would hardly think that would be anything new."

"Ah, yes, I've always been rather smitten with myself, I will confess, but it has been quite the tumultuous love affair. I've found a better understanding with myself, perhaps."

Canna nodded at that and smiled sadly. "If you have this new outlook—and I am glad to see it in you—are you not perhaps turning it in the wrong direction? Should you not focus on finding someone to truly love?"

"Oh, I'm not at all convinced I'm much good at that," I said. "You wouldn't recommend it if you knew who I've most recently bedded." And so I told her all about the admiral. For all that she'd obviously been aware of my affairs with men, I had never actually spoken to her of such things. It was oddly freeing to do so.

Admiral Rostrum was a well-known public figure in Summer, so Canna was quite aware of his professed opinions on family values and traditional ways of life. She was all incredulity that I would ever so much as think to lie with him, offering up as shocked and horrified a reaction as I might ever have wished to provoke. In the end though, she began to laugh about it. She laughed a good deal in fact, almost hysterically, for what stretched on to become an uncomfortably long time.

I did not mind. It was lovely to see her so full of mirth, and I certainly could see the humor. Though my choice of the admiral was perhaps a sad statement on my lack of regard for myself at the time, it already felt like the past, something I had moved beyond and need not affect me anymore. Funny how my time with Jack still did not feel that way, not even after seven years.

"In all seriousness though," I told her when she began to calm down, "I do think that one day I might fall in love again. But that is not for me to conjure such hot feelings into being, and in the meantime, I must gather warmth where I may. I have the highest respect and esteem for you, Canna—no, no, that's not what I meant to say at all. I mean to say I *love* you, Canna. Not as you'd wish to be loved, perhaps, nor as you deserve to be loved, but I do. I love you."

Canna smiled, and at last she believed my sincerity in this. It did not escape me that she did little to reciprocate my overtures. She shared no confidences of her own and professed no affections. But for the moment, it was enough that she simply accepted my efforts. We sat together in companionable silence for a time—until Zinny and Little Brother came back in, each toting multiple kittens and filling the whole apartment with a flurry of frenetic movement.

LITTLE BROTHER WAS NOT eager to meet his mother. He must have gleaned from my mind that she had mixed feelings on his existence, and dragons of both sexes are solitary creatures, at least from their own kind. In some ways, it was not natural for a hatchling to know his mother.

But I was stern on this point and insisted, for both their

sakes. I was not at all convinced that dragons knew what was good for them in these matters. It was plain to me that they were as lonely and desperate for connection as any human, but they were worse than even most humans at dealing with it.

Descending into Summer's lair, I was struck anew by just how crazily colossal she was. Spending time around other dragons had habituated me to a lesser standard, but nothing could compare to my magnificent dragoness. Little Brother cowered at the first sight of her silver coils, so I was obliged to scoop him up and carry him the rest of the way. I deposited him right down in front of Summer's sensational head.

The dragoness considered the drake without moving at all. Even her pupils did not contract or expand. At first Little Brother cringed back from her gaze and shivered, but as the scrutiny continued without any sign from her, he turned defiant. Ultimately he was a proud and impetuous little peacock, and it was not in his nature to quail before others. He stood himself up on his hind legs and stretched to sniff the top of her snout. Then with a flap of his wings to propel him, he clambered right up onto her head.

Summer reared back in surprise, but Little Brother spread his wings and kept his balance. He returned her gaze and took his own measure of her. Summer's feelings warmed wildly in all directions—outraged by his insolence and yet impressed by his fearlessness. The sleek grace of his wings drew her admiration as well, for she had no such appendages of her own, and dragons are always more easily won over by beauty than anything else. I knew then that they would be fine.

Little Brother would surely come to have a place in Summer, though I could not yet guess what it might be.

OF COURSE THE DAYS to come still held many challenges for me. Lengthy conferences with the military leaders and the nobles would fill much of my time for months, but I did not dread such business as I once had. I belonged in my role; the dragon had chosen me, and no one could gainsay it. I had as much right as anyone to have opinions on how we ought to run the island and organize her defense, for I *was* Summer.

I did not forget nor underestimate the threat of the Kittevers who were still out there. They had made it my business, and I intended to see it through. Not only was I keen to expand our naval force, but to modernize it: to ensure that Summer's forces could face off with the ships of a new era. Brook's efforts certainly helped there, for he sent on much material on technical matters—schematics and manuals of the highest quality—along with his general observations on the state of things in the otherlands. I received a good deal of approval for the foresight of positioning him so strategically, though of course I deserved no such credit for the thought or the action.

Some of the officers and nobles were initially startled by the energy and enthusiasm I now brought to these discussions, but they quickly adjusted. In truth, I might have liked a little more resistance, for there was a distance in their deference that I perceived would not easily be breached. It was no wonder that Summers of times past had gained their reputations as brooding loners. Whatever it was that people saw in my eyes, they turned from it. Just when I most wished to forge bonds to other people, I found that new connections were nigh out of reach for me.

The exception, perhaps, was at night—while I slept. In my dreams, I wandered the minds of many, and for a time at least, I knew them as I know myself. This was how Summer herself experienced the land, I came to realize, flitting from mind to mind as passing thoughts might entice or alarm her. The pursuit was not limited by distance, not within the bounds of Summer at least. I might fall into the rhythm of a fisherman digging for oyster beds on the eastern shore at dawn just before being pulled into the concerns of a coffee farmer on the southern slopes of the mountain.

I knew no way of stopping these nightly roamings, and selfishly, I did not wish to. It brought me comfort, this communion with the land of Summer, and I was convinced that this power was meant to be within my gift as Summer. Occasionally, I wondered if anything about this bond to the land ever went in the other direction, in the way that my bond with the dragon went both ways. There was much that I still had to learn about being Summer.

YET EVEN AS I began to feel good about all my progress, another matter weighed more and more heavily upon me. Zinnia was still not content. I had thought that she might simply need time to adjust to the changes, but I could see it was not so. She remained out of sorts even months after our return, and I was certain her unease centered squarely on me.

So I selected an afternoon to cancel all my engagements and focus my attention solely on Zinnia. Even Little Brother was left behind, much to his jealous dismay. I took her out to a bit of forest on the border between two sprawling orchards, and we set up a picnic on a flat rock overlooking a pleasantly babbling brook where I had once played as a boy. Spring had given way to full summer, and it was one of those charmingly drowsy days that make one feel that a nap in the sun would be just about the peak of human delight.

Zinnia sat with her legs dangling over the stone ledge and watched the water striders dart this way and that.

"You have not been happy, my darling," I said to her. "I can see it in you."

Zinny shrugged and did not look at me. "There's a lot in my head now," she said.

"Is there?"

"There's me, and there's Summer, and now there's you."

"You can sense me in your mind?"

"Uh-huh. Can't you?"

"You mean, can I sense you, my darling? No more than anyone else in Summer, I should say. I can feel everyone a little now, at least when I focus on them. But it sounds as though this is different. How often does it happen?"

"All the time."

All at once I was very glad I had not taken a new lover since I had broken things off with the admiral. I cleared my throat. "Perhaps there is something to be done to help with it, something the loremasters would know about. Many previous Summers have written about their experiences. Perhaps there is some trick to suppressing it that is normally taught from one Summer to the next. I was never an heir like you, so I would not know."

"I don't mind it so much." But she continued to stare at the water, her outer calm belying shadows shifting below the surface.

"It seems as though you do," I said gently. I wished to batter her with questions about the exact nature of what she could perceive of my mind, but I forced myself into silence and waited for her to be ready.

"What if there is no me?"

"What? I'm sorry, my dear, but I don't follow."

"There's so much in my head, what if there's no more room for me?"

"Oh, darling, that's not how it works. You can't run out of space in a mind. If you could, people my age would be frightfully out of luck finding a spot for all our memories and useless knowledge."

"But if I do something, how do I know I did it?"

"You mean like making choices? You want to be sure that your choices are your own?"

Zinnia nodded.

Such as if you were to choose a lover who looked almost identical to your father's longtime lover? I spoke no such thing, of course. But I suddenly felt that I understood something more of Jack's problem with his father Leo and how it may have tainted our relationship from the very start. To me, it had been a curious yet ultimately inconsequential coincidence that our parents were also lovers, a thing altogether separate from my relationship with Jack. But to Jack . . . no wonder he had never seemed entirely certain what he truly felt for me.

I tried to refocus my thoughts on the problem at hand, but purging Jack from my mind never came easily. Then it occurred to me that I was coming at it the wrong way around.

"Zinny, have I ever spoken to you of my friend Jack? From before you were born?"

At last Zinny looked up at me, her big, dark eyes giving me her full attention. She must have had some gleaning of what Jack meant to me from her sense of my mind, though she couldn't possibly know the details even so. I was sure it could not work that way.

"Jack had the same problem as you, I think. He felt he was tangled up with his father, who was Summer before him, and it caused him a great deal of anxiety. His father Leo was not a very good person, you see, and I suppose Jack was afraid of being like him." I paused and gathered my thoughts. "But Jack was wrong. I knew both of them, both Jack and Leo. A lot of people said they looked alike or that their manner was alike, and there was some truth in it on the surface. But in essentials, the two of them could not have been more different. Jack was a good man, kind and gentle and generous. He worried needlessly about becoming like his father."

Zinny's little brow furrowed as she took that in and turned it over. "I'm glad you're not a bad person," she said at last. "So I don't have to worry about that."

I smiled. "Well, there are still a few things I'm worried about," I told her. "But I feel certain we can figure it out together, now that you've told me what's wrong."

We relaxed for the rest of our afternoon together and did not speak more of the issue. Yet almost at once, Zinnia seemed happier and less anxious after we had discussed it. I found that I felt lighter too. A weight on me lessened when I spoke of Jack, as I seldom had with anyone since his death. Zinnia and I played in the creek, basked in the sun, and laughed together with all the ease that we had once enjoyed.

That night was lovely too. I slept over at Canna's, with Zinnia and with Little Brother too. Canna had accepted the dragon hatchling more readily than I ever could have hoped; she seemed to regard him as one more cat about the place. I suppose that was not so very far from the truth, though he was growing at a rather more alarming rate than a typical feline. Snuggled together with all of them there with me in Summer's palace, I felt more content than I can ever recall.

PERHAPS THAT IS WHERE I should leave off with this tale, at least for now. Now, my dearests, you mustn't go and gloat that I have given this account to the two of you rather than to your brother, though he is the one who asked for it. Brook is quite right that these matters ought to be set down for posterity, but not in his way, not yet. You may publish this when I am dead or when I am too ancient and venerated for a little youthful flirtation with regicide to be held against me. But you, my dear children, I trust in all things, and you may yet profit from the knowledge of my follies and my triumphs.

Yet when I think back on the whole business, it occurs to me that many of the things I learned or realized were things that I already knew on some level. Perhaps that is the nature of the middle years. A man of forty ought to know most everything he needs to know to be getting on in life, should he not? But sometimes one has to dig out the things he has buried out of sight or refused to look at for too long. I wonder what might be the next curiosity I shall have to haul from my closet and dust off? Whatever it may be, I can only hope it will have come back into fashion.

AN END

ACKNOWLEDGMENTS

MUCH THANKS AND APPRECIATION to:

Brenna English-Loeb, my agent, who was the first in the publishing industry to see this book's charm and who provided invaluable insights and support throughout the entire process of bringing it to publication. And the rest of the team at Transatlantic Literary Agency, including Stuti Shah, Sandra Edwards, and a special mention to Amanda Orozco for passing along my query letter to Brenna.

Diana Pho, my editor, who really understood what I was going for with this book and helped to bring out all of its potential. And the entire team at Erewhon Books and Kensington Publishing, including Viengsamai Fetters, Cassandra Farrin, Martin Cahill, Erin Roll, and Kelsy Thompson.

Stewart Spilkin, who not only provided necessary feedback but also listened patiently to all my endless complaints and doubts on this journey. Beth Radke-Farabaugh, who was the first to read the book with genuine delight and shared in my joy at its success. Bill Radke, who made so many things possible for me to be the person who would write this book, and who read the thing despite it being very far from his typical interests. Sharon Pavlik, who has always been incredibly supportive of everything I've written. Rosy Radke and P.G. McKinley, who provided much-needed emotional salve and inspiration. Cynthia Tuck and Spencer Tuck, who encouraged my love of science fiction and fantasy when I was a child.

And *you*, reader. None of it would mean much without you.

DISCUSSION QUESTIONS

These suggested questions are to spark conversation and enhance your reading of *An Accident of Dragons.*

1. How would you describe Teddy's connection to Summer the dragon? How does their relationship change throughout the course of the novel?
2. Would you want to live in Summer under the arrangement the island has with its dragon?
3. Early in the book, Teddy seems convinced that many people don't like him or are unhappy about him being Lord Summer. Do you think that assumption is true? How does people's attitudes about Teddy as Lord Summer reflect upon what is acceptable or not in their society?
4. Why do you think Teddy starts an affair with Admiral Rostrum, whom he clearly dislikes? Besides being a bad personal choice, do you think he was treating the admiral poorly as well?
5. Why do you think Teddy has such a hard time connecting with his stepson Brook?

6. From the reminiscences of Teddy's early life, what revelation surprised you the most?
7. Teddy repeatedly asserts that he is not very brave or heroic. Do you agree? Why or why not?
8. How would you characterize Summer the dragon and her interactions with her islanders? What are the benefits or disadvantages does she experience?
9. Zinny relates to Summer and other dragons in different ways than Teddy does. Why do you think that is?
10. Teddy relates several stories about his relationship with Jack and the adventures of their youth. Are there signs that his memory of Jack is seen through rose-colored glasses? Do you think Jack was a good person? Do you think Jack loved Teddy?
11. What do you think is the connection between cats and dragons in this world? Why are the cats always hanging around dragons?
12. What do you think will happen to Sally Hollow-Light and Tom Hollow after the events of this novel?
13. At the end of the book, do you think Teddy will truly be happier now after all his realizations? Why or why not?